FIGHTING THE MOON

TALES OF THE ROUGAROU BOOK 3

JULIE MCGALLIARD

Fighting the Moon
Goth House Press
Copyright © 2021 Julie McGalliard

Edited by Shannon Page
Cover Art and Design by C.S. Inman
and Julie McGalliard

Library of Congress Control Number: 2021900952
ISBN:978-1-951598-04-4

For the city of New Orleans
Someday we'll see each other again

PART I

NEW ORLEANS

CHASING THE WOLF

"**A**bby, did you locate the animal?" Barney's voice comes over my headset.

"I did. We're having a bit of a standoff. He's guarding his kill from me."

"Bon Dieu, he killed something? Please tell me it wasn't a person."

"It was a Lucky Dog cart. He's got it turned on its side, all the hot dogs spilled out in a pile. Little bit like intestines."

A moment, then he bursts out laughing. "Abby! Don't do that to me. Where are you?"

"Top floor of the shopping mall. Café area."

"I'll find you. Try to get him under."

I glance around, make note of the dozen or so people gathered in a loose circle, a wary but curious distance from the wolf. The wolf has apparently decided I'm not an immediate threat after all and gone back to gobbling up hot dogs as fast as he can manage.

"Stay back everyone, I'm going to try to knock him out." My voice echoes loud off vast, glossy expanses of polished stone. It's evening the day before Thanksgiving, and the space feels empty, only about half the café slots occupied, a movie theater that appears to be shuttered for good, a large carpeted space that looks like it was intended to be something it never became. At least it isn't crowded. Big crowds would make this that much harder.

I load up my tranquilizer gun, take aim, and—

"Hey what's going on here?" A man comes up behind my right elbow.

I swivel the gun up to the ceiling, hiss "shhh" at him, but it's too late. The wolf snarls at both of us and runs off, claws skittering on the slick floor. I try to drop into a crouch and get ready to chase after, but the man grabs my shoulder. Instinctively I growl and try to shake off his hand. But my own wolf has been gone for three months and the growl comes out more like a small, annoyed grunt.

"Miss, I'm going to have to ask you to leave, we don't allow weapons here."

He folds his arms, awkwardly over what might be a bulletproof vest, and looks down at me through mirrored sunglasses.

"Leave? Mister, I'm from Snarlaway, you called us here to deal with the animal."

I point to my olive green jumpsuit, with its patches that identify me as "Abby" and my employer as "Snarlaway Rabid Animal Control."

He sniffs, frowning. "But you have a gun."

"Right, a tranquilizer gun. To deal with the animal." I stare intently into his eyes. With a wolf, when I do this, my eyes flash green and the person I'm staring at melts a little under my gaze, relaxes, becomes suggestible.

This guy just shakes his head. "Where's your supervisor?"

Barney arrives then, dressed like me and dragging an enormous animal carrier. "Did you get him?" he asks.

"No, I got interrupted." I glare daggers at Security Guy, who hasn't bothered to introduce himself.

Security Guy focuses his attention on Barney. "Young man, does this girl work for you?"

"We both work for Snarlaway. We're tracking the animal." He gestures at the carrier trailing behind him. "We drug it, get it in the carrier, and take it to a secure location."

"Huh." Security Guy grunts. "All right, go on."

I don't have time to be mad that it took my male co-worker for this guy to listen to me. Instead I glance at Barney, we nod, and I take off at top speed in the direction of the wolf's scent trail.

My speed is nowhere near what it was three months ago, but my sense of smell, at least, seems nearly as strong. The Varger, my werewolf relatives, tell me that's typical. Even if my wolf is gone for good, it's likely that I'll never fully lose my enhanced sense of smell.

The wolf has gone to Bourbon Street. Naturally. He's found another Lucky Dog cart and is showing his dagger teeth and dripping jaws to the wide-eyed vendor.

I call out. "Sir! Hello? Sir? Lucky Dog?" The vendor turns toward me. "Sir, I'm with Snarlaway Rabid Animal Control, and we're trying to take care of this animal for you." I start aiming the tranquilizer gun. "Please, step away from your cart slowly to give me a clear shot at the animal. Don't run."

Apparently the only part of my instructions that got through his fog of terror was the word "run," because that's what he does. He takes off at full speed right down the middle of Bourbon Street, dodging tourists and empty plastic cups.

This is a problem. If you run, to a wolf, you become prey.

The wolf chases after the hot dog vendor.

"Merde," I mutter, and sprint toward the wolf at my current top speed, which seems frustratingly slow, as if I'm running with weights tied to my ankles.

New wolves have a powerful instinct to hunt, and that includes wolves who appear unexpectedly in urban environments where humans are plentiful and elk are scarce. While most urban strays end up going after ducks, pigeons, geese, squirrels, rats, or other city wildlife, sometimes they do end up killing a person. Worse, if a wolf hunting for the first time takes a human as prey, sometimes their wolf gets the idea that humans are the best prey, and from that moment, their wolf will go for humans every single time.

All of us on the track and chase teams have a command: keep the new wolf from killing humans by any means necessary, even if you have to kill the new wolf.

Strapped to my back, in addition to the tranquilizer gun, I have a gun-gun, and an axe.

I really hope I don't have to use them.

The wolf is almost close enough to bite the man's heels. Burst of speed, but I'm too far behind and take a wild leap, hoping to land on the wolf's back.

Instead I crash face-first onto Bourbon Street. This not only hurts, it also smells really bad. But my outstretched fingers brush the wolf's tail, and this gets his attention. He whirls around to snarl at me, ignoring the Lucky Dog vendor. Face down on the ground, I can't get to most of my equipment, but I can get to a pocket containing a bag of drugged venison, and dump it out onto the street.

The wolf gobbles it quickly, barely giving me time to push myself up and into a crouch. He growls, demanding more, and I put out another bag, then another, while I sort of crab-walk backward. It probably looks ridiculous, but I need to get him off Bourbon, away from the crowds, as soon as possible.

Barney's voice through my earpiece. "Abby! Where are you?"

"Giving the wolf drugged meat and trying to lead him away from Bourbon Street."

"Bourbon Street. Merde." He sighs.

"He really wanted some more of those Lucky Dogs. Wait, can you get more? Like, buy a whole bunch off a cart or something?"

"Sure. What's your cross street?"

"Iberville."

"I'll find you there. How's the drugged meat working?"

"Pretty good so far. He's calmed down a lot. But he's bitten, so I don't expect it to last."

"Bitten? Are you sure?" Barney sounds shocked. "And you didn't have to kill him?"

"Barney! What a thing to ask."

"Well, he's a bitten wolf, on Bourbon Street, on almost a holiday weekend, are you sure he hasn't attacked anybody?"

"I'm sure! I was right there. Just meet me at Bourbon and Iberville with the carrier and a bunch of Lucky Dogs, okay?"

I turn my full attention back to the wolf, who does seem a lot calmer. He's tall and light-colored, a lanky blond wolf, which probably means a lanky blond person. I put out some more drugged meat. While he's eating, I stand up. He follows my movements but doesn't growl or freak out. He just watches me.

"Hey, boy." I hold out my hand the way you'd meet a dog. He sniffs cautiously. I kneel, putting our heads at the same level, keeping my hand held out. I'm hoping he'll get close enough for me to scritch his neck ruff of extra thick fur, which the born wolves usually like. If I inject him back there, he probably won't even feel it.

Closer. Closer.

"Oh my God, is that your dog? He's so big!" A very drunk woman, wearing Mardi Gras beads in November, lurches toward us, her body language clearly signaling that she wants to give the wolf a big sloppy hug. But the wolf finds that threatening. He snarls at her and runs off.

She's frozen for a second, then screams. "Oh my God! Oh my God! Did you see his fangs? What kind of a dog is that? Oh my God! Holy shit!"

"Probably a wolf-dog hybrid," I say. "An escaped pet. Excuse me."

I chase after the wolf's scent trail again. He's heading toward the river this time. That's good. There's a park along the waterfront and he's likely to find something good to hunt there.

I call in to Barney. "Hey, Barney? I lost him again. He got spooked by a drunk tourist and ran toward the waterfront."

"Understood. I'll head there. I've got the Lucky Dogs."

I find the wolf in another standoff, this one between him and a small, fierce terrier straining at the end of his leash. The terrier's owner clearly has no idea what to do. I'm not sure either. Maybe this is a good place to use my catch pole? But that will definitely break the fragile trust building between me and the wolf.

"Ma'am? Your dog?" The woman looks at me, eyes wide and worried. "I'm Abby from Snarlaway Rabid Animal Control. We're here to take care of the stray animal."

"Is it rabid?"

"We have to assume he is, ma'am. Now, I'm going to engage the animal, which should distract him from you and your dog, but as soon as he is distracted, you need to start moving away from the area. Move rapidly, but don't run. Do you understand?"

"Yes." She nods. "Engage the animal how?"

I inhale. Exhale. Shake myself a little. "Like this." I dive to all fours and gallop toward him, head down, in the physical attitude of a canine who wants to play-fight. He responds in kind, and now we're wrestling in earnest. He's biting at me, not intending to break the skin, but he might anyway. It won't heal instantly the way it would if I had my wolf, but it won't do me any permanent harm, unless he goes for my jugular, which he's not likely to do.

I don't think.

In terms of strength, without my own wolf, I'm completely outmatched, and he discovers this quickly, straddling me in a "ha-ha, I win!" posture. He's figured out where the drugged meat in my jumpsuit is stashed and starts pawing at it, growling at the velcro as it sticks to his fur.

At this rate I'm going to run out of drugged meat. I reach for the pocket with the syringes, dodging his paws and nose. I'm absolutely covered with bitten-wolf saliva now and I wonder what that would do to a regular person. What if you get saliva rubbed into a cut, does that have the same effect as a bite?

One syringe into his neck ruff. I was right, he doesn't notice.

Barney arrives with the Lucky Dogs. The wolf runs toward him. He startles and dumps the Lucky Dogs, mixed with capsules of sedative, onto the ground. The wolf scarfs up the hot dogs and the sedative without noticing the pills at all. While he's busy, I jab him with two more syringes.

"I can't believe he's not down yet," I mutter. I've been told the bitten need more sedative than the born, especially on their first night out, but this is incredible.

Another syringe and finally, he goes under. Barney and I take the long, thick leather straps out of the carrier and use them to bind the wolf's limbs tightly against his body. We maneuver him into the animal carrier and shut the door.

Barney pulls the carrier behind him as we walk rapidly toward the French Quarter maison, at Bienville and Burgundy. We enter the courtyard through a narrow brick passage, barely wide enough for the carrier. Etienne comes rushing out of the main house.

"You got him alive, good job." Etienne nods toward the carrier, nostrils flaring. About five years ago he got a severe head injury and, like me, hasn't transformed since. But he's still the best scent tracker among the Varger, and he's become my mentor in how to use the gifts of the wolf most effectively even as they fade. "I'll get the garage open for you."

He punches the code into the lock and flings the doors wide. We call it the "garage" because that was its official purpose when it was built in the 1950s, but it was always intended for this: a reinforced, padded, secure room for new wolves. It gets used as a sparring and workout room the rest of the month.

Barney pulls the carrier inside and Etienne shuts the doors. His nostrils flare again and he frowns. "Bitten?" I nod. "You'll need more sedative and drugged meat then."

"And beer," Barney says. "We'll need beer."

Etienne smiles. "Of course. I'll be right back."

I open the carrier door to check on our wolf. Fine, but already stirring a bit. I jab him with another dose of sedative, muttering, "Unbelievable."

"The infected are basically rabid, aren't they?"

"Barney, please."

He rolls his eyes. "Sorry, I meant bitten. Infected is considered offensive now, is it?"

"Well. Yes. Anyway, you know that's a person you're talking about, right?"

Etienne returns with a cooler full of beer, sedative, and drugged meat. He sets it in a corner, nods toward the carrier. "How's he doing?"

"Fine so far."

Barney grabs one of the beers and sinks against the wall. "Etienne, could you get us some dinner too? After all that running around, I'm starving. Those Lucky Dogs made me hungry and I don't even like Lucky Dogs."

"Of course. Quartermaster okay? I can have it delivered."

"Sure. That meatloaf platter if they've got it. What about you Abby?"

I'm definitely hungry, but hesitate, torn between the urge to ask for something vegetarian, and the knowledge that I haven't really been a vegetarian for at least three months, not since I got hurt. My wolf family convinced me that I would never heal my injuries properly without meat protein, and I believed them. But I'm fine now.

"Mac and cheese?" In New Orleans, that's vegetarian most of the time.

"Be right back." Etienne nods and takes off again.

I grab a beer myself and sink down next to Barney, clink bottles with him. "Phew, that was exhausting."

Now that the adrenaline is wearing off, every cut and bruise and strain is starting to make itself felt. I inspect my body and clothes for damage. One of the safety pins hemming the cuffs of the jumpsuit popped open during the tussle and scratched my ankle. Even though I've been training for this all month, for some reason nobody checked to see if the jumpsuit fit me until about five minutes before moonrise. While living out in Bayou Galene I got out of the habit of carrying a sewing kit around.

Barney sighs. "Exhausting is right. But we did it. Cheers." We clink again, drink. "He looks like a proper wolf, I didn't even know he was infected until you mentioned it."

"Bitten."

"Whatever. I never brought one in before. I thought they looked weird, you know? That kind of half-wolf look. Like in the movies."

"Sometimes they do. There's a lot of variation in the bitten that you don't find in the born." I say this like I'm an expert, but most of what I know is from interacting last summer with my half-brother Jaime and Reina, his bitten-wolf girlfriend.

Growling and movement from the carrier, and by the time I realize what's happening the wolf has already knocked it over. I dive to hold it still, keep him from escaping. "Barney! He's storming already, I need more sedative!" .

Barney grabs one of the needles, hesitates. "I need to open the door to get the needle in, but he's got his mouth free, I don't want to get bit."

"Just hand it to me." I position myself in front of the door, then open it just a bit. The wolf snaps and snarls, trying to force his way past me, but I get the sedative jammed into his nose and he goes under again. I rewrap the straps, paying extra attention to his jaws, and close the carrier. "This design doesn't seem ideal for the bitten. It assumes the wolf inside is going to sleep through the night."

"Well, yeah." Barney shakes his head. "What was that? You called it a storm?"

"It's something the bitten often get on their first couple of moons. Even if you sedate them heavily, every couple of hours they go into a frenzy and you have to sedate them again."

"Every couple of hours?" He looks dismayed. "Seriously?"

"Don't worry, I'll take care of it." I smile with more courage than I feel. "Just, please get me another beer? Most of mine ended up on the floor." I sink against the wall again. It's going to be a long night.

DISTANT HOWLING.

My wolf, where is she? We can't hear each other now. Where is she? I need her for something, we have to—

I wake up.

The howling continues, telling me it's almost sunrise, almost moonset, and the wolves are coming home to sleep. I glance at Barney, slumped against the padded wall, trickle of drool in the corner of his mouth. I yawn, stand up, stretch, go check on the wolf. Sleeping, but his ears twitch. Does he hear the howling of the other wolves? It's been a couple of hours since the last storm, and I need to make sure he sleeps through the rest of the morning.

I get another syringe and open the door of the carrier. He's curled against the far edge, forcing me to crawl inside to get access to his body.

Behind me, Vivienne thumps her body against the door,

the wolfy version of knocking. I ignore it and continue trying to inject the new wolf.

"Huh?" Barney wakes up, checks the camera that shows the outside of the door. "Oh, it's Viv, I'll let her in."

"Barney, no!" I shout but it's too late. Vivienne rushes into the garage and toward the new wolf, growling and ferocious, while the other wolf races past me to erupt from the carrier and challenge Viv, eyes flashing yellow, fangs dripping.

"Merde!" Barney exclaims. "What do I do?"

"Sedative, Barney!" I wrap my body around the new wolf to keep him away from Viv and hold out my right hand. Barney puts a syringe into it and I inject. Another syringe. And another. Finally he passes out.

I step back a little, preparing to reassemble his straps. But now Viv darts toward him, wide open jaws heading straight for his neck.

"NO, BAD WOLF!" I leap onto Viv's back and wedge my forearm into her open jaws. She could probably bite the arm right off me, bone and all, but she doesn't. Her teeth close enough to break the skin, which hurts like hell, but the smell of my blood seems to cause alarm and she whimpers, slinks out of combat mode, backing away from the other wolf and trying to shake me off her back, gently. I continue to hang on, and she eventually curls up underneath me.

I feel an enormous atmospheric pressure, close my eyes. Ozone or something tickles my nose. A feeling of excitement and release sweeps over me, like a wind. Viv's body shakes and twists for a moment, then I'm grasping skin instead of fur.

"Ugh, get off me, Abby." Viv sits up and I tumble off.

Danger over, I lie on the floor, wrecked from the adrenaline hangover of two big battles in one night. Above me, Viv pulls on a robe, seeming dazed. "What's going on, Abby, who is that?"

"New bitten wolf," I say. We all stare, as he begins his transition back to human.

For the born, the transformation happens in an instant. But with our new wolf, it seems to take forever. He shakes all over, twitching and quivering. He whimpers, as if it hurts, throws back his head and howls in pain. He strains against the straps, growling and snarling, and with every tortured gesture, seems less wolf and more human, a grotesque, malformed mixture of the two. His fur ripples and blisters, then smooths down into human skin that looks red and irritated. His howls subside, becoming whimpers and finally purely human panting.

A naked man lies before us, sweaty and exhausted. He exhales, seems to truly relax for the first time. As expected, he's lanky and blond. Pale skin, no freckles. Short hair, pretty features in a sharp clean-shaven face. No obvious wolf sign. Looks about thirty-five.

"We should get the straps off him," I say. But the instant I touch him, he startles awake, sitting up, thrashing against the straps.

"What the hell?" He groans in pain, clutching his abdomen. Then he vomits up a shocking quantity of half-digested Lucky Dogs.

2

ANDREW

"Buddy, you okay in there?" My brother Nicolas raps on the door of the bathroom, where our new wolf has been holed up for quite a while.

The door opens a few inches, releasing steam and the olive-oil smell of the soap we use at the maison. The man peers out through the mist, eyes darting rapidly from Nic, to me, back to Nic. He smells stressed out. "I'm sorry, does somebody need the bathroom?"

"No, dude, you're fine, we were just worried about you." Nic smiles.

"Right. Right." The man runs his fingers through his wet hair. "And who are you again?" His voice is sharp, suspicious.

"I'm Nicolas. Nic."

"And this is your place?"

"I live here, yes."

The other man's nostrils flare. "We didn't hook up last night, did we?"

"No, we didn't."

"I'm sorry, I just don't understand why I'm here."

"We found you last night, wandering the city in a vulnerable state. We took you back here to keep you safe."

"Safe. Right." He glances at me. "I know you. There was something… why don't I remember?"

"Something extraordinary happened to you last night." Nic gives him a big, artificially jolly smile.

"Extraordinary, right." He frowns. "What do you mean by extraordinary?"

"Complicated question. There's a robe in the bathroom, why don't you put it on and come out and let us explain?"

"Sure. Yeah. Okay. Just give me a few minutes alone."

"Of course. Come on, Abby."

I follow Nic back to the main sitting room, where Viv and Etienne are drinking coffee, perched awkwardly on the vintage furniture. The sitting room doubles as the business offices of the Snarlaway Rabid Animal Control company, and the room is dominated by an enormous wooden desk with a computer, old-fashioned telephone plugged into the wall, letter tray, and other assorted detritus of a nominally active business. The telephone gets answered promptly during the nights of the full moon, less promptly at other times. Although, for the sake of cash flow and general appearances, during the rest of the month Snarlaway does act as a real animal control company, doing things like trapping mice and coaxing raccoons out of attics. I began my apprenticeship at the beginning of November, right after I didn't transform during the October full moon. During the last four weeks I, personally, have removed from people's homes a boa constrictor (friendly, escaped pet), tarantula (also an escaped pet, less friendly), bat (adorable, terrified), family of rats (relocated to a park), abandoned puppy (adopted), and a brown recluse spider (so far the only subject of my calls to end up dead).

"How's he doing?" Etienne asks.

"Not great." Nic shakes his head. "He seems confused and emotionally hostile."

Viv grimaces. "That's probably my fault. My wolf's first instinct was to consider him a threat and challenge him." She nods in my direction. "Without Abby intervening, we might have fought, and he'd probably be dead now."

Etienne gives me a brief hug. "It's good that you were here, Abby."

"Thanks. I take it that hostility isn't typical for the born wolves?"

"No. There seems to be some kind of kinship instinct that kicks in with them. They hunt beside the senior wolves all night and in the morning, even if they don't remember it clearly, they have an emotional bond with us." Viv shrugs. "Of course, born wolves appearing for the first time are usually teenagers. That probably makes a difference."

I sit down at the desk, pour myself coffee, stifle a huge yawn.

"You can go to bed, Abby," Etienne says. "Barney already has. We don't expect you to be up all night during the full moon and then up all the next day too."

I yawn again, sip some of the coffee, find it unpleasantly bitter, on the burner too long. "But I'm apprenticing. Isn't what you do the next day part of what I have to learn?"

"We have a whole team, you don't have to do it all."

"I'll make some fresh coffee." I hold up the pot. "This stuff has turned into toxic waste."

I head to the modern kitchen, a small room that used to be a staging area for dinner parties back when all the food was cooked in a big, brick oven in a separate building. It was modernized in the mid-1960s and I swear some of the equipment dates back that far, including the manual coffee grinder. Zoning out to the repetitive act of turning the crank, inhaling the pleasant smell of freshly ground coffee, staring out the window, it takes me a moment to realize what I'm seeing.

Our new wolf, wearing just the terrycloth robe, runs through the courtyard to climb up and over the brick fence.

I drop the coffee grinder and chase after him at top speed. With both of us human we're more evenly matched and I scramble over the fence, catch up right away. My first instinct is to drop him by tackling his legs, but we're on a hard brick surface and I don't want to hurt him. Instead I leap onto his back and wrap my arms around his shoulders.

I hiss into his ear: "You're a werewolf."

"What the hell? Get off me!" He reaches awkwardly backward, twisting and flailing.

I continue to speak right in his ear. "That thing that happened to you last night that you can't remember, is that you're a werewolf. Last night was the full moon."

He stops trying to fight me, stands still for a moment, then bursts out laughing. "Okay, what?"

"You know all those Lucky Dogs you threw up? That's because the human digestive system can't handle everything a wolf eats. Like, little bones and cartilage and a million hot dogs and things like that."

I sense he's intrigued enough not to run away, so I hop off his back, move so that we're facing each other. He folds his arms, give me an amused look. "So what are you? Vampire? Zombie?"

"Also a werewolf. Those other things don't exist as far as I know. We took you in last night to keep you from hurting anybody or getting hurt yourself."

"We." He folds his arms. "Meaning you and that extremely handsome ginger Black man, you mean?"

"Right. The man is Nicolas and the red-haired woman is Vivienne, and a couple of other people you didn't meet, we're all werewolves. And we want to help you."

He rolls his eyes. "Well, this is more entertaining than 'I know where you got them shoes,' I'll give you that much." He tightens the robe, looks around as if perplexed. "Wait, where is this?"

"French Quarter Courtyard Inn. Do you remember how you got here?"

He frowns. "I climbed the fence."

"You practically levitated over that fence. Could you have done that yesterday?"

He looks troubled. "Well, I do work out a lot."

"But could you have done that yesterday?"

"I don't know." He frowns. "And you were right behind me. Climbing the same fence."

"Right! Because, also a werewolf."

"You jumped onto my back."

"To keep you from running off. I'm sorry. I know you don't believe me yet, and it sounds like a crazy thing I'm telling you. But it's vitally important that you accept the reality of your, you know, your condition. If you don't work to manage it, you could end up really hurting somebody next full moon. Or getting hurt yourself."

"You do seem sincere." He sighs, shaking his head. "Which means you're nuts. Or a good actress. What do you people want from me anyway? I don't really have any money. Is this some kind of internet stunt? Am I being filmed?" He glances around suspiciously.

"I want you to believe I'm telling you the truth."

He shakes his head and starts walking away. I panic and leap onto his back again. "Fight me."

"What? Oh, honey, no. Don't be ridiculous."

"You don't want to do it because you think you'll pulverize me. Right?"

"That's about the size of it. I'm not only a foot taller than you, I'm also trained in several martial arts."

"And I'm a werewolf. So fight me."

I hop off his back and get into a combat-ready crouch. I'm not well trained in this kind of fighting, but I have watched the other Varger spar with each other and I can imitate what they do.

He shakes his head, folds his arms. "You are really committed to this bit, I'll give you that. But I need to get my phone and wallet back from the gym, I don't have time to arm wrestle a little girl."

"What can I do to convince you?"

He chuckles. "You know, that's a good question. How do you prove somebody's a werewolf? Shoot them with a silver bullet and see what happens?"

Silver doesn't do anything, but he's given me an idea. It's a terrible idea. I check the pocket where I stashed my knife last night. The knife is still there, heavy, hard, a little cold. I take it. Flick out the blade.

"I'm so sorry," I tell him.

"What?" He looks confused, then notices the blade. "Oh, shit, no—"

He takes a step backward. I rush forward, blade out, sink it deep into his gut.

Instinctively, he reacts with a deep-throated growl, eyes flashing red. He seizes me by the back of my neck and tosses me all the way across the courtyard. I crash hard into iron porch furniture and it hurts. Keeps on hurting. Stupid no-longer-instant healing.

I disentangle myself from the furniture. He comes toward me with a concerned, distraught look.

"Oh, honey, I'm so sorry, I didn't know my own strength there, but you came at me with a knife, you have to understand, please."

"Look at the wound."

"What?"

"Where I stabbed you. Check it out."

He looks down, sees the blood. And then, with a look of wonder, runs his fingers over his skin. "It's already almost healed."

"That's right."

A woman strides impatiently out of the main building, dressed in a suit and carrying a large ring of keys. She stops, hands on hips, to give us a stern look.

"I heard that. You loup-garous get on back to y'own place, don't be fighting in my courtyard. And put the furniture back the way you found it!"

She marches inside again. Sheepishly, I start moving the furniture back to its original position, as close as I can remember.

He frowns. "Wait. What was that she called us?"

"Loup-garous."

"That's French, isn't it?"

"Uh-huh."

"For werewolf?"

"Uh-huh."

"Well. Damn. Maybe you are telling me the truth."

"I'M SORRY, I REALLY WASN'T BITTEN BY ANYTHING LIKE A large dog four weeks ago." Our new wolf, Andrew Collins, sits on the couch with a cup of coffee. He wanted butter instead of cream in it for some reason, but seems happy enough to be drinking it. He's wearing one of the dark gray track suits that we keep on hand for new wolves, who usually turn up naked.

"The full moon was October 28," Etienne says. "Does that prompt anything? Do you keep a personal calendar?"

"I know what I was doing. I was in a theatrical version of Dracula. We had two shows that day."

"Did you go to a party or anything afterward? Drink heavily, lose any time?"

"No, I don't do that kind of thing."

"What about sleepwalking?" I ask. "Or stage hypnotists?"

"Stage hypnotists?" Viv gives me an incredulous look. "Abby, where do you get this stuff?"

"Just trying to think of all the ways you might have something happen and not remember. Did you maybe fall asleep in a theater? You know, watching a boring movie or something?"

"Abby, really."

Andrew chuckles. "Not on that night. Two shows kept me pretty busy. Although I think I would still notice getting bitten by a big shaggy wolf creature."

"It does tend to be memorable." Viv nods. Arms folded, she's got what I think of as "Skeptical Lawyer Viv" face on. I think she doesn't believe him about the party and assumes he did get drunk enough to lose time.

"Did you maybe think it was somebody in costume?"

"I would still have noticed getting bitten, hon."

"Hey, how's it going in here?" Nic walks in the door with a big smile and a bag of beignets, which he sets on the desk.

Andrew brightens. "Hello again." He closes his eyes. "My God, you do not want to know how good those donuts smell."

"So have one," Viv says, taking one herself, brushing off the signature powdered sugar that gets absolutely everywhere. "Nic brought plenty."

"I can't." He sighs. "I'm an actor in my later thirties, I can't do carbs at all."

"It was the full moon last night, eat whatever you want."

"Well, I already had all those hot dogs, though."

"Bon Dieu, just eat the donut!" Babette calls out from the stairway. She enters the main room, yawning, grabs a donut herself. "I can't believe I missed all the excitement around here," she grumbles, pouring herself some of the coffee. "Y'all brought in a brand new wolf. What did I do last night? I ate a squirrel and scared a couple of tourists. Hi, I'm Babette." She offers a hand to Andrew, who shakes it, looking a little uncertain.

"Like Abby, she's training with us," Viv explains. "Unlike Abby, she has an active wolf and spent last night en loup, as we say. Or sometimes en morph."

"Oh." Andrew nods but continues to look confused. "So that means…?"

"In wolf form." Nic smiles. "Idiomatically. All the fractured French confuses me too. It's a Louisiana thing."

"You're not from here?"

"Nope, I'm from Berkeley, California. I was visiting New Orleans when my wolf appeared for the first time, though, so I kinda stuck around. Oh, here are your things from the fitness center." He hands him a plastic bag branded with the hotel.

Andrew pokes through it, flips through his wallet, laughs. "Everything seems to be here. But I had two hundred dollars cash in my wallet. Now I have twenty."

Nic chuckles. "That's New Orleans for you. They took your money, sure, but they didn't want to leave you totally stranded."

Viv says, "You might want to get your cards canceled and re-issued anyway, even if they're still in there. Sometimes crooks will take down the information and leave the card where it is so that you don't know right away that it's been compromised."

"Do you want more coffee?" Nic offers.

"How about some with bourbon in it? That's what I'm getting." Babette hops up with her un-bourboned coffee and heads into the kitchen.

"Could I get some water?" Andrew says.

"Sure, sure." Nic looks over at me. I'm standing nearest the water cooler, the old-fashioned kind where the bottle gets put in upside-down and it goes glug-glug-glug whenever you use it. "Abby?"

I give Andrew a cup of water. Nic hands him a pen and a pad of paper. "If you could recall everywhere you went on October 28? Even things like coffee shops. If we go to the location and find a trace of another wolf, that could help figure things out."

"A trace? You mean something like hair?"

"Scent traces, most likely."

"You'd be able to smell something from an entire month ago?"

Nic makes eye contact with Etienne, chuckles. "We could demonstrate. Let's pick just one place you went a month ago, go there together, and show you the way your own scent trail is still there."

"You're coming with me to Idaho?"

"Idaho?" we all say, more or less in unison.

"Yes, Idaho." He laughs. "Why is that so surprising? "

"Because there's no traditional wolf presence there," Nic says. He calls up a map on the computer. "Where in Idaho?"

"Meriwether. Right on the Washington State border."

Viv studies the map. "Looks like a full day's drive from Seattle, it's probably not practical for the maison there to handle it."

Etienne says, "If we set up a temporary maison, it should be a good exercise for the ones in training." He gestures at me and Babette.

"There's a maison in Seattle?" I say. "Why didn't they find me the first time I transformed?"

"Because it wasn't there yet. It's another temporary, set up to deal with the people bitten by George." She sees the look on my face, stops. "You didn't know, did you?"

"No. I guess nobody thought it was worth telling me that I personally started a bitten wolf epidemic in Seattle."

"Hey, cher, I think you need some of this." Babette offers me her coffee, at least half bourbon. I take a small sip and hand it right back.

"This is wolf-strength, Babs, I can't drink it right now. Viv, how many people did George bite?"

"I don't have an exact number on that." She looks down, deliberately evasive. Then she looks up with a forced smile. "Well, Andrew, guess what? It looks like we are going to Idaho with you."

3

THANKSGIVING

"My phone is ringing." I announce this in surprise, because I had forgotten I'm even carrying a phone. It's in one of the pockets of my jumpsuit and is protected by an extremely heavy-duty case. Good thing too, because I'm pretty sure I landed right on top of it when I face-planted on Bourbon Street. It's still intact when I pull it out, Steph calling. "Hello?"

"Hi sweetie. Sorry to call you like this, but you weren't responding to texts. I'm sure you're busy dealing with your new job, but my brother really wants to know if you're joining us for Thanksgiving dinner?"

"Oh, shoot, right, that's today, isn't it? Just a second." I pull the phone away from my ear, glance around at the others. "My Aunt Steph just called to remind me it's Thanksgiving. Are you all okay without me?"

"Of course." Etienne nods. "We've been doing this since before you were born, Abby. Go have fun."

"Thanks." I put the phone up to my ear again. "Steph? I'll be there soon."

o ⚜ o

Nic drops me off in front of Steph's house. Normally I would walk there, but I decided to dress up for the holiday and I'm just as happy not to walk two miles in brand-new ankle boots. For the last month, as I've been training here in town, Viv has made it her business to improve my wardrobe. It's my own fault, really. She made some disparaging remark about my clothes and I said, "Well, I grew up in a cult wearing prairie dresses and getting my head shaved periodically, it's not like I learned anything about fashion." Ever since then I've been her project, whisked around to dressmakers and hairdressers and cobblers. I spent hours one day letting a little old French lady manhandle me in a matter-of-fact way, taking measurements and writing things down in a notebook, insane little details like the circumference of my wrists and the distance from the bottom of my chin to the hollow of my collarbone.

The upshot: I'm wearing nice shoes, a short, tailored dress in warm gray, a vintage swing coat in an eye-popping yellowish-green called "chartreuse," and an actual structured underwire bra. The bra was picked out by the little old French lady with the notebook, so I assume it's supposed to fit like this. But it feels disconcertingly like I've got my boobs stacked up on a display shelf and a metal spike poking into my armpit.

I wave goodbye to Nic, step onto the porch, inhale. The smell of Steph's family is welcoming, but I only called this house home for about three weeks back in August. Since then I've lived two months in Bayou Galene and one month in the New Orleans maison, and I've gotten used to them. No werewolf would ever let me stand on the porch for this long, they'd have already noticed by smell that I was here and thrown open the door. Humans need you to knock, I guess.

I knock.

Steph answers, baby Terry on her hip, although he's getting so big at six months, hardly a baby anymore. He reacts right away, holding out his hands and saying "Bah-bee! Bah-bee!" which is his version of my name.

"Abby!" Steph hands me the baby and envelops both of us in a big hug. "It's so good to see you. Is that a new dress?"

"Yep. Another Aunt Viv special." I hand Steph the baby, step away and twirl around. Viv likes to dress me up a bit like a sixties hipster, in very short A-line dresses and opaque tights. The short skirts are functional in most respects, but I have to be careful how I sit down.

"You know, I'm still not used to you looking so grown up. I keep expecting a skinny little girl, not a gorgeous young woman.'

I blush. "Steph, please."

"I know, I know, your aunties are so embarrassing, aren't we? But you really do look beautiful." Her eyes tear up and she hugs me again. "I was so scared for you after you got hurt last summer. Your family said you would recover, but it was hard to believe it. You seemed so fragile, I was afraid to hug you too hard. And just three months later—well, here you are. A little taller, I think, or is that just the shoes?

"No, you're right. I'm at least an inch taller. Five one and something. They're gonna want me on the basketball team any day now."

Courtesy laugh, then she beckons me inside. "Well, come on. I warn you, it's a full house. My mom's church friends, my dad's musician friends, my brother's hunting friends, and my bartender friends. We are all sworn not to talk politics, national or local, or any other controversial topic. So far, that's left us talking about food and Saints football."

Morgan greets me with a platter. "Abby! I made duck skewers."

"Thanks." I take one. Eat it. There's a long pause, as if he's trying to think of something else to say, or waiting for me to say something. "They're good."

"Well. Thanks. It's nice to see you."

"You too."

He wanders away to offer skewers to another guest. Morgan used to tease me relentlessly about being a vegetarian and I teased him back for being a carnivore, but now that he can offer me a duck skewer and I accept, it feels like we never have anything to say to each other anymore.

Steph's dad greets me next. "Abby, my girl. How's things out there in the bayou with your grandfather's people?"

"Pretty good. But you know I've been living here in town for the last few weeks?"

"You have? Then why haven't you tossed any money in my hat?"

Steph's mom comes up to roll her eyes and kiss his cheek. "Oh, now, Roderick, don't be silly." She shakes her head. "He's been busking on Royal again with some of his buddies. He claims it's better money per hour than he makes with the symphony but I'm not sure I believe him." She takes a look at me. "Miss Abby, you do look sweet in that little dress. Your people know how to take care of you, it looks like."

"They do, Mrs. Marchande."

"You want to help me with the biscuits?" She walks into the kitchen, puts on an apron. I follow, hand her things as she asks for them. Flour, butter, salt.

"Did you do much cooking while you were growing up, Miss Abby?"

"Well, I helped my mother and my older sister sometimes." A visceral memory of picking bugs out of the flour and having my mother say, *no, honey, we just grind them up, it's okay, extra protein.*

I gasp, feeling inexplicably panicky. "Excuse me, Mrs. Marchande, I think I need some fresh air."

"That's all right, I've got things settled here." She looks concerned. "You're turning a little green, did you eat something that didn't agree with you?"

I head out into the yard, where people are smoking and

drinking. All men. Everything at New Harmony, the cult where I was raised, was strictly gendered because of how Father Wisdom interpreted the Bible, using a doctrine called Christian patriarchy. But here in the outside world, things often end up getting gendered almost as strictly, according to rules I haven't figured out yet.

"Miss Abby, isn't it? I'm Pete Landry, remember me from last summer?" I don't, but I nod anyway. "You want a beer?" He holds out an Abita Amber and I take it.

"Thank you." With only men in the yard I get shy about sitting in the short skirt and lean against the fence.

"So, the ladies didn't manage to force you to work in the kitchen, huh?" one of the men says, to general laughter.

"Young people don't do much cooking these days, I hear. You're a millennial, right?"

"I don't know."

"No, she's too young to be a millennial. How old are you, hon?"

"Eighteen." I give the age on my ID card. I'm really closer to sixteen and a half, but when Steph and I went to get me an official legal existence, we made me eighteen to simplify the issue of my guardianship. At the time we thought I had no living parents, and I would hardly want my biological father Leon to have legal custody of me anyway. Steph would have been willing to formally adopt me, but why bother with all the paperwork when I'm going to be eighteen for real in a year and a half?

"Yeah, see, millennials, they're pushing thirty. My kids, now, they're millennials."

"You don't say. Pushing thirty. So, what are you, hon?"

"What am I... what?"

"What generation are you?"

"I don't know."

All the men laugh at that. "She don't know! Generation I dunno!"

"Is that you? Generation I dunno?"

"Sure." I smile tolerantly.

The men continue to chat for a while, mostly about Saints football. I know my Seattle friend Edison has played college football, so I feel like I ought to care, but they're describing games I haven't seen and none of the terms mean anything to me. Although I do stifle a giggle when they mention a position called "tight end." I wonder if that's what Edison played. He does have a very—uh—

Never mind.

Sheila Durocher, one of Mrs. Marchande's friends from church, comes out of the house, puts her hands on her hips and scans everybody in the yard. "Herman, you come on inside, I need you for a minute." She spies me and her eyes narrow. "What are you doing out here, Miss Abby? Drinking and smoking with the men?"

"Drinking." I hold up the beer. "I don't smoke."

"Hmm. You don't cook either, I suppose?"

"Not really."

"Kids your age don't, I hear."

"Well, this is where I came in, see you guys later."

I head back inside, setting the empty beer bottle down. I caught that look from Ms. Durocher. That look that said, "Hey, you teenage floozy, what are you doing out here talking to my husband?" Is that what I get for trying to dress better? A bunch of middle-aged New Orleans wives take one look at my short skirts and underwire bra and conclude I'm trying to steal their husbands or something?

The kitchen is now mostly occupied by Morgan, checking the temperature on a huge turkey. "Hey, Abby. I think we're just about ready to take this baby out of the oven."

"Do you need help?"

"Sure, lay out a bunch of potholders on that part of the counter there so I can put the pan down and let the turkey rest."

I snort-laugh, even while doling out the potholders. "Rest? It's dead, Morgan, it doesn't need any rest."

"It's a cooking term. You can't just start carving right away, the juices will all spill out."

"Juices? What kind of juices? Blood, sweat, tears?"

"Meat juices." He chuckles. "I know you'll eat this turkey but you still have to make it sound disgusting, don't you?"

"Sorry. All the vegetarian propaganda I was raised with, I mean, it's kinda true, right? We are eating the corpse of a dead animal?" I put two fingers to approximate where the turkey's head would have been, then do a little turkey voice. "Help me, it's so hot in here!"

Morgan tries to look stern, then bursts out laughing. "Just, don't do that kind of thing in front of my mom, it'll make her start thinking you're a weirdo again."

"She doesn't think I'm a weirdo now?"

"Not in that dress. She seems to think you're all grown up or something. Like, wow, that Abby has really blossomed into a lovely young lady."

"Blossomed, huh? It's probably the bra."

He laughs again. "Well, I'm sure that's part of it. And the hair, and the dress, and the shoes—I mean, do you remember how often last summer you would simply walk around without shoes?"

"Well, it was August in New Orleans, Morgan. Who wants to wear shoes in August?"

"Good point." He leans against the counter, wipes sweat off his forehead, pours himself a glass of wine, leans against the counter. "So."

"So?"

"Oh, just wondering, how's it going out in the bayou? You're—" He drops his voice. "Living with a whole town full of werewolves, what is that like?"

I laugh. "Pretty normal, actually. I mean, except on the

full moon, they pretty much do what other people do. It's a very small town, though. I prefer being in the city."

Steph comes into the kitchen. "Morgan? I told everybody that we're not having a formal sit-down dinner, because there's too many people to fit around one table. So, whenever you say it's time to cut into the turkey, we'll just start letting people get their food and eat wherever they can find space."

He looks surprised. "But what about the, you know, the giving of thanks?"

"I thought you didn't care about that."

"I don't, but Mom does. Father Landry is here, she always makes him say grace even though he's retired."

Steph glances at me. "Uh. I talked about it with my mother. She, uh, she thought it would be fine to—you know, not have a formal blessing. This year."

I jump in. "Steph, I appreciate the thought, but if you're doing this for my benefit, you don't have to. I'm not going to have a big freakout just because you guys say grace."

"You sure?"

"Yep. Absolutely." I take Terry from her and dance him around the kitchen while he giggles. "Because Terry and I are going to be out in the yard while you do it."

She hugs us. "Thank you, Abby. I think that will be easiest all around."

I head out into the yard, and Terry and I do our favorite thing, which is me walking around and showing him stuff in nature. When he was an extremely fussy newborn I used to do this with him in Seattle all the time, just walk around and look at stuff. And I don't know if he remembers it or not, because six months in a baby's mind might as well be forever, but he seems to appreciate it just as much now as he did then. Look at the tiny lizard, inhale the flowers of the sweet olive tree, pat the soft moss.

Wait. Pere Claude is here.

I take the baby back inside. "Are you all done talking to God in here?"

"We are, and I was just about to come get you, what is it?"

"My grandfather." I hand her the baby and rush to open the front door, reveal Pere Claude standing on the porch wearing a red flannel shirt and carrying a cloth sack in his hands, like a burly Cajun Father Christmas.

"Granddaughter." He welcomes me into his arms, and a bear hug from Pere Claude is astonishingly like being hugged by an actual bear.

"Come in." I lead him into the living room. "You remember my grandfather, Claude Verreaux?"

I'm not sure if Steph's parents actually met him last summer, but they act as if they remember him, and everybody's friendly enough, it doesn't matter much. Terry obviously remembers him, holding out his hands and saying "papa!" which is also what he calls Steph's father.

"May I?" he says to Steph, who hands the baby over with a smile. Terry gets slung up onto the tallest shoulders he's ever ridden around on, shrieking with delighted laughter. After parading Terry around the living room a few times, heavy steps rattling the glassware, he hands the baby back to his mother and opens the sack.

"For your Thanksgiving feast, and the Yuletide to come." He starts pulling out a variety of sausages and smoked meats and seafood, setting them on one of the folding tables. "We make all of these in the traditional way in Bayou Galene, from our own hunting grounds and livestock. This andouille and this boudin should be cooked before eating, everything else can be eaten now. Most of these meats will be familiar to you, however, this one—" He smiles and holds up one round, blackened sausage with a peculiar sharp, musty smell. "Might be unique to our own village. We call it granpere cour boudin, meaning grandfather-heart sausage, and it is, I am told, an acquired taste."

Morgan picks it up, obviously intrigued. "How is it made?"

"It is, to start with, a sausage of blood and organ meats, which these days people find rather unusual. Then it is fermented, which gives it a unique pungency. After that it is smoked. Oh, and it is quite spicy."

"It sounds like a dare!" one of the men calls out, to general laughter.

Pere Claude gives him a tolerant smile. "It is, as I said, an acquired taste. I also brought this." He pulls out a leather-wrapped package. "It is a traditional-style knife that we call the agnara. We have a small forge where it was made." He opens up the package, reveals a curved knife of a style that I know from its use in trauma-morph training. Morgan regards it with a kind of awe.

"This is absolutely beautiful, Mr. Claude. Beautiful." He tests the edge of the blade, winces, sucks his finger. "Is it a cooking knife? A hunting knife?"

"A knife can be used for anything a knife can be used for, no?" He winks. "Now, can I borrow my granddaughter for a moment?"

"Of course," Steph says. "Our dinner today is very informal."

Pere Claude and I leave by the front door to walk around the block. "I will not keep you too long from your party, Abby. But I wanted to congratulate you for your work in bringing our new wolf home alive. It has been a long time since any of us has done that."

"I know. And I'm not sure why the Varger haven't managed it, when the Cachorros—" I stop myself. Last summer, several of the Varger met several of the Cachorros, but it was under very strange circumstances. A massacre engineered by my half-sister Opal, for some Russian mobsters who call themselves the Strigoi, who were hoping to get bitten but not killed by some real loup-garous. Pere Claude and Leon were both shot full of berserker drugs and fought each other in wolf form. But berserker drugs interfere with the memory, so I don't know what either of them recalls about that night. We haven't talked about it much. I get the impression it's a touchy subject.

He nods. "The Cachorros. My son's Los Angeles pack. I know that they count several bitten wolves among their number."

"Have you and Leon been communicating?"

He sighs, shakes his head. "We have exchanged a few emails."

"Is that good?"

"I don't yet know. But, please don't worry, whatever I do, it will be what I think is best for all our people." He gives me a quick one-armed hug. "I hear that Vivienne and Etienne are going to take you to help them set up a temporary maison in Idaho?"

"Oh, they already told you about that? Wow. Any pointers?"

"Based on last night, your instincts in the matter seem good." He smiles. "But do be careful, granddaughter. Until your wolf returns, you are vulnerable to many injuries."

"Until. You all talk like you know for sure that she's coming back. But you don't know."

"I do know." He makes eye contact with me, not quite a dominance contest, but something close, a certain intensity, as his eyes flash red. "Your wolf is sleeping now, as she does in our children before she comes for the very first time. If she had never come before, I would say to you that she was readying herself for her first appearance. All the usual signs are there. Including, I must say, a growth spurt."

"A growth spurt, ha." I roll my eyes. "Some growth spurt, when I'm still the shortest person I know, except for the baby."

"An inch and a half in three months is quite significant,

child." His eyes twinkle. "You are, I believe, very nearly the size of your grandmother when I met her."

"What? My grandmother was short? Why don't people tell me these things?"

"I suppose it never occurred to me you didn't know." Another big bear hug. "You will do well in Idaho. I have every faith in you."

We go back into the house, where we find Morgan and a few of the men daring each other to eat the grandfather-heart-sausage and laughing.

"It's good," Morgan insists. "You just have to wash it down with a beer."

They all stop when Pere Claude enters, and look embarrassed, like naughty children caught in the act.

"Happy Thanksgiving and good Yule to everyone," Pere Claude booms out, and everyone responds with well-wishes in return.

He leaves. Rooms always feel very empty when Pere Claude leaves them.

"So that was your grandfather," Steph's mom says. "A lovely man. We should invite him over more often."

PART II

MERIWETHER

4

AIRPLANE

When I woke up this morning, I was absolutely beside myself with excitement: today is the day I ride in an airplane for the first time. But after almost two hours in traffic and forty minutes standing in this security line, the excitement has started to wear off. I shift position and knock my shoes against the floor. Viv notices. "You still aren't sure about the heels, are you?"

"Well, you know me, I'm not too sure about shoes anyway."

"They're barely heels, Abby. You should see some of the things I've worn."

"I do see the things you wear, Viv. And Babette too. What is it about tall women that you always wear heels to make yourselves even taller?"

Babette grins at me. "Work with what you've got, cher." Today she wears slip-on flats, in anticipation of being made to take off our shoes in the security line. My ankle boots have zippers for quick removal.

Barney and Etienne are with us too, but if they have any thoughts about shoes, they keep it to themselves.

At last we're up at the counter. Vivienne goes first, indicates that we're all traveling together.

"One way to Seattle?" The agent frowns at her boarding pass. "Are you moving there?"

"We're thinking about it," Viv says, smoothly. Actually, we're planning to land in Seattle, buy a used van, and drive to Meriwether.

He nods, as if satisfied, and begins initialing our boarding passes. I'm last in line and when he gets to me, the agent pauses, staring at my ID for a long time.

My heart races. The ID is still fairly new, and it's technically fraudulent, so it always makes me a little nervous to present it for some kind of authoritarian inspection. He holds the ID up to look at it next to my actual face, squints. "You let your hair grow out," he says, finally. When I got the ID three months ago, my hair had been shaved entirely off about three weeks prior, and was still very short and spiky looking. It grows fast, so it's already long enough to start getting in my eyes. "It looks good." He finally hands the ID back to me. "Very flattering."

"Uh. Thanks." Is that normal, to get a compliment from the TSA agent? It seems weird, but maybe he was just trying to make up for being so suspicious about whether it was really me in the ID picture.

I put my suitcase and shoes on the conveyor belt and step through the metal detector. It buzzes. They pull me aside.

"Any change or keys in your pockets, miss? Large pieces of jewelry?"

"No, nothing like that."

A female agent runs a wand over my body. It starts making noise when it passes over the new bra Viv made me wear. The agent sighs. "Right. Sorry, miss, I have to pat you down."

"Oh. Um. Okay."

I hold my breath while she brushes her hands lightly over

my breasts, then nods. "Okay. Don't wear an underwire next time. Try a sports bra instead."

I nod, rush to get my suitcase and shoes from the end of the conveyor belt, hurry to catch up with the others. Now that I'm past security I let some of my frustration show.

"Viv, that bra you made me wear set off the metal detector!"

"It did?" She looks confused, then laughs. "Oh, right, I've heard underwires do that sometimes."

"You knew? Then why did you make me wear an underwire bra to the airport?"

"I'm sorry, little one, I didn't think of it until now. I'm wearing an underwire too. But mine never set off the metal detectors."

"Why did mine?"

"At a guess? It might be made of a different material, or have more metal in it. I did buy you a very nice bra. The finest one Madame Lajaunie had in stock."

"I'm sure you did. But why do underwires even exist, anyway? Who thought it was a good idea to jam a metal rod up under your armpit?"

"Underwire bras exist for the same reason all foundational garments do, which is to help give your body the correct fashionable shape under your clothes."

"But what if I don't care about having the correct fashionable shape under my clothes?"

"It was your words, my dear. 'I don't want to spend my whole life dressing like a weirdo who grew up in a cult.'"

"I don't think those are my only choices, Viv."

"No, of course not, I'm just teasing you." She gives me a quick one-armed hug. "Just be glad I didn't make you wax your legs."

"Wax my legs? Why would I do that?"

"Wax is used to remove the hair, little one. The wax is applied when warm and soft, then hardens at room temperature, so when removed, it takes the hair with it, plucking it out by the root, which gives a smoother finish than shaving."

"Plucks the—Bon Dieu, Viv, that sounds horrible! Doesn't it hurt?"

She chuckles. "Really, Abby, after everything you've been through, getting your legs waxed sounds like it would be too painful?"

"So, what happens—you know, at the full moon?"

She clears her throat. "Not here, Abby."

"Right, sorry, okay."

"I don't wax either," Babette tells me. "What's the point, after all? You just have to do it again."

Barney clears his throat, as if uncomfortable, but doesn't say anything.

When we get to the gate, Viv says, "Let's go up to the counter and see if we can rearrange our seats at all." Since we bought at the last minute, we're all scattered around the plane. Vivienne apparently has a lot of frequent flier miles or some sort of thing, and they offer her, but only her, an upgrade to first class.

"Sorry, little one," she tells me. "You're stuck in that middle seat."

"What's wrong with the middle seat?"

Babette snorts laughter. "Oh, cher, if you have to ask."

"They don't give much elbow room, you see," Etienne says. "You're small enough you might not find them so bad."

"I've got a middle seat too," Barney grumbles.

"Seniority," Babette says. "I snagged an aisle seat and I am not giving it up."

The traffic and security line delayed us long enough that the plane is ready to start boarding shortly after we get there. But boarding seems to take a long time. Viv, in first class, gets on the plane a full twenty minutes before they start loading my section. I wave to her as I pass through first class. When I get to the main cabin, I see what they were all talking about: the seating in the main cabin is two groups of three narrow seats with an aisle down the middle. The middle seat puts you right between two people with no elbow room.

The man with the aisle seat is already there, legs and arms splayed out. He smiles as I approach, sits up straighter. When I reach to put my backpack in the overhead bin, he hops out of his seat. "Wait, let me get that for you." He wrestles the bag out of my hands and shoves it into the overhead bin. I sit down in my seat and the man sits down in his. "I'm Thomas Harrington. You can call me Tom." He shakes my hand. "I know I'm a little old-fashioned, but I just hate to see a petite lady like yourself struggling with those overhead bins designed for tall men like me."

"Abby. Thank you." I give what I sense is the correct response, out of habit, but right away I'm annoyed with myself. Being too nice will just encourage him, and I'm pretty sure I'm not interested in talking to the kind of dude who identifies me as a "petite lady" and wears way too much of some aggressively masculine cologne, a blunt force attack of musk and patchouli. Although Etienne has been coaching me in general scent tracking and identification, Babette has been training me in identifying colognes specifically. This, I think, she would peg as a man who started wearing one of those "body spray" scents as a teenager and never changed his scent habits. Thomas "Tom" Harrington looks about forty to me, graying, clean-shaven, trim figure, moderately well-made gray suit. Because wool jackets need to be dry-cleaned, they often provide a powerful scent record of where people have gone and what they've done while wearing them. Unless I'm way off, I believe Thomas "Tom" Harrington has spent a lot of his time in New Orleans drinking in strip clubs.

Now that we're both sitting down, he relaxes into his seat, splaying out into both the aisle and the arm rest we share. I don't know what the rules of arm rests are, so I don't fight him for it. I just fold my arms and think unflattering thoughts about his cologne.

From my smaller satchel I pull out my travel reading material, one of the *Teen Mode* magazines I picked up when I was at Steph's for Thanksgiving. After they did a profile of me in their September issue, I stayed on the subscription list and they mail one every month to Steph's address. The man leans toward me, bringing a fresh waft of patchouli that I can taste all along the back of my throat. "What are you reading?"

"Uh. This?" I hold up the magazine.

"You're a teenager, huh? What, sixteen, seventeen?"

"Eighteen."

"Are you in school?"

"No, I'm working."

"What do you do?"

"I catch rabid and dangerous animals."

He grins broadly. "No shit? What is that like?"

"Not as exciting as it sounds."

We're interrupted by the arrival of our third person and stand up to let her by. She's an older woman, plainly dressed, a little heavy. Tom gives her a brief look of disdain, then turns that into a jolly smile. "Isn't that always the way, huh? Of course the person with the window seat is the last one to get here."

She gives him a courtesy laugh before dropping into her seat and beginning to rummage for her seatbelt. "Sorry, dear," she says to me, as her elbows invade the space of my seat. "There we go." She locates the other end of the belt and fastens it, then leans against the window, folding her arms to yield me that side of the arm rest, and apparently drops off to sleep right away.

Just a few moments later, the plane begins to move, driving slowly away from the gate. The flight attendants do a pantomime, where they point to the emergency exits and demonstrate things like how to put on the seatbelt and use the oxygen masks if they drop down from the ceiling. Most people aren't paying attention, but I've never seen it before, and I'm oddly fascinated by the small ritualized gestures they make.

They go through the cabin, stop at Tom. "Seat fully upright, sir."

He grunts and puts it up. "I don't know why they make us do that," he says to me. "If we crash, what difference is it going to make?"

The plane starts moving forward swiftly, faster and faster, and I know it must be going more than a hundred miles an hour, but it feels like being in a car. Until the moment when the plane leaves the ground, then it doesn't feel like anything I've ever experienced before. I'm flying. I'm literally flying. I crane around the woman in the window seat and look out, see New Orleans rapidly shrinking below us, the whole city laid out, bounded by Lake Pontchartrain and the Mississippi River.

"Wow," I say. "It's like a map, only alive."

"I remember the first time I was on an airplane," Tom says. "I thought it was the most exciting thing I'd ever seen."

"It's pretty cool."

"Traveling on your own?"

"No, I'm with my aunt, but we bought at the last minute and couldn't get seats together."

He nods thoughtfully. "Well, I'm traveling alone, Abby," he says. "Do you like your aunt?"

That seems like a weird question, and the true answer is way more complicated than anything I want to get into with a stranger on a plane. "Yeah, I guess."

"I bet she likes to tell you what to do, huh?"

"Sure."

"I had an auntie like that," he says. "She acted like my mom sometimes, when my mom wasn't around. What about your mom?"

"Uh. Dead." It feels awkward to say it like that. I probably should have said "passed away" or something.

"I'm sorry to hear that. That's rough, isn't it? Losing a parent so young?"

"It was rough losing my mom."

"What about your dad, is he in the picture?"

I laugh. "Nope."

"You say that like it's a good thing, like you don't want your father in your life?"

"No, I guess I don't."

"Why, what did he do wrong?"

"You know that Temptations song, 'Papa Was a Rolling Stone'? Basically that." And that's only what's wrong with my biological father, my stepfather was even worse.

He chuckles. "I hear you, Abby. My dad was like that too. You know what the Irish call that? They call it playing the wild rover. I'm Irish. What about you? You look Irish, with that red hair and freckles."

"People tell me that, yeah."

"You mean you're not Irish? What are you then?"

"American."

"Oh, a mutt! Yeah, me too."

"I thought you just said you were Irish."

"My name is Irish. But my family comes from all over."

We're interrupted by the arrival of the drink and food service. I order a fruit and cheese box and a ginger ale and he orders two of those little single-serving rum bottles, and a Coke. He pours one of the bottles into his Coke and offers a sip. "You want? Or I could just give you the other bottle to pour into your ginger ale."

"No, thank you."

"Come on, Abby. Your auntie isn't going to know."

I laugh at the idea that I could possibly drink an alcoholic beverage and not have Vivienne notice. Even regular humans typically have no trouble spotting alcohol on somebody's breath, so the idea that one of the Varger wouldn't know is laughably ridiculous.

But wait. All of a sudden, I know what this guy is trying to do. He wants to insinuate himself with me, make me think he's my buddy, and then, when we land in Seattle, he's going to use that to try to get me away from my controlling auntie, take me somewhere it's just the two of us. Maybe all he wants is the chance to pester me for sex, but if he were a serial killer, it would be exactly the same script.

Well, what should I do? I've been reading a lot about serial killers, sociopaths, and criminal predators ever since almost getting killed by my half sister Opal, a serial killer who styled herself the Frat Boy Killer. No matter what this guy wants from me, he's not going to get it, not with Viv and Etienne around. Feeling safe, I'm curious to study his methods.

"Sure, give me the other rum." I pour it into my ginger ale, take a sip.

He smiles triumphantly. First hurdle past. "So, Abby, where did you grow up?"

"I was raised in a cult."

"No kidding? I was raised Catholic. But I don't believe in that stuff anymore. Especially not all the anti-sex stuff. What about you?"

"I don't think you understood me, Tom. I was raised in a *cult*. Place called New Harmony, on a compound miles away from everything. We tended our own sheep and wore these weird little prairie dresses and got tortured regularly, and at the end of July, when the police raided the compound on suspicion of child abuse and homicide, everybody almost suicided like in Jonestown. The big meltdown was the top story on CNN for almost a whole week."

He frowns. His script has clearly been thrown off. Then he laughs, makes kind of a tossing-away gesture. "You're pulling my leg, kid. But I like it. You're a free spirit, just like me."

"I'm not pulling your leg. Tom." The issue of *Teen Mode*

that profiled me is stored on my phone, so I can access it easily, and I pull it up. "See? That's me on the cover."

He grabs my phone, rudely, and looks from the picture to me and back to the picture. "Okay, she kind of looks like you, sure."

"She looks like me because she is me."

"But your hair is so short here."

"Because they shaved it at the cult." I ruffle my current mop. "This is almost four months of growing out."

He flips through the article until he gets to another photograph of me, pauses, flips to the next photograph. He grins and tries to take control of the conversation again. "You look pretty good in these photos, but you look a lot better now."

I can tell I'm supposed to say "thank you" and this will get things back on his preferred track, where he flatters me into doing whatever he wants. Instead I say, "My aunt tells me the same thing."

Awkward pause. "Well. She's right."

"She's often right, but even when she isn't right, she tends to win the argument anyway. She's a lawyer, you know."

"Yeah? A lawyer. Wow. Is that what makes her so bossy?" He grins.

"You've never met her, how do you know she's bossy?"

"You said she was bossy."

"No, I never said that."

A pause, while he tries to gather up the reins of conversation again. "How do you like your drink?"

"It's okay."

"Do you want another one?"

"I haven't finished this one yet."

"I mean, when you've finished that one, do you want another one?"

"I won't know until I've finished this one."

A pause. He's getting annoyed because I'm not cooperating

with his script. But he can't display that he's annoyed, because that will blow the game completely. He inhales broadly and says, "I'm going to Seattle for a business trip. I travel a lot. What about you?"

"I thought we established this is my first time on an airplane?"

"I meant, why are you going to Seattle? Do you live there?"

"No, we don't."

"So what are you doing when you land? Is your aunt taking you to a motel or something?"

"Probably," I say, and realize I'm not sure. Are we going to spend a couple of days in Seattle before picking up the car? Will I have a chance to visit my Seattle friends?

"That sounds boring, doesn't it? Land in Seattle, go right to a motel? Don't you want to go out and have a little fun in town first?"

"What kind of fun?"

He gets eager. This is the sort of question he wants me to ask. "You know, dinner, drinks."

"Tom. I already told you I'm eighteen, you cannot buy me drinks in a bar."

He grins broadly. He's ready to reel me in. "Well, I can buy drinks at a store or something and we can drink them elsewhere."

"Elsewhere like where?"

"Like my hotel room."

"So, that's your idea of having fun in Seattle? I go to your hotel room and drink?"

"Sure. Doesn't that sound fun?"

"I'm not seeing how going to a hotel room with you is any more fun than going to a hotel room with my aunt."

"I'll buy you drinks."

"My aunt will buy me drinks."

He pauses. He hit a roadblock. He fills the pause by flagging down one of the flight attendants for another couple of rum bottles. "You haven't finished your drink," he says.

"No, I haven't."

"If you finish, I'll get you another one."

"You mentioned that."

"Come on, what are you waiting for?"

"You bought me a drink, and I'm drinking it. What's your problem?"

"Nothing. I'm going to the toilet." He gets out of his seat, body language sullen and unsteady, and marches down the aisle toward the bathrooms.

"Dear." The woman to my right is looking at me, eyes open, wide awake. "I noticed that man was being awfully pushy with you. Do you want to switch seats with me?"

"You know, I think I do. It's my first time in an airplane, after all. I want to look out the window. Thank you."

"You're welcome."

When he comes back to his seat, Thomas "Tom" Harrington is visibly angry to find out about the seat switch. He tries to keep up the conversation with me over the head of our companion, but it doesn't work very well and eventually he puts in headphones, angrily, and begins watching one of the inflight movies. I secretly take a picture of his face. He might not be a serial killer, but it couldn't hurt to put him on the Varger watch list anyway. Eventually I fall asleep myself.

5

A SMALL, PIOUS TOWN

*S*he stands on the opposite shore, staring at me with brilliant green *eyes. Her fur is a deep burgundy red, not a natural color, no true wolf looks like that, only the rougarou. She paces back and forth, cut off by the river.*

Call me over, she says. Call me over and we'll hunt together.

Not yet, I say, and I feel sad as I say this, as if I'm letting myself down in some way. But still I say: not yet not yet not—

"Abby, did you want to see?"

Viv's voice startles me and I sit bolt upright in a panic. "What? What's happening? Where am I?"

"You're in a van heading into Meriwether, Idaho. We decided to take the scenic route down the hill, and I thought you might want to see."

I look out the window. We're at the top of a hill and I can see we're on a road that spirals down a steep, mostly treeless hillside into a river valley. "Sure, thanks."

We didn't stay in Seattle long enough for me to visit my friends. The used car place was right next to the airport.

Except for a few bathroom and food stops, we drove straight through the night, Viv and Etienne trading driving duties. Babette and Barney both have licenses, but were just as happy to sleep instead of drive.

I don't know what I expected from Meriwether, but it's still a bit disappointing. Knowing it's not that far away from Seattle, and built at the intersection of two rivers, I was expecting things to be more lush. But it seems treeless and dry, like the landscape through inland California. Just as in New Orleans, everything's already decorated for Christmas, but the themes here seem more openly religious: angels and manger scenes and banners that say things like JESUS: THE REASON FOR THE SEASON or LET'S KEEP THE "CHRIST" IN CHRISTMAS!

"There seem to be a lot of churches here," I say.

Viv, who is driving, glances back over her shoulder at me with a worried look. "Are you bothered by that, Abby?"

"No, of course not. I just thought it was notable." I try to turn it into a joke. "Anyway, if we have to go into a church as part of the investigation, we can make Babette do it."

She lowers her sunglasses to look at me. "Of course, cher. As long as we can make you be the one to get the rats out of the walls."

We drive through the city center, which doesn't take long, then start heading up the hill on the opposite side. The farther up we go, the more dreary the landscape becomes: barren, partially developed, as if intended for grander things it never became. There's a vast paved-over shopping center gouged into the hillside that looks strangely aggressive: piles of blasted rubble, the mountain damaged and wounded. Only about three businesses are open. A sign identifies the plaza as Nez Perce Hills Galleria.

We wind up past a nursing home of low, rambling pink buildings, meander past a closed Walmart and a church that looks like a shopping center. Finally, we drive through an enormous gate into a housing development called Orchard Estates, although I don't see a sign of an orchard, or many trees of any kind. Like the galleria, the development seems only half built and sparsely occupied, sitting on an infrastructure designed for something bigger.

We pull into the driveway of a shambling two-story house. Like the nursing home it's painted in shades of pink, and I think, maybe, it's trying to look like an Italian villa? It has a lot of pillars and arches and vaguely Baroque details: a single row of extremely tall, narrow windows; turret covered in fake bricks; white-painted balcony too small for a person to actually stand on.

We all look at each other in dismay and confusion, then Viv laughs. "Yes, it's a total McMansion, but we're getting it cheap for the amount of space. The rental agents should be inside already."

"Why does the air smell like that?" I ask. "Like... spoiled lunchmeat, maybe?"

"Paper mill," Etienne says. "Sulphur compounds used in manufacturing, probably sulphur hydroxide."

"Is that going to throw off our scent-tracking?"

"I don't think so. When scent-tracking, we already have to ignore any steady background smells, do we not? You have tracked in southern Louisiana, does the smell of the oil refineries make that impossible for you?"

"I guess not. But right now it seems like all I can smell is that damned paper mill."

"Because you dislike it. A strange thing about being a human scent tracker, no? A wolf, a bloodhound, they recognize scents, but don't so much have opinions about them."

I sigh. "Are you telling me I'm doing it wrong, Etienne?"

"No, I was expressing sympathy. We wolves have a divided nature. The human feels disgust or displeasure at many kinds of scents, but the wolf feels only interest, curiosity. Scents are information. Not all information is pleasant."

We walk up onto what I think is the front porch, a large half circle with pillars arranged so close together they make the porch dark and claustrophobic. I notice a place where the stucco crust of the pillar has been broken, and the interior—

"Is that pillar made out of *Styrofoam?*"

"Polyfoam," Viv says, with a smirk. "Styrofoam is a brand name. But, yes, for this type of construction, polyfoam is often used as a decoration element."

"But I don't understand. How can you make a *house* out of that?"

"Decorative elements only."

Etienne laughs. "It is quite the estate, isn't it?"

We knock, and a husband-and-wife real estate team opens the front door, welcomes us inside with big smiles and effusive talk about what a marvelous great bargain we're getting and pushing the paperwork toward Etienne. He frowns at it, nostrils flaring. "Before we sign the lease, we must inspect this house. Babette, you and Abby take upstairs. Barney, the garage and yard. Vivienne and I will inspect the main floor."

The agents seem taken aback, but can't technically object to us wanting to inspect the house before signing a thirteen-month lease. I don't know what they're worried we're going to find. It smells strange in here, not like wood, more like... hand sanitizer? Babette and I climb the grand staircase to the second floor, push open elaborate double doors, get over-whelmed with a dank, moldy smell.

"Bon Dieu," Babette says, nostrils flaring. "They thought they could hide this level of water damage from us?"

"Well, they don't know we're werewolves."

"You do not need a wolf's nose to smell this, cher."

"I suppose not. But I'm still a little surprised a house in an area that seems as dry as Meriwether got enough rain to get water damaged."

She laughs. "The construction seems very poor, maybe one rainstorm was all it took."

We explore the bedrooms and upstairs baths, see some of the obvious signs of mold and water damage, although there are also signs they tried to scrub it away, including that overpowering hand sanitizer smell. The house seemed huge from the outside and does technically have five bedrooms, but many of them are laid out oddly, with sloping ceilings more appropriate for an attic room, little cubbies and nooks that make even large bedrooms seem claustrophobic.

"This window doesn't even open, cher, look!"

"Oh, this is where you get to that balcony that isn't big enough to stand on. Why would you build something like that?"

"This bathroom is huge! But notice how the floor seems spongy? I would be afraid to take a bath in here, I'd think the bathtub might burst right through the floor!"

We join the others downstairs, where the agents are slumping, defeated, in their pastel suits, while Viv and Etienne negotiate a lower rental price.

WITHOUT FURNITURE, AND WITHOUT WANTING TO VENTURE upstairs, we camp out in the living room, eating takeout pizza and a couple of whole, small, roasted chickens from the grocery store. I get a text from Andrew:

> Back in Meriwether, should I come over?

"Andrew's back home, Viv, should he come over right away?"

She nods, I text back with the address, and about twenty minutes later, Andrew walks up to the porch and I throw open the door, eager for a new distraction. "Andrew, welcome to the maison. You know everyone here."

"I do." He nods. He enters with a slight smile on his face.

"Orchard Estates, really? Do you know the history of this development?"

"Native burial ground?" Babette suggests.

She's joking, but he nods. "As a matter of fact, yes. The whole hillside was claimed by the Nez Perce tribe to be sacred land, but a federal court ruled against their claim. Then, when this development was started, they found human remains. Nobody could prove the remains belonged to members of the Nez Perce tribe, and it didn't change the federal ruling at all, but it seemed to sink nearly all the planned development for this hillside. The shopping center was never completed. The Walmart was completed but went out of business. And Orchard Estates—well, you can see for yourselves."

"We're here for thirteen months," Viv says. "I've spent longer in worse places. So, Andrew, how are you doing?"

"Well, I have to admit, until I walked up here, I was half convinced that everything in New Orleans was a dream."

"It's like that at first," I say. "Your brain just sits there going 'I'm a werewolf, seriously?' on endless repeat. Like it can't possibly be real. But it is real, so eventually you do get used to it."

"Have some wine," Babette offers. "It's pink and it has a screw top and I got it at the gas station convenience store, but it's making my day better."

Andrew shakes his head with a small smile. "No, thank you. But I'll have some of the chicken, if you don't mind?"

"Of course not." Viv pushes it toward him.

He pulls off a drumstick, digs in. "Oh, my God, thank you for this. I didn't know how hungry I was until I smelled the chicken. They never have any decent food on airplanes anymore." After he's finished the drumstick and a wing and another drumstick he pauses. "Do you know, do people like us have special dietary requirements?"

Viv smiles at him. "Meat protein." She gives me a sidelong look.

"I don't have a wolf right now, Viv, don't hassle me. Anyway, Andrew, don't you already do some kind of low carbohydrate or paleo type of diet?"

He nods. Viv says, "The buttered coffee was a dead giveaway."

"I do the Centurion Diet. It's a Hammerfit thing. Hammerfit is my gym."

"Hammerfit. Is that like Crossfit?"

"Yes and no. We do a workout with sledgehammers, which I've never seen anywhere else." He pauses. "Is there a recommended fitness routine for people like us?"

Viv looks thoughtful for a moment. "I don't know if this is true for bitten wolves, but born wolves often find that we really enjoy recreational combat against other wolves. That could be tough for you, to find other wolves."

"I'm sorry, did you say, 'born wolves'?"

Everybody stops. Looks at each other. You can almost hear the record scratch.

"You didn't know?" Viv says.

"Obviously not. I don't understand, how can you be born like this? From a mother who was bitten?"

"I'm not aware of that as a possibility," Etienne says. "When we say born, we mean, genetic. Inherited. But we don't start transforming until young adulthood."

I raise my hand. "That's where a lot of the bitten wolves come from. A wolf raised by outsiders, so they don't know what's going to happen, and they transform for the first time somewhere crowded."

He looks thoughtful for a moment, then smiles. "Abby, is that what happened to you?" I nod. "Biter or bitee?"

"Um. Biter."

"So you were raised on the outside. That's why your accent is different. Like Nic."

"An awful lot like Nic, actually. We had the same biological father."

Vivienne gestures at herself, me, Etienne, Babette. "We are all born wolves."

"I'm not." Barney holds up his hand. "I mean, I'm not a wolf. My father married into the pack when I was a little kid. I have a wolfy younger sister, and a brother who's too young for a wolf anyway, but my father is wolfless like me."

"What? I assumed you were one of the born wolfless." I goggle at him. "Your father married into the Varger and he never became a bitten wolf?"

"Of course not. Why would his own wife bite him?"

"I can't believe this hasn't come up before. That seems so weird—what's it like growing up among all these werewolves, knowing you'll never be one of them?"

"I never experienced anything else, so... anyway, you're one to talk, it doesn't get much weirder than growing up in a hyper-Christian torture cult."

"Maybe. But everybody knows Christian weirdos exist, not everybody knows about werewolves."

He laughs. "Everybody I know, knows about werewolves."

Andrew's nostrils flare. "I can smell the difference between wolf and not-wolf, it seems. But I'm not sure if I can tell bitten from born. Should I be able to? Is there a difference? Can all of you tell?"

Etienne smiles. "Scent acuity is highly variable even among our own people."

"To me, all wolves are very peppery, but bitten wolves are a little more sulphur," I explain.

"Sulphur?" Andrew looks dismayed, smells his own armpit. "My God, I smell like the pulp mill? That's terrible!"

"No, no, that's not what I meant at all," I say. "You smell fine. It's just, if I'm trying to identify how you smell different from a born wolf."

Babette jumps in. "You know the art of parfumerie, yes? You sometimes wear Santal 33 from Le Labo, I notice, which is quite a high-end scent."

He nods. "I got it on a trip to New York. But I haven't put it on for days, I didn't even bring it to New Orleans, how did you——" He shakes his head. "Never mind, I just realized this whole time you've been talking confidently about picking up smells from a month ago. You smelled it in my clothing, my luggage."

"Correct." Babette smiles. "Well, in perfumes, not all the smells are sweet, taken on their own. Some are musk or sulphur or ammonia or dirt or mold, so strong that if you were to smell a vial of just that——" She pantomimes smelling something and then retching. "But in a perfume that uses it properly, without it, the perfume would be insipid. It would lack punch and depth and savor, like a Thai curry without fish sauce or a clam chowder without clam nectar. Do you understand?"

He laughs. "I don't eat clam chowder, but your point is taken. You're telling me I don't have to worry that everyone I flirt with from now on is going to think, 'My God, you smell terrible?'"

"Not at all." Babette puts an arm around his shoulders and leans in with an air of camaraderie. "Cherie, the smell of your sweat will intrigue, not repulse. I guarantee it. Your love life will be more successful than you ever could have dreamed. However, you might want to shift your cologne choices. I trained in Paris, I can help you with that."

Viv sighs. "Babette, can we focus, please? Andrew. We have the list you made of your activities during the day of the last full moon. Can you help us map those properly onto the actual locations?" She gestures toward the wall, where she's pinned up a gas station map of the area, covered with a sheet of plastic so we can draw on it.

"Of course. Well, let's see. The coffee shop I went to is here…"

We spend a while tracing his locations onto the map with a red marker. Assuming his memory is accurate, we get about six places to check and start making concrete plans for how we're going to do that.

Something occurs to me, and I raise my hand. "Viv? Etienne? Have you considered that he might have been exposed by a trauma morph?"

They give each other looks of horror. "No," Etienne says. "As a matter of fact, that had not previously occurred to me."

"I'm sorry, trauma morph?" Andrew frowns, shakes his head, finally takes some of the wine from Babette. "What are you people talking about now?"

"Sorry, werewolfing with these guys is just full of insider jargon," I say, with a smile. "Their, uh, their pack has been around for more than three hundred years. They've got special terms for everything. What they call a trauma morph is a werewolf who also transforms when badly injured, not only at the full moon. A trauma morph might have bitten you at any time in the last month, not just during the full moon."

He looks thoughtful for a moment, then shrugs. "I don't remember being bitten by a large dog on any other day either."

"But it means we have to widen the search a great deal." Etienne sighs. "You could even have been exposed in New Orleans!"

Andrew looks pained. "Are you seriously asking for a list of everywhere I went for the entire past month?"

"Why don't you check your credit or debit card report?" Viv suggests. "Unless you pay cash for everything?"

"No, most of the time I use a debit card." Small smile. "Except for a few select businesses that only take cash. It's, um, sometimes it's hard being a gay man in such a small, pious town."

"Gay bar, sex toy shop, or strip club?" Babette asks.

"Babette!" Etienne says.

"What? You all know that's what he's talking about.

Right?" She turns to Andrew. "That is what you're talking about?"

He laughs. "Bar. A small place I quite enjoy, but the owner doesn't want, as he puts it, 'the man' to have an accurate record of who went there at what time. So, he doesn't take credit cards."

Babette continues, "Do you ever go to a sex toy shop or strip club here in town? And can you tell us where they are?"

He chuckles, blushes, shakes his head. "I only do that kind of thing on trips to New Orleans, hon. But not on this particular trip." To Viv he says, "I'll work on an extended list. It's a small enough town, the extended list might be identical except for the New Orleans locations." He winces. "Oh, and my visit to Seattle, that was right after the last full moon."

"Seattle?" My heart leaps. If we have to do some tracking in Seattle, maybe I'll get to see my friends there after all.

Viv sees my reaction and smiles. "I saw that look, Abby. If we do end up sending people to Seattle, I don't see why it can't include you."

"You know, we drove all night to get here, and I'm already feeling tired," Etienne says. "Andrew, why don't you go back to your home, and we'll reconvene here tomorrow morning?"

Andrew nods. "What time?"

"Eleven," Babette says.

"Eight," Viv says.

"How about nine-thirty?" Etienne suggests.

"All right." Andrew nods. He smiles, but he's nervous. "Thank you all for your help." Hugs, then he leaves, struggling for a moment to close the slightly out of skew front door.

6

HAMMERFIT

The next day, as a group, all four scent trackers plus Andrew run through everything he did on October 28, in geographic rather than chronological order:

The house where he lives.

The grocery store where he shops.

The school where he teaches.

His favorite coffeeshop.

The theater where he played Dracula.

"Viv, why are we all trooping around as a whole pack? Wouldn't we cover more ground if we split up?" I wonder out loud.

"Don't split up! That's how the axe murderer gets you," Babette jokes.

"In a larger town, or with a tighter deadline, we would split up as you're suggesting. But Meriwether is so small, and you and Babette are still training, so we're doing it this way."

We start heading to the final location, Andrew's gym, Hammerfit. All of us pick up on it right away. "What is that?" Andrew frowns, nostrils flaring. "It's—it's wolves, isn't it?"

"Wolves." Etienne nods. "Bitten."

Viv smiles. "Well. If there are bitten wolves who go to

your gym, that could certainly explain your exposure, couldn't it?"

"Could it?" I wonder. "People in gyms don't generally bite each other, do they?"

"And why are there so many bitten wolves at this one gym, anyway?" Babette says. "Did they send out a memo?"

"The scent trace is the memo," Etienne says. "I've seen this happen before. Bitten wolves form a kind of—a kind of found pack, I suppose you'd say—based on noticing each other's trails."

Andrew frowns. "And these packs, are they—what are they like?"

"Usually very supportive." Etienne is reassuring. "They get together in order to help each other."

Andrew takes a deep breath and pushes open the doors of Hammerfit. We follow him into a large reception room transformed into a demented Roman fantasia, with columns of fake marble, statues, more of that pasted-on decoration that I now know is made of polystyrene foam.

But Andrew seems happy to be here. "Lauren, hi!" he says to the receptionist, a perky blonde with a smooth tan and a bouncy ponytail, long legs in white shorts.

"Mr. Collins, hello," she says with a bright smile. Then she frowns at the rest of us. "And these people are?"

"Friends of mine, Lauren." Big smile. "They're in town for a while, can we get them all temporary memberships?"

"All of them?"

"We're starting a franchise of the Snarlaway Rabid Animal Control Company," Vivienne says.

Lauren frowns for a moment, then gets a big, I'm-getting-a-commission smile. "Would you like a company membership?"

And that's how the Snarlaway Company of Meriwether, Idaho gets a group Hammerfit account at the full Emperor level. Viv looks frowny for a moment, presumably at the price, then shrugs and signs the paperwork. "We're saving enough on the rental, this should be fine."

"Welcome to the ultimate fitness experience." Lauren hands each of us our badge, various pamphlets, and a copy of a slim book: HAMMERFIT: THE DIETS. The front cover resembles the lobby design, Roman motif of columns and grapes surrounding a white statue of an extremely athletic-looking, half-naked man.

"That's where I got the Centurion Diet, but they have others," Andrew taps the cover.

"You know back in Roman times those statues would have been painted in bright, even garish colors," Babette says.

I flip it over, check out the back. "Viv, look!" I show her the authors and founders of Hammerfit, Roman and Rufus Hammond, two large, golden-haired men who look astonishingly like young and extremely fit versions of Pere Claude.

"Bon Dieu." She flips over her own copy of the book. "You don't think—more of your half siblings?"

Lauren speaks up with a practiced air. "Roman and Rufus Hammond are local boys with a passion for fitness who made good, born and raised right here in the Meriwether area."

"Are they still here?" I ask.

She frowns, sighs. "They recently moved out to be closer to Seattle, where they're opening a new Hammerfit, part of their deluxe spa clubs opening in larger western cities." She smiles big. "But they still come out here often. It is their hometown."

I whisper to Viv, "The Seattle maison, can they try to make contact?"

"We'll see," she whispers back.

Andrew smiles. "I'll show them around, Lauren, you don't have to do it."

She smiles. "Thanks, Mr. Collins."

We scan our badges and the door unlocks. After three months recovering from my injuries, then training to be on the

track and chase teams, I'm familiar with the general parameters of a gym: elliptical machines, treadmills, stair climbers,
stationary bicycles. The Roman fantasia theme persists, with
statues, columns, fountains, pretend grape vines. I can see
from the expression on Viv's face that she's suppressing an
urge to mock. Eventually she leans over to whisper, "It's like a
gym theme park."

I snicker, even though my only experience at a theme park
was the ruined Six Flags in New Orleans that the Cachorros
were using as a base of operations last summer.

We follow the strongest wolf scent trails to one of the
classrooms. Andrew says, "This is where they do the sledgehammer workouts. See, there's a code lock. You type in the
code, there's a warning, then a ten-second delay before the
door unlocks. That way everybody inside knows to stop for a
moment, make sure a stray sledgehammer doesn't hit you in
the head."

"It also gives them a chance to stop doing anything suspiciously wolfy before outsiders see," I observe.

Andrew types in the code and the door buzzes. Ten
seconds later it buzzes again. We enter what seems to be a
Varger-style sparring room, with padding on the walls,
although they don't go so far as to have a padded ceiling. It's
thick with bitten wolf smells of memory, plus the two men
currently in the room.

They watch us enter, postures wary and nostrils flaring.

"Oh my God," says one of them, a smallish man with
graying brown hair and a demeanor that screams 'accountant.' "Who *are* all you people?"

7

THE PACK

"We call ourselves the 'hammerpack,' I know it's cheesy, but we try to have fun," a Hammerfit wolf named Melissa is telling us.

We managed to convince the first two Hammerfit wolves that the rest of us meant no harm, so they called the final member of their little pack and we gathered at the nearby Dante's Underground, the bar portion of a fancy-ish restaurant called Butcher's Steak House. Both the bar and the restaurant are decorated like a 1950s Italian restaurant, with deep mood lighting and red booths of studded fake leather. The bar is a few steps down from the restaurant and is even darker than the restaurant, with no windows. A small plaque on the wall explains its history as a speakeasy.

I'm too young to be in here, but since I didn't ask for any booze, just an espresso, our server gave me a knowing nod and moved on.

"And you swear you weren't bitten?" Etienne says. "This is extraordinary."

Melissa shakes her head. "Nope. It was a ski trip. I was on a retreat and got snowed in with one of my co-workers. She told me exactly what was going to happen, but, you know how you can't possibly believe it until you've seen it? When she tried to leave, I thought she was just nutty from cabin fever. That's how I got scratched up so bad, because I was fighting with her when the moon came."

"Did her saliva get into the cuts?" I ask.

She shrugs. "Maybe. I didn't notice. I had other things on my mind."

"When I was bringing in Andrew, I noticed, at a certain point, that I was absolutely covered in his saliva."

Andrew snickers at me. "Sorry about that, hon." He's seemed a lot more relaxed since starting to make friends with the hammerpack.

I smile back. "It's fine, buddy. It's just, I remember, even at the time I was wondering what would have happened if I were an exposable human. There was just so much…slobber."

The hammerpack and Babette all laugh uproariously at that, but Etienne and Vivienne look troubled. Etienne shakes his head. "Well, this is extraordinary. I suppose it makes sense, but we have no record of a saliva-to-cut transmission happening before."

"Where's your co-worker now?" I ask.

"She relocated to Los Angeles, to work in the new Hammerfit there. We said we'd stay in touch but of course we haven't. I think I do have contact information if you'd like to talk to her?"

"We would like that, yes," Viv says. "Would the rest of you mind sharing how you were exposed?"

Kevin Bell, the accountant type who was in the room when we first arrived, speaks up. "I was in Seattle when it happened. I had gone there for a concert." He gives us all a slightly nervous look. "And then I, uh, I…"

"You were picked up for drunk driving, man, don't beat around the bush." His friend Francisco, who was in the spar-ring room with him, is stern in words, but pats him on the back in a sympathetic fashion.

Kevin buries his face in his hands for a moment, then raises his head with an almost defiant look. "Yeah. Okay. I'll own it. I was heading home from the concert, and I got picked up by the police for drunk driving."

"Oh no," I say. "You were bitten during the prison riot, weren't you?" He nods. "Bon Dieu, that makes you my wolf grandson!" Everybody laughs at that. "I'm so sorry."

He laughs. "Don't be sorry, kid. I've been okay." He holds up his drink. "I mean, I can drink now. Without—well, you know. It barely does anything. I still go through the motions, mostly out of habit."

"My friend, if you want to know how to get truly looped as a loup-garou, talk to me, I've got—"

"Babette, no!" I say. She rolls her eyes, but goes silent and sits back in the booth, takes a defiant sip of her gin and tonic.

Francisco says, "Me, I was in San Diego. Newly arrived to this country from Mexico City and a little disoriented. The next day there were some people like you, experienced wolves, who helped me. But I was already planning to meet family here, so I didn't stay. I suppose I was the anchor of the hammerpack. The first one, who drew the others to me."

"What about you, Andrew?" Melissa asks.

"I don't know how I was exposed. I went to New Orleans to escape my family for Thanksgiving, as usual, and I woke up —like this."

Francisco looks shocked. "New Orleans? How on earth did you survive the rougarou?"

"Hey, sitting right here." Babette slurps loudly from her drink.

"You?"

"Of course me. Rougarou, that's just what the Cajuns call us, you know? Anyway, how did you hear about us?"

"I'm not sure. It must have been in San Diego. I heard that the New Orleans pack was called the rougarou and that you were very territorial and very deadly."

Babette laughs. "But so are all wolves, isn't that right? When we walked into that sparring room, that was your territory, yes? And you were ready to try to kill us, were you not? Until we convinced you we were not a threat. And now, here we are, all having drinks as friends." She plunks her drink down, loud, and catches the eye of our server. "Another round for the table. On me."

Etienne says, "Babette, it's not on you, it's on Pere Claude."

She shrugs. "If he wants to argue with me over the cost of one round of drinks, he's welcome to do that."

Etienne shakes his head, sighs. "Very well. I suspect, Francisco, that the caution was well meant. Had you visited New Orleans in human form, we might have kept an eye on you, or even made contact. But if you had become a wolf there, while we also were wolves? Especially if we had not made contact previously? We might well have fought. With deadly consequences."

Francisco thinks for a moment, then nods. "I think I see the issue. Yes."

A moment of uncomfortable silence. Then Babette raises her glass. "Well, you all survived that first moon, did you not? And there's very little to threaten you now. So, cheers."

The hammerpack clinks glasses with her and we move on to talking pleasantly about random things. As the evening starts to feel like it's winding down, Etienne speaks up.

"Members of the hammerpack—will you help Andrew through future moons?"

"Hell yeah," Kevin says, prompting a brief group hug involving only Hammerfit wolves. "We have a cabin in the mountains. It's nice. The only challenge is that full moons don't always occur on the weekend."

"Weekend." Andrew frowns. "Shoot, I'm an actor, what am I going to do?"

"Understudies?" Viv says. "I've worked as an actor, and

unless things are really different these days, they're just grateful to have somebody show up when they're supposed to, sober and knowing their lines. Full moons are easy to schedule around. And you're unlikely to need any other kind of sick leave, so it balances out."

Andrew looks intrigued. "We don't get sick?"

The hammerpack all look at each other. Melissa says, "Wow. You know, I really can't remember the last time I got a cold or anything. I never even thought about it being related to the wolf."

Etienne holds up his hand. "I haven't transformed for five years. I got a cold or something a few months ago. I lost a good portion of my sense of smell for a few days. It was the worst experience of my life. But it had never happened before."

"You haven't transformed?" Andrew frowns. "Did you mention that? How is that possible?"

"It can happen when you get shot in the head at close range," I say, miming the bullet going into the back of my head where I still have a small scar. "Which happened to me. Is that what happened to you, Etienne?"

"A metal spike got driven through the back of my head during a fight." Etienne gestures at me. "Because Abby is still very young, we assume her wolf is coming back fairly soon. Mine, we assume is never coming back. After thirteen moons with no transformation, that's when we assume it's permanent. Abby has only been wolfless for three moons."

The Hammerfit wolves goggle at us. Francisco says, "So, neither one of you is transforming right now?"

"No," I say. "And the crazy thing is that if you don't transform for a prolonged period, you start to lose your superpowers."

The hammerpack and Babette laugh, but Viv rolls her eyes. "Abby, really."

"Well, what would you call them?"

"Gifts of the wolf, as I believe you know."

"Right. And those gifts are superpowers. Aren't they? Enhancements in strength, speed, senses, and healing?"

She sighs. "It's not that you're wrong, exactly." She shakes her head. "You've talked to my father. You know he believes 'superpowers' is the wrong way to look at what we are. Reductive. Disrespectful to the spirit of the wolf."

"I know that, and I see his point, but most people these days understand what 'superpowers' means. You know, they've seen all the comic-book movies. They get the idea that powers bring responsibilities. They understand the idea of having that one kryptonite thing."

The hammerfit wolves nod. "Silver," Melissa says.

Now it's my turn to goggle. "I meant the 'what am I going to do during the full moon?' kryptonite. Silver doesn't do anything."

Melissa takes out one of her earrings, holds it in her palm. "Silver doesn't kill us, I know, but these are stainless steel for a reason."

"No." Viv has an expression on her face of somebody whose mind is being blown. She takes out one of her own earrings. "These are silver. They do nothing."

"But silver jewelry causes irritation," Melissa says.

"And ingestion causes great discomfort," Francisco says.

"When would you eat silver?" I ask.

"Oh! Those little balls they put on pastries sometimes?" Babette guesses.

Francisco nods.

"But silver doesn't *do* anything," Viv says, and the expression on her face is pure "existential crisis."

Kevin sighs. "Here. I'll show you." He picks up one of the silver-plated butter knives that has been sitting at the table, unused, since we didn't order food. "Just holding it like this, it would take several minutes for anything to happen. But if I do this—" He picks up a steak knife with a wooden handle and makes a shallow cut in his wrist, then quickly inserts the silver-plated butter knife. He grimaces in pain, and his skin reacts by turning red and blistering. He drops the silver knife and the cut heals, but the skin remains raw and irritated.

"Bon Dieu." I'm as gobsmacked as Vivienne. "I made that exact same test when I realized what I was. Nothing happened." A thought occurs. "Say, do any of you have crippling obsessive-compulsive counting disorder or frog-phobia?"

They look at each other, then burst out laughing.

"No, just the silver."

"It must be bitten vs. born," I say. "Right?"

"That's a good working hypothesis," Etienne says.

"What if we added something like colloidal silver to the sedation mix?" I say. "It sounds like it wouldn't kill a bitten wolf, but it might make you less fighty?"

"You know," Babette says, slurping her drink. "It seems to me that perhaps—just perhaps, mind you—it would be beneficial if we all spent a bit more time comparing notes with other wolf groups."

General nodding, then Vivienne speaks up, seemingly to change the subject. "It sounds like everyone in the Hammerfit pack has your wolf really under control. None of you exposed Andrew without knowing it."

"I don't see how it could have happened, no," Francisco says.

"But somebody must have exposed him. Have you all ever noticed any other wolves in town? Not any of us, but also not a member of your own pack?"

"Sorry. No," Francisco says, and the others nod.

Viv and Etienne look at each other and sigh. "All right," Etienne says. "Thank you all so very much for talking to us like this. We will be in town at least thirteen moons, looking for the source of Andrew's exposure and also seeking to control any new wolves who might be a result of the wolf who exposed him."

The server shows up. "Sorry, guys, it's a weeknight, we're closing up pretty soon."

"Absolutely." Babette takes the bill. "Thank you so very much." She looks at it, whistles. "We should always drink in small, pious little towns, the booze is so cheap."

8

SNARLAWAY

We go back to the maison, where Barney has spent the day setting up the Snarlaway Office: wifi, computers, desk, phone, big screen for teleconferencing, coffee maker. He's playing a video game on the big screen, wearing headphones, and doesn't notice us enter at first. He catches us out of the corner of his eye and startles, ripping off the headphones and tumbling out of his chair.

"Bon Dieu, don't sneak up on me like that! These noise-canceling headphones really work, by the way. Abby, I left you a note over on the desk, you have a Snarlaway job tomorrow."

I pick it up. "Tomorrow? But we're not even advertising yet, how did we already get a Snarlaway job?"

"It was a wrong number, but when I answered 'Snarlaway Rabid Animal Control' they talked about having a black widow problem."

"Ugh, why is it always spiders?"

"Because people are afraid of spiders," Babette says, unscrewing another bottle of pink wine from the convenience store.

Viv picks up the headphones, inspects them with a frown. "Barney, did you pay full price for these?"

"It's on the expense sheet."

"There's an expense sheet?" I ask. "Should I be entering things into an expense sheet?"

"You're under twenty-one, Abby," Viv says. "Giving you access to the company credit card would have involved certain awkward changes to the paperwork, so we didn't. When you need to purchase things, we give you cash and that goes into a 'petty cash' line item on the expense sheet. Barney, are we fully ready for remote conferencing with other maisons?"

"Sure," he says. "Isn't it a bit late back in New Orleans though? Shouldn't we call in the morning?"

"We call now," Vivienne says. "Pere Claude, Nicolas at the French Quarter maison, and we should bring in Theo at the Seattle maison too."

"Got it." Barney grabs the keyboard and mouse and begins to pull the other locations into a group conference. Pere Claude leads the meeting, even though his satellite connection seems to be glitching a bit, with sound and picture stutters and delays.

Pere Claude says, "Meriwether maison, you have a day of investigation to report?"

"We do," Viv says. "We have discovered many things, although not our primary objective, how Andrew was exposed. His preferred gym turns out to be home to a small group of bitten wolves, and they welcome him as one of them. However, their wolves are all well under control. They spent last moon in the wilderness and did not expose anyone."

He considers, nods. "What else?"

I speak up. "There's a bitten wolf at Hammerfit who was scratched, not bitten."

Nicolas frowns. "Saliva to bloodstream is the only vector we've ever found."

"You can get saliva in a cut, Nic."

"Enough to cause a transforming wolf?"

"Obviously, since it happened. She was fighting with her

co-worker when the moon rose, and got scratched by her claws, so it was probably a fairly deep cut. I've fought a bitten wolf, it got really messy."

He nods. "All right. We'll add that to our understanding of transmission vectors. But it still doesn't seem to explain Andrew?"

"No," Vivienne says. "But we learned something else quite astonishing. Silver apparently sickens the bitten."

"No," Nic says. "Really?"

"Well, the Hammerfit pack members at least all report such an effect. It may not be universal."

"Viv, tell them my idea about the colloidal silver."

"Oh. Yes." She gives me one of those looks that says, "You're out of line but technically correct so I'll let it go this time." "Abby had the idea that if we add colloidal silver to the sedation mix we use for newly appearing wolves, it would do nothing to the born, but might make the bitten easier to control. As you know, the biggest challenge with the bitten is that, especially on their first moon, they are extremely difficult to sedate."

Pere Claude draws in breath, a sign that he's thinking, and we all go quiet. Then he speaks. "I believe that is a good idea to explore. But I am somewhat concerned it might affect the born in ways we do not anticipate. Theo, what is your thinking?"

Theo is a medical doctor. He too thinks for a long moment, then speaks. "I would hate for this to be the way we discover that injected colloidal silver is actually harmful to the born under certain circumstances."

"Well, can't we test it?" I say. "If a born wolf injects a whole bunch of colloidal silver and nothing happens, doesn't that tell us it's safe?"

"Not necessarily," Nic says. "The sedatives tend to be used on the first moon only, and that might change the equation. We still don't really know if it makes a difference for the wolf to be sedated at all on the first night. There's some evidence that it might make the wolf less powerful, permanently."

"What? Why? How would that even work?"

"We don't know how exactly it would work, there's just some evidence that it might work that way. But our numbers are too small to be certain."

"So, what you're saying is, we don't know if the sedatives themselves are harmful, so we're not going to add silver to them because we don't know if that's harmful either?"

My frustration is obvious, and Nic gives me one of his "tolerant big brother" looks. "Abby, we didn't say no. We're just being cautious."

Pere Claude says, "Very well, the silver matter is under investigation. Nic and Theo, I expect you to work together to determine whether adding colloidal silver to the standard sedation mix would be safe and effective."

"Look what else we found," Viv says, holding the back of HAMMERFIT: THE DIETS up to the camera. "These are the founders of Hammerfit."

"Oh, my," Pere Claude says. "Sons of Leon, do you think?"

"We do think," Viv says. "Theo, they're setting up a Hammerfit in Seattle. If it's open for business, you should see if it's become a haven for bitten wolves. Also, we heard the twins recently moved to the Seattle area, so if you could track them down for a chat, that would be great. At their age it seems unlikely the twins themselves would be direct vectors of exposure, but if they've created any bitten wolves more recently, that could be our source for Andrew."

"We'll do that," Theo says. "Thank you."

There's a pause. "Does anyone have anything else to say?" Pere Claude asks. "Three of you at Meriwether are apprentices, do you have any thoughts?"

"The wine selection here is bad." Babette holds up her pink bottle.

"The wifi is okay," Barney says. "Not great."

Everybody looks at me. *I kinda hate it here*, are the words that tumble across my mind, but I suppress them. "I, uh, it's interesting to train for scent tracking in a town with a paper mill."

o ⚜ o

THE BLACK WIDOW, IT TURNS OUT, IS A SINGLE ARACHNID, though a fairly large one. Unlike the brown recluse, the black widow strikes me as pretty: its carapace is an intense glossy black and the lurid red-orange of the telltale hourglass stands out against it with stunning vividness. It's living in a planter outside the front door, so instead of blasting it with the brown recluse concoction and sucking it up into a shop vac, I capture it in a mason jar.

"Oh my God, oh my God, oh my God," says the young woman, recently married, I think, based on the wedding detritus I glimpse and the pointed way she calls herself "MRS. Joel Camper." "I can't believe you just went right up to it like that and put it in the jar, aren't you afraid of getting bitten?"

"I'm immune. It's part of why I have this job." Although, come to think of it, I don't know that even a fully functioning wolf would insulate me from the effect of spider venom. I should ask.

"You didn't spray it or anything."

"We try to use non-toxic methods whenever possible."

"And you're taking it somewhere in the jar?"

"Well, when we set up a franchise in a new city, we like to track the creatures we encounter and find out what we can about them. It really helps us know what to expect."

She nods, smiling. "You're really good. The man on the phone said you take cash?"

"We do." I pause, realize I never asked Barney what this particular job was supposed to cost.

"All right. Here's forty. Thirty-five, plus a five-dollar tip."

"Thank you very much, Mrs. Camper." I stuff the money into a pocket of the green jumpsuit. "You're our first customer here in Meriwether and I hope this bodes well for our business here."

There's an awkward pause, then she throws her arms around me. "God bless," she says.

"You too," I say, automatically, although the words "God" and "bless" get my heart pounding. I head back to the rental car, where Barney is enjoying his noise-canceling headphones and startles when I enter.

"Damn it," he says, "you wolves are stealthy. Success?"

"Success." I hold up the jar, gratified when he scrambles backward.

"Holy shit, that's really a black widow!"

"It is."

"And it's fricking huge."

"Is it? I don't know how big they usually are."

"Why'd you put it in the jar?"

"It just seemed easier than bringing out the whole killing-it apparatus. And I thought it was pretty. Do you think we can keep it as a pet?"

"Well, you have to poke holes in the top or it'll suffocate. I think. Or maybe that's crickets."

"No, that sounds right." I take out my pocketknife, make a few small holes in the top of the lid. "What do you feed it?"

"Insects, I guess. Abby, you're not really keeping a black widow as a pet, are you?"

"I don't know. I guess I'm taking it back to the maison to see what the others think."

He shakes his head. "You're nuts. Well, we have one more call, and then we're going to go around town putting up flyers and all that."

"Another call? How do we have two calls before we even put up the fliers?"

"Apparently we're one number off from a local pizza joint. It's funny, our conversion rate is really high, maybe we should always make that part of our marketing strategy. We have ads coming out in the next issue of all the local publications. One newspaper that comes out twice a week and a monthly they do at the state college. Oh, and a few church bulletins." He gives me a slightly evil grin. "Apparently church is where you go in this town if you want to find people."

I roll my eyes. "Did you get on those one-sheets of bad jokes they put on the tables at grandpa restaurants?"

"Actually? Yes, I think we did. It's called the Merry Coffee Break."

"Why do we do all of this anyway? I mean, it's not like we're really trying to get a rabid animal control company off the ground, is it?"

"Actually, it is." He shrugs. "The maisons are expensive to run and we need to offset that any way we can. Plus, a lot of places offer tax breaks and things to small businesses. We want to explore as much of the city as we can, which includes scent tracking houses and businesses, right? And we also want people to have a phone number to call when they see something that might be a wolf, so we want a good reputation."

"I guess that all makes sense. So, what's this other call?"

"Rats. Not super dangerous, most of the time, but they can be pesky. Chew on things."

The rats, it turns out, are like the black widows: just one and I can remove him easily using non-lethal means.

"I don't understand how you did that." The male half of the couple, the Reverend and Mrs. Jerry Franklin, stares at me. "It looked as if you caught him with your bare hands and just put him in the cage."

"Well, at Snarlaway, we know a lot about animal psychology. It's our specialty. I know how to sneak up on rats. It's hard to learn, but once you've got the trick, it works just about every time. We'll take this little guy out to the wilderness. He doesn't really want to be in your house anyway."

"You're not going to kill him?" Mrs. Reverend Jerry Franklin, a woman with what I can only describe as extremely religious hair, gives me a grateful look. "I'm so happy you're not going to kill him. Poor little thing."

"Nope." I hold up the cage, make eye contact with the gray rat, who gives me an alarmed look and cowers against the rear of the cage. Okay, I guess it must have been wolfy eye contact even if I didn't mean it to be. "Thank you, we'll take it from here."

Once again, I get forty dollars in cash, with five dollars as a tip. I put it in the increasingly thick pocket of my jumpsuit along with the other cash.

In the car, I put the rat in the back seat, far away from the black widow. They don't seem to notice each other.

"Hey, Barney, how do we set our rates?"

He shrugs. "I don't know. In New Orleans there's a book, but here I just made it up."

"I think we must be cheap, because they keep paying in cash and then tipping me."

"Cash?" He grins. "It's all yours then."

"What? No. Really?"

"It's how I do it. If they give me cash, I pocket the whole thing."

"Isn't that…" I struggle for the word. "Stealing?"

"Look, are you drawing a regular paycheck from this?"

"No. No, I'm not. I mean. Viv explained it as being like an unpaid internship."

He shrugs. "Well, there you have it. If they're not paying you, the cash is yours. There's a petty cash jar like in New Orleans if you just feel too guilty keeping it for yourself. I never do."

Nervously I pat the money. "So, where to now? Plastering fliers everywhere?"

"Yep," he says. "I'll probably want you to navigate, here's a list." He texts me the locations. Restaurants, coffee shops, campus locations, hardware stores—and churches. So many churches. I make him go into the churches.

He laughs at me. "Really? You're going to avoid churches like some cheesy vampire?"

"It's a traditional rougarou characteristic, do your homework."

"Well, all the other wolves can go into a church, I think it's just you." He's teasing.

"It is me." I shrug. "So what?"

"You should confront your fears," he says.

"I'm not afraid of church. I'm afraid that I'll go into church and have a big freak-out that'll be hard to explain to people."

"Abby, that's being afraid of church."

"Fine, I have church-phobia, happy?"

He grins. "Yes. It's the first thing I've found that you're scared of."

We finish the list, drive into the hills to release the little rat, head back to the maison. Everyone is gathered in the tiny back yard, around a newly purchased grill, aromatically roasting an assortment of cattle parts and a few vegetables. I assume the vegetables are a nod to me. Even though I grudgingly accepted that I need meat protein in order to be fully healthy, or at least to recover from getting shot in the head and losing a foot, I'm not content to eat nothing but meat.

Etienne tends the grill, Vivienne wears a pair of little reading glasses and studies her laptop computer, while Babette is drinking another bottle of that pink wine and playing songs through her phone and a bluetooth speaker.

"What did you find?" Babette asks. "I got nothing. The only wolves in town are the ones at Hammerfit, I'd swear it."

"Don't leap to conclusions too early," Etienne says. "We conduct our investigations in a certain systematic way. If we rely too heavily on first assumptions, we miss things. Follow the process."

She rolls her eyes. "Fine, but, I'm right and you know it. What about the Seattle team?"

"They discovered the Seattle Hammerfit is another mini bitten wolf haven. Just like the one here, it's got a traditional sparring room and lots of other wolfy touches. But, also like here, the wolves are under control, no biting incidents in the last month," Etienne says.

"Oh, wait, I almost forgot." I go back to the car and retrieve the black widow, still in its jar and apparently alive. "I got us a pet today."

"Abby, why?" Viv says, shaking her head.

"I think she's cute," Babette says. She taps on the glass and the spider responds by rearing up its front legs. "She's saying hi, look!"

"That's probably an attack mode, actually."

"Abby, no," Viv says. "I'm not letting you keep a black widow as a pet."

"What? You don't like it, do you?" I bring the jar close to Viv and she shrinks away from it, distress spiking.

"Stop it." Etienne grabs the jar. "We do not deliberately torment other members of the maison." He leaves the yard, to kill or release it far away.

"I'm sorry, Viv. I really am. I honestly had no idea it would bother you."

She sighs. "I'm just phobic, don't worry about it."

Etienne returns and the conversation moves on, but it continues to bother me: why is Viv scared of spiders? And why didn't I know that?

Much later, as we're all getting ready for bed, I take her aside. "Viv, I'm really sorry about the black widow thing."

"Abby, I already said it was okay, I know you didn't mean it."

"But I don't understand why."

"Why? Why I'm afraid of spiders, you mean? I said it was a phobia. You know what a phobia is, right? Spiders are one of the common ones, it's why we get all those calls."

"But they can't hurt us, right? Or can they?"

"No, they pose no threat to those with an active wolf. And even the most fearsome spiders aren't as deadly as their reputation would have it, they almost never bite a human and their bite is almost never fatal."

"So you weren't ever hurt by a spider?"

"I wasn't, no." She pauses for a moment, her face wearing a complex happy-sad look. "Not unless you count the times when we were kids and Leon would dangle spiders right in front of me to watch me jump."

"That was mean."

"I suppose it was. He thought it was funny."

"I'll never do that to you again, Viv, I swear, it was an accident. I just didn't know. I didn't think the older wolves were scared of anything."

"No?" A small chuckle, as she pats me on the shoulder. "Everybody's afraid of something, little one."

PART III

SEATTLE

9

CHEZ LUNATIC

Over the next couple of weeks, things settle into a pattern: Snarlaway jobs, scent mapping, and brainstorming conference calls with the other maisons. We get so many Snarlaway jobs that it's almost like having a regular job myself. I deal with raccoons and rats and squirrels, a litter of surprisingly aggressive (but not rabid) feral kittens, a couple of bats, and one really enormous (but entirely harmless) giant house spider. I feel a little bad for killing it with the spray and the shop vac, but I went in prepared for a brown recluse, which the customer claimed it was when he called us.

"It's brown, it looks like this, come on," he says, seeming angry, holding up a photo that actually doesn't look anything like the spider in his apartment. "It's a brown recluse!"

"It's fine, sir, we can eliminate the arachnid either way. I just thought you'd want to know that this particular arachnid is probably harmless." He continues to seem so angry that my urge to have a satisfied customer briefly overwhelms me. I force a smile. "Of course, it can be really hard to tell the difference if you're not an expert. We do this for a living at Snarlaway. It's good that you called us. It easily could have been a brown recluse."

He goes from seeming angry to seeming satisfied. For my part, I feel a little cheap. But I leave, with the dead spider in the shop vac, and hopefully a customer who's going to give us a good rating online.

But, after almost two weeks, we seem no closer to finding the source of Andrew's exposure. On the conference call I suggest: "Well, the Hammond twins are still ignoring us too. What if Andrew and I went over to Seattle? We can check out the places he went during his trip and I can try to talk to the twins. If they're my brothers, it shouldn't seem too threatening for me to just show up at their door, right?"

There's silence on Pere Claude's end. Is he considering saying yes? Or is he considering telling me to simmer down? I press on. "And if I go out there with my loufrer—my non-wolfy friends—it should seem pretty harmless, right?"

Viv gives me a knowing look. "I see what you did there, Abby."

"Am I wrong?"

Pere Claude clears his throat. "No, Abby, you're not wrong. Your plan sounds good to me. Vivienne, you and Abby should accompany Andrew to Seattle."

"Abby gets to go to Seattle and I'm stuck here?" Babette says. "Excuse me!"

"What are you complaining about, Babs? You spent a year in Paris, I should get to go to Seattle for a few days."

* * *

We start driving in the darkness of the middle of the night, arrive in Seattle late morning. Viv and Andrew drop me off outside "Chez Lunatic," the University District rental house shared by Deena, Izzy, and Edison.

"You and your loufrer will be ready to head out to the twins' place tomorrow morning and report afterward at the maison?" I nod. Viv kisses my cheek. "Have fun with your friends tonight. Don't drink too much. Remember, without the wolf, everything hits harder than you think it will."

"I'll be fine, Viv." I grab my backpack, get out of the car, wave as Viv and Andrew drive away. The weather is pure Seattle: cold enough to make me glad of my wool coat and thick tights, but well above freezing, with a wet, clean sharpness to the air and just a hint of ocean. The houses on this street, a block or two away from what they call Frat Row, are older and a little shambling and unkempt, but with yards full of tall trees. Above me, a thick evergreen spreads its branches overhead. I reach up to grab a pine needle and crush it for the pungent citrusy scent. Seattle, I missed you. Not only because my loufrer are here. I lived in Seattle for months before I even met Edison, before I knew Deena as anything other than the one Saint Sebastian girl who bothered to talk to me, but because she was always cracking jokes, I couldn't tell if she wanted to be friends or if she was just making fun of me. I called her Smoking Girl and she called me Gator Girl. It's funny to think back that far. It wasn't really so long ago, just last summer, but it feels like ages. Everything before the wolf came seems impossibly remote now.

Seattle was my territory when the wolf came, and I think it will always feel like home. The thought brings an unexpected rush of tears. Inhaling that sparkling silver-gray air, it hits me: Seattle was the first place I ever went that didn't feel like New Harmony, that didn't smell like southern Louisiana. Seattle doesn't just smell like home, it smells like freedom. New Orleans and Bayou Galene are, in most ways, nothing at all like the cult where I was raised. But they've got the same air. The same weather. The same landscape.

I'm still staring up at the branches of the tree when the door of one of the houses flings open and Edison comes rushing out. "Abby!" He throws his arms around my waist, picks me up, whirls me around. "I didn't know you were in town already."

"I texted you, you big dork, don't you ever check your

phone?" Giddy, I laugh, bubbling like I'm full of champagne inside, touch of melancholy forgotten.

"Come on inside. I'll get your bag." He takes my backpack in one hand, puts his other arm around my shoulder. "How are you?"

"Still wolfless."

"I'm sorry about that." He squeezes my shoulders. "Not forever, though, right? She's coming back?"

"That's what they tell me. I don't think they know." I take a second look at him. He let his hair grow out since the summer, and it's extremely tousled. He came running out of the house barefoot, in gray UW Huskies sweatpants and a vintage leather jacket and nothing else, as if he just got out of bed...

I blush, look down at the sidewalk. Blade of grass. Chewed gum. Empty Pabst Blue Ribbon can, partly crushed.

Edison leans over to kiss my neck. "It really is good to see you, Abby," he murmurs into my ear, breath warm. "I'm sorry I'm not better at long-distance communication."

"It's okay," I whisper, glad he's not a werewolf, because another wolf could smell how into him I am.

He stops walking for a moment, exhales a long shuddering breath. He's interested too, I think. "Say, are you hungry? You want some breakfast?"

"The last thing I had was a fast food breakfast wrap on the road, I could eat."

"Let's do it." He takes my arm and we walk up into the disheveled house, our path thick with scent trails of my loufrer and their friends.

I follow him into the kitchen. "I didn't know you cooked."

"I didn't until living with Izzy. Because she's, like, the granddaughter of one of the most famous chefs in the world, for the first couple of weeks she told us it was fine if Deena and I didn't cook, as long as we did all the dishes and took out the garbage and went to the grocery store when she didn't feel like it and that sort of thing. Then she snapped. She said it was completely unacceptable for two adult humans to be incapable of feeding themselves and started making us do some of the cooking. Nothing fancy. I still can't make an étouffée or whatever. But I can scramble eggs and leftover steak."

"Steak?"

He pauses, plastic container of steak in hand, gives me a worried smile. "I thought you stopped eating vegetarian when you got hurt?"

"True. But without the wolf I've been drifting toward it again."

"You want eggs without steak?"

"No, it's fine. I want whatever you're eating. I was just surprised. I don't even know why I was surprised. Carry on. Do you need any help?"

"No, I've got it, thanks. Just, you know, sit there and enjoy."

I do enjoy, watching him enact small, everyday movements like opening the refrigerator for tomatoes, putting the tomatoes on a cutting board, slicing the tomatoes in half, getting a paper towel and bending down to wipe where the tomato juice spurted onto the floor. With every move he exudes grace and presence, a sense that he knows exactly where his body exists in space. He's not some jerk who's going to hog more than his share of the middle seat on an airplane. The pan sizzles and he begins stirring the contents with a spatula, starts singing to himself. Not a song I recognize, but he has a good voice. He has a good everything. Is he somehow more perfect now than he was three months ago, or did I just forget?

He divides the eggs, steak, and tomatoes in half, slides each half onto a plate, puts one plate in front of me. "Do you want toast or anything to go with it?"

"No, I'm good."

He places Crystal pepper sauce and sriracha in the

center of the table, douses his eggs with the sriracha. "The Crystal is Izzy's idea, it's pretty good. Like Tabasco, but cheaper."

"I know what Crystal hot sauce is, Edison."

"Of course you do." He laughs. "I'm sorry, I forget you're from there too. I keep thinking of you as a displaced Seattleite."

Tears prickle my eyes again. He's right. I *am* a displaced Seattleite. How did he know?

I stab at my tomatoes with the fork. "Well, I'm not from New Orleans the way Isobelle or Steph are. I didn't grow up with hot sauce."

"You didn't? I guess they didn't have it in the cult, did they?"

"No. We barely had salt, honestly. I mean, my mom made the best of things, but... I don't know, it doesn't matter. I'm not starving now, right?" I take a bite. "Hey, it's good, I guess you did learn to cook."

He leans forward with a serious air, looking right into my eyes, so hard that I get uncomfortable, blink and look away.

"You don't like making eye contact," he says.

"I guess I don't. Not unless it's a dominance contest, which I would lose right now anyway." I glance up at him, try to smile in a reassuring way. "It's okay. Don't worry about me. What about you, though?"

"I'm good. Never better."

"Really?" It sounds like an overstatement and I'm skeptical. "You still don't remember getting kidnapped and almost killed by my sister Opal?"

"I don't. She drugged me with so much alcohol, it just feels like I got way too drunk at a party and forgot a bunch of stuff." He grins. "I was incredibly hung over when I met your grandfather the next day, I do remember that."

I take his hand, as if his skin will tell me if he's telling the truth. "What about when wolf me bit you?"

He looks down at his arm, where the scars of her teeth would be. "Nope. No problems at all."

"What about lingering effects? From Reina's cure?"

"No, nothing." He looks down and away, and I'm almost sure he's lying, which brings a surge of guilt. There probably is some lingering effect, but he's trying to spare my feelings by not talking about it.

"Edison, it's okay if there's something."

He takes a bite of egg. "Is it okay if there's nothing?"

Deena shuffles into the kitchen, yawning and smelling of hair dye. One half of her hair has been colored bright red, the other half, bright green. Christmas colors.

"You made steak and eggs, but you couldn't be assed to make coffee?" she grumbles at Edison. "Oh, hi Abby. You look fantastic, by the way. Love the dress, is it vintage?"

"Good eye. My aunt Vivienne helped me pick it out from this store that's all vintage designer stuff, most of it barely worn."

"Vivienne, did I meet her?"

"I'm not sure. She's very close to my grandfather, works as his lawyer? Tall, likes to wear heels, long auburn hair that she usually puts in a severe bun?"

"Oh, yeah, I remember her." She fills an electric kettle with water, turns it on. "She looks just like this legendary 1980s scream queen, Roxy Void, did I ever make you watch any of her movies?"

"I don't think so."

"Some of them are really good, we should put them on for the party tonight." She pulses the coffee grinder, then dumps the grounds into an X-shaped coffee maker. "Right, did I tell you we're having a party tonight?"

"A party?"

"In honor of you being here." The kettle shuts off and she starts pouring the water over the coffee. "It's going to be mostly the same crowd you know from the Howl and that party where you punched out Colin Ambrose. Anyway, Brad has a T-shirt or something he wants to give you. Honestly, the bros cannot stop talking about the New Orleans trip. Apparently having spent a fun evening partying with a serial killer is good for one's dating prospects." She grins and divides the coffee into four pint glasses. Edison takes one, then she pours milk into two of the remaining glasses. "Izzy's got me drinking cafe au lait, you want? Or do you drink it black?"

"I drink it however it's offered."

"Here you go then." She gives me one that's half milk, finishes pouring, grabs the other two. "I'll just take these back to the bedroom." She turns to go, but Izzy comes in, yawning.

She leans over to gives me a hug. "Hey, Abby, how you doing?"

"Pretty good. Now that you're all here—wait, are there any non-loufrer around?"

Deena shakes her head. "Nope. The party starts around eight, officially, but only the band is going to show up that early. Maybe the posse for decorations. I decided this was going to be our Nightmare Before Christmas party, which is basically just a Halloween party in December. Have you been to a Halloween party yet?"

"No, I haven't."

"Well, there, you see? We'll have costumes and those tiny little chocolate bars, you'll love it. Now, I hear we're driving you out to Enumclaw tomorrow, what's that all about?"

"I guess I told you the plan but didn't give you the full backstory. I'm here as part of an investigation. We got a bitten wolf last moon in New Orleans, Andrew, but he's from Meriwether, Idaho, and we can't figure out how he got bit. Then we found out there were likely Leon offspring originally from Meriwether, but recently moved to Enumclaw. They've been ignoring our emails, so the plan is to send me out there with you guys, under the assumption that me, as family, and you, as non-wolves, will make the visit seem friendly and non-aggressive. But the real goal is to find out if they know anything about Andrew's exposure. For example, did they make any bitten wolves recently who they lost track of?"

"Okay, I think I've got it."

"Does it have anything to do with this?" Izzy holds up her laptop and shows a brief, blurry clip of the wolf in the mall.

"It does! How did you know about that?"

She grins. "I wrote an algorithm for one of my computer classes. It scrapes social media and news sites for anything that looks like werewolf activity. Then I wrote a completely different algorithm for the actual assignment because I got nervous that turning it in to the professor would somehow get back to the loup-garous and piss them off. Do you think the loup-garous would like to see the first algorithm?"

"I'm pretty sure they would."

"Good. My grandma Charli cooked for y'all and you protected her these many years. I want the same deal, only I code, I don't cook. You get me?"

Deena comes up, sets the coffees down, puts her arms around Izzy's neck, kisses her cheek. "Oh, babe, that's harsh. You cook better than anybody I know except my Italian grandma."

"Well, I still code better than I cook."

"Right, that's the harsh part. I mean, I bet you code better than anybody I know too, but I lack the means to judge that." She kisses her again, then pulls away. "Oh, check this out." Deena pulls up her phone and shows me a video clip identified as "drunk girl face plants on Bourbon Street" which is me, in the exact moment after I failed to catch the wolf. I notice the video was uploaded by username bdog467.

"That's Barney! I'm gonna kill him. I think he was the one who circulated that clip of wolf me trying to get out of the corset, too."

"But that's a classic! People still use that gif all the time," Deena says. "This one is good too. Your butt looks fantastic in that jumpsuit, in case you had any doubts. And that sort of utility green is an ugly color on most people, but you're such a classic ginger, it looks great on you."

"Thanks, I guess."

She takes a big sip of the coffee. "So, how's things out in the swamps?"

"It's a bayou, not a swamp."

"And the difference is?"

"I have no idea. I just know that whenever I said we lived in a swamp the other Varger would correct me and say we lived on a bayou, not in a swamp."

"Okay, so, how's things out on the bayou?"

"Not bad. Better than I thought they would be. It's almost like, take anything that was true about New Harmony, and Bayou Galene is the complete opposite of that. They're basically pagans."

"Really? Don't they celebrate Mardi Gras and all that?"

"They do. But they don't follow it with Lent."

"Wow, imagine that, Mardi Gras with no Lent." Deena nudges Edison. "Remember that time we both gave up sugar for Lent? It's not fair, by Easter I was a gibbering wreck of my former self, but this dude basically never ate sugar again." She smiles at me. "I don't know if you know this, Abby, but our families are still excruciatingly Catholic. And I don't even know if I'm ready to come out to them. I mean, sometimes I daydream about doing it at the big Christmas Eve lasagna feast in front of everybody, and sometimes I daydream about just running off to New Orleans with Izzy and never seeing my family again. Because your family already knows, right, babe?"

"Grandma Charli knows, I'm not too sure about everyone else. But she's the one who really matters. If she's okay with it, nobody's gonna go against her. And she's okay with it." She squeezes Deena's hand.

And then.

Edison reaches out very casually to squeeze my hand.
Almost unconscious.

Like it's the most natural thing in the world.

I swallow, hard, try to calm down. I don't have a lot of cool to start with, but I seem to lose every last bit of it around him.

"Say, Edison, have you ever been to Hammerfit?" I manage to squeak out.

"You mean the gym? No. It's supposed to be super fancy though."

"The one in Meriwether is kind of a werewolf gym. and according to the Seattle maison, the one here is the same."

"There are werewolf gyms?" Deena is delighted. "How can you tell?"

"The scent trails would tell any wolf that other wolves go there. But Hammerfit has a bunch of wolfy touches by design, like a padded sparring room. The chain was founded by the brothers we're going to go see tomorrow." I pull out HAMMERFIT: THE DIETS, show them the back cover.

Deena goggles at it. "Wow, they look so much like your grandfather."

"That's what we all thought. We're going to be shocked if it turns out they're not Leon offspring, right?"

She flips through the book. "You've been in Idaho for the last couple of weeks. Is it still super conservative over there?"

"Pretty much. A lot of churches. But the Hammerfit pack is cool, they've really accepted Andrew even though he's gay."

"Yeah? That's good. I always feel bad for the queer kids who grow up in any place less tolerant than Seattle's Capitol Hill. Which is, basically, everywhere, right?"

"New Orleans isn't too bad," Izzy says. "What about Bayou Galene, Abby?"

"Well, the surrounding area is pretty conservative, but the Varger themselves don't have a lot of taboos related to sex and gender."

Deena flips through the book. "Edison, remember Wildwood? That Idaho church camp we used to go to sometimes?"

"Oh yeah. We pretended to be dating so that everybody would leave us alone."

"And on the bus out there we'd always pass that series of super right-wing billboards, remember? That one that was always about the end of the world? And that one about how LGBTQ rights are a plot of the Jews? And all the gun shops?"

"Yeah, I do remember that." He frowns. "Why?"

"I don't know, just thinking. Remember that diner in Meriwether where you had to go through the bar to get to the bathrooms and the mirror behind the bar had this oh-so-hilarious cartoon of a cowboy roping and tying a sexy woman silhouette as if she were cattle?"

"Ew," I say. "That cartoon is still there."

"What? No. Really?"

"Yep. Barney and I were going around town putting up Snarlaway ads, and that diner has a community bulletin board. They were doing line dancing in the bar when we stopped by, which got me to go over and look, and that's when I noticed the mirror. Kinda dusty. Still there. Which reminds me—" I take out some of the Snarlaway Meriwether business cards and hand them over. "Have you guys seen these?"

"No!" Deena is delighted. "I love the logo. Do you have T-shirts?"

"I don't think so. I could probably get you a patch like the one on my jumpsuit."

"I would say they're extremely retro, except, you guys have probably just had the same logo since 1962, right?"

"I think so, given that everything else in the office seems to be that old."

"What happens if I call the national number?"

"That phone gets answered in New Orleans and then transferred, if there's a more local office. If not, they try to determine if it's a wolf-related call or not."

"What if I call this number and ask to speak to you by name?"

"I guess they forward it to my cell phone? I don't know."

"Do you get a lot of Snarlaway calls?"

"In Meriwether, we have. There seemed to be strong pent-up demand for a way to get black widows out of your planter and rats out of your church building."

Somebody new walks up onto the porch. Edison and I both snap our heads toward the front door a second before we hear the knock. He says, "That's our new drummer, Kennedy. They're even tinier than you, Abby, but they can really thrash the hell out of their drum kit. Let's go help load it in."

"Got it." Edison and I both hop up to open the door. And then I realize: that's the second time today that Edison knew somebody was outside before they knocked, and knew who it was before opening the door.

Just like the wolves do.

10

NIGHTMARE BEFORE CHRISTMAS PARTY

K ennedy is, as promised, even smaller than I am. They have a delicate, almost fragile look, which reminds me—of me. When I first left New Harmony, I looked a bit like that. The shaved head, the giant eyes. But they seem to have no trouble carrying their drum kit equipment. As soon as we're done setting everything up, they ask, "So, what's the leftover situation right now?"

"We've got jambalaya," Izzy says, pulling a container out of the refrigerator, setting it on the table, then setting out plates and cutlery.

"We pretty much always have jambalaya," Deena says to me, as an aside. "Apparently word gets around."

Shortly, the bass guitarist Nora, an English-Indian woman with blazingly blue hair and an accent that I would call 'cockney' but I'm probably wrong, arrives and they all play a test set while adjusting the sound. I enjoy the chance to watch the band without any other distractions. Edison changed out of his raggy sweatpants into a pair of roughed-up jeans (with a good, uh, fit) and is now wearing the leather jacket over what looks like a vintage T-shirt for a band called the Fastbacks. The song ends.

"Well that was a corker," Nora says. She grins at me. "Abby, how's the sound, love?"

"Good. It sounds really good. Loud."

"We should get you a tambourine, put you up on stage with us. Can you sing?"

"Not really. I can dance though."

"Definitely a tambourine, then. We'd come off like a sixties cartoon band. You in that little mini skirt, and your hair just too, too red."

They put their equipment away and crack beers. The posse arrives next: Deena's friends from Saint Sebastian, Nina, Claudia, and Portia. Claudia, who dresses very Gothic, is carrying a big box of Halloween decorations. Nina, wearing plaid flannel as usual, grabs a beer right away. Portia gives me a hug.

"Abby! Deena told us you were coming!"

"I heard you moved to New Orleans?" Claudia sets down the box and comes to takes my hands. I nod. "So jealous. When Deena went out to visit you last summer, my only consolation was that it was August, but in November I imagine it's perfect."

"It's okay. What's been going on in Seattle?"

"Nothing much." Nina hands me a beer. "We're seniors now, so we spend most of our time daydreaming about college. What about you? You going to school back in New Orleans?"

"Right now? I guess you could say I'm seeing tutors. I was home-schooled before Saint Sebastian, and I guess I never really got the whole school thing figured out."

"What are you studying?"

"A lot of chemistry. Animal biology. Exercise physiology." All true, but I'm not learning any of it in what you would call an academic setting.

Close to party start time, Deena takes me aside. "You need a costume, let's go." She pulls me into the large bedroom she shares with Izzy. "I'm a terrible roommate, I'm afraid. She's basically got only the amount of clothes that will fit in a large suitcase, and I've got—well—this." She gestures toward a packed, chaotic closet full of vintage items, starts ruffling through it, tossing things on the bed. "I don't know why I always buy these cool things in thrift stores that don't quite fit me, you know? Like, I try them on and think, 'oh, I don't have to button it' but then in real life of course I need to button it. Or I can get it on in the dressing room but the instant I sit down or anything I split a seam. Here we go, this is what I was looking for, check it out." She holds out a slinky black velvet dress. "Like, what was I thinking? I can't even zip it. Was I imagining that I'd always wear a coat over it? No idea. Well, try it on, see what it looks like."

I still find it weird to change clothes right in front of people, but it's what the Varger do, so I'm trying to get used to it. Deena, for her part, looks away while I wriggle into the dress. I can zip it up without trouble, but it's pretty snug, I can see where Deena wouldn't have been able to wear it zipped.

Because of where the straps fall, I have to take off my bra. It makes me feel self-conscious. Is that the kind of thing Edison is going to notice?

"Done," I say.

She turns around. "Oh, perfect! Now, gloves." She hands me black velvet elbow-length gloves. "And pearls." She hands me a choker of plastic fake pearls. "Okay, let me sweep your hair up with this tiara I got in New Orleans—are you going to mind hairspray?"

"Yes, but do it anyway."

"Hold your breath, and—okay, done! Now, can you see in these?"

She puts some large sunglasses on me. It's startlingly dark for a moment, then my eyes adjust. I guess I still have good night vision. "I can see."

"All right! You're almost done. Open your mouth."

I do, and she shoves in fake teeth. I run my tongue over them. "Are these fangs?"

"They are definitely fangs! You're Audrey Hepburn in *Breakfast at Tiffany's* only a vampire! Holly Go-Biteme!" She cracks herself up laughing, then looks vaguely apologetic. "Sorry. Did you notice I'm a big dork? Oh, one more thing!" She hands me a long cigarette holder. "Get on out there, you look great."

"I'll take your word for it." I laugh, feeling a rush of nervous excitement. Do I look great? Will Edison think I look great? I wander through the party, trying to find him, to show off my outfit. He's left scent trails absolutely everywhere. At the back porch, for example, Edison was here recently, but isn't here now, although someone else is: a man, approaching from the yard.

Oh. Oh no.

It's Colin Ambrose, the jerk I punched last summer after he groped me.

"What are you doing here?" I ask.

"I was invited, sweetie."

He doesn't appear to recognize me. Well, why would he? I'm literally wearing a costume.

"I doubt that. You should leave."

"Yeah?" He starts walking up the stairs to the back porch. "Why do you say that, cutie? Do I remind you of your ex-boyfriend or something?"

"Deena? Izzy? Edison?" I call out, as loud as I can. "You guys around? Do you want to tell this jerk to leave?"

He gets up to porch level. He pauses to loom over me, then starts laughing. "Wait, I know you. You're that little redhead who punched me last summer. You got lucky that time, you wanna try it again? We could wrestle. It'll be fun."

I clench my fist. I do want to punch him again. I want to punch him right off this porch into the thorny bushes below. But I don't know how much power is behind my punch right

now. The last thing I want to do is punch him and have…
nothing happen.

I call out again. "Edison! Deena! Izzy! Chez Lunatic!
Colin Ambrose thinks he's welcome at your party, you want to
come here and explain it to him?"

He tries to move around me, into the porch. I block him.
He moves again. I block him again.

He puts his hands on my shoulders to move me out of the
way. I have an impulse to growl at him, but it comes out as a
grunt. I shake him off, but it's hard. The power isn't there. I
can feel it. The wolf is gone.

Edison comes out of the house behind me. "I'm sorry,
Abby, Deena was doing my costume, I didn't hear you at first.
What's wrong—oh, it's you."

He and Colin look at each other. "Yeah, bro, it's me. This
chick here is telling me I'm not welcome at your party. I was
telling her I think I am." He holds up a twelve-pack of beer,
with a baggie of marijuana on top of it.

"You're not welcome here, Colin. Abby's not the only girl
you grabbed without permission. Although I think she is the
only one who ever punched you out for it."

"Bro, come on." He holds up the baggie. "This is the good
stuff, extra-high THC content."

Edison stares intently at Colin. I notice that Deena has
costumed him by attaching latex prosthetics and applying
makeup to create the illusion that chunks of broken glass are
embedded in his skin, as if he's been in a terrible car accident.
It's creepily realistic. He inhales, and his body language
changes dramatically. All of a sudden he looks hulking and
tense. I see this power there, this menace, and it reminds me
of when the wolves challenge each other, so much that I
almost expect to see his eyes flash.

Wait, *did* I see his eyes flash?

Colin smells terrified all of a sudden. Puts up his arms.
Backs away. "Whoa, dude, I don't want any trouble."

"Then leave." Edison's voice is low, rumbling, almost a growl.

Colin stumbles over himself, tumbling down the stairs again and running out of the yard.

"Huh, he left the beer and the pot," Edison says, totally his normal self, leaning over to pick it up. "That was fun."

"Thanks. I didn't want to try punching him or anything myself, just in case it didn't work."

He hugs me. "It's okay. He shouldn't be your problem to deal with. We've tolerated him way too long just because he always shows up with beer. Anyway, the band's about to start."

I follow Edison back inside, where the bros have arrived: Ward, Brad, and Reed. They already look less uniform than they did last August. Brad looks a little chunky, Reed looks sort of hipsterish, while Ward looks, somehow, older than his friends, as if he's all of a sudden thirty-five while they're still in their early twenties. Ward has a woman with him, attractive in a very polished, rich-looking way.

"Abby, so nice to see you again," Ward says, taking my hand with a slightly courtly air. "This is my fiancée, Brooke. Brooke, this is Abby, Edison's girlfriend in New Orleans."

"Fiancée? Wow, congratulations!"

"Thank you." She dangles her hand, with a huge sparkly diamond, in front of me.

Brad gives me a big bear hug. "Abby! Dude! I heard a rumor you were going to be here. This is gonna be one epic party."

I laugh, a little uncomfortable. "Brad, last summer we played a drinking game that put you in the hospital."

"Right. Epic." He drapes his arm around my shoulders, gives an enthusiastic squeeze, looks out at the room, as if he's presenting me to everyone. "This chick here is, like, unstoppable. You party with her, man, you know it's going to be legendary. Oh, I've got something for you." He hands me an oversized T-shirt in burgundy and silver, which announces me to be:

Ψ Φ Θ
Psi Phi Theta
NUMBER ONE PARTY ANIMAL

"I know, it'll be kinda big on you, but I figure you can sleep in it, right?"

"Thanks, Brad." I look around for where to put it, and Deena holds out a hand. "I'll put it with your backpack."

Reed gives me a small, awkward smile. "Hey, Abby. Love the outfit."

"Thanks. Deena picked it out." I'm not sure where I stand with him. He bought me drinks all night last summer but then he also did a weird thing where he insulted me and then asked if I wanted to make out. We've never talked about it.

Edison excuses himself to go pick up a guitar, Kennedy bangs their drumsticks together, and the house explodes with music. The floodgates open and within about fifteen minutes the house is almost too packed to move. I originally wanted to watch the band from right in front, but it turns out to be too loud for comfort and I let myself get buffeted by the dancing masses to the other side of the room, and then, eventually, into another room entirely. Reed and a few people I don't know are drinking cocktails. I'm torn for a moment. I was enjoying the band, but the relative quiet seems like such a relief.

"Abby." Reed greets me by holding out a flask. "You like a good single malt, don't you?"

"Usually." I sniff the flask before taking a sip. "Talisker?"

"Good nose."

You don't know the half of it. "My grandfather is a Scotch enthusiast. I've been living with him, I guess it rubbed off."

"You like that stuff?" says one of the women I don't know.

"I think it tastes like dirt and campfires."

"Oh, that's what I like about it."

Everybody laughs.

I start passing the flask back and forth with Reed.

"So, what are you doing here in Seattle? Move or visit?" he asks.

"Visit. I'm here with family, basically just for the weekend. It's nice to see everybody though."

Brad enters the room. "Abby! Dude!" Hey, you wanna do shots? We could have a rematch. I've been practicing." He pats his belly, lets loose a large belch.

"Nice one, Brad," says campfire girl, rolling her eyes.

"I don't think so," I say. "I don't want you going to the hospital again."

"Oh, it doesn't have to be a contest or anything. Just shots. You know. For old time's sake. Come on." He gives me an enthusiastic one-armed hug. "No other girl I know parties like you."

"You've obviously never met Babette."

"Who?"

"Somebody I work with. You'd like her."

"You're working?" Reed asks. "Doing what?"

"I work for Snarlaway Rabid Animal Control."

"Rabid Animal Control, no kidding. What's that like?"

"I don't know, it seems like I meet a lot of spiders."

Brad tries again. "Come on, Abby. We'll let Reed make the drinks, he can try out all his weird ideas on us. He's a professional."

"A professional? You mean you're working as a bartender?"

He nods. "It's at the top of a swanky hotel tower in the University District. The kind of place you take your parents so they can look out at the Seattle views and feel good about how much money they're spending on your education."

"Do you like it?"

"Mostly. There are worse jobs."

"Yeah, I get rabid raccoons out of attics."

"Do you dislike that?"

"Not really, it was a joke. To be honest I kind of like it. Working with animals. I don't know, when I do go back to school, I might want to study to become a veterinarian." Wow, where did that come from? I guess I just didn't want to sound like a no-ambition loser in front of the bros. Can a werewolf become a veterinarian?

Reed says, "Sure, I'll make you guys shots. Anybody else want in?"

"I'll take a shot but I'm not doing any contests," campfire girl says. "I'm Elaina, by the way."

"Abby. Nice to meet you."

Her face lights up with recognition. "Wait, you must be Hoodoo Abby! I thought you'd be taller."

"I'm sorry, you've heard of me?"

"Everybody on the team knows Edison is dating a redhead from New Orleans."

"The team?"

"You know, Huskies football."

"I thought Edison wasn't going to play this year?"

She shrugs. "I guess he changed his mind. And a good thing, too. Without him, there's no way they would have made it to the Rose Bowl. I swear, if it were possible for a running back to win a game all by himself, he'd do it."

"But where does the hoodoo come in?"

"It's just a joke. You know, he goes off to see his girlfriend in New Orleans and comes back and the team starts winning? So we joked about him getting some hoodoo done, and he joked about you being the one to do it... I'm sorry, it seemed really funny before, but with you sitting right there it's starting to seem a little disrespectful. So, shots?"

"Shots."

Unlike the "death shots" game last August, Reed's goal is

to make shots that actually taste good and show off his bartending skills. We get layered shots and finessed shots and high end liquor shots. After a few, I'm surprised to notice that I'm starting to feel it. I also realize the band has stopped playing.

"Whoa. Okay, Brad, I think you win the rematch. I need to take a little walk."

"What? Already? In New Orleans we went all night."

"Come on, Brad, you won. Just gloat. Now, I'm going to go find Edison."

Brad snickers. "I didn't win. You're just thirsty for something other than alcohol, I get it."

I wander through the party feeling unsteady, as if I'm on a boat, tipping and rolling. Finally, I make it out to the yard, find Edison leaning against a dilapidated fence, sucking on a joint and drinking a can of Pabst Blue Ribbon.

"Hey Abby," he says, without turning around. "You want?" He turns around now, holding out the joint. I give it a try. It tastes like burning weeds and makes me cough. I hand it back. "Thanks, but I don't think I get the appeal."

He shrugs. "Well, if you're really curious, you could try some edibles before you give up entirely. But maybe it doesn't do much, not to people like you anyway, I don't know."

"Without the wolf I am getting a lot more drunk." I make a show of stumbling against him. "Whoa. I think I need you to hold me up."

He laughs and opens his arms, welcoming me into them. Starts by nibbling on my neck and I think I'm going to lose it, my body is just going to dissolve. He scoops me up in his arms, holds me with my legs wrapped around his waist, presses me up against the fence, and we're kissing and his mouth tastes like pot and cheap beer and pizza and it's the best thing I've ever tasted and then—

We're falling into space.

Half a second later I realize the sensation is physical reality. We tumble onto broken concrete and blackberry vines and it hurts, almost as much as bullets. He lands on top of me and I'm crushed under the solid, fleshy reality of his body.

"Oh, God, Abby, I'm so sorry." He scrambles off me. "How badly are you hurt?"

"I'm okay." I sit up, testing. Everything is sore but nothing important seems broken. I cough. Ow. "Maybe a cracked rib? It's okay. I still heal pretty fast. What about you?"

"I fell on top, you got the worst of it. Oh my God. I'm not light, Abby. I could've crushed you."

"No way. I've had guys way bigger than you try to crush me, I'm uncrushable."

"That was when you had the wolf. Don't move, okay, not until I've checked you for serious injuries."

"Fine." I sit still while he explores every inch of my body with his fingers, pressing gently, and even when he hits a bruise or a scrape, it's possibly the best thing I ever felt. By the end of it I'm feeling so relaxed I could fall asleep right here.

"Well, nothing seems broken. Which is pretty amazing."

"I told you, I still heal pretty fast. Look, we broke the fence." I point up at the fence, which is shattered and hanging in pieces.

He laughs. "Yeah. Well. I'm carrying you inside, okay?"

"Sure. Carry me anywhere."

He carries me into the house and Deena meets us at the back porch. "Oh my God, what happened?"

"We were leaning against the fence when it broke. We both fell, but Abby got the worst of it."

"I'm fine."

"You want a drink?"

"I do. Yeah."

Edison carries me, and my drink, to the couch, where he sits down and I'm sitting in his lap and this feels totally natural. I could stay here all night.

Except that I have to get up to go to the bathroom.

"I'll be right back," I tell him. He nods absently. I move through the hall, notice the party is far less crowded, and I'm very sore and also really drunk. Way more drunk than I can get with the wolf. Everything is blurry and my head is swimming.

I'm not sure I like it.

I leave the bathroom, try to keep steady, almost collide with Reed, who also seems drunk.

"Oh my God, what happened to you?"

"Well, you know that fence that used to be out in back above the carport?"

"Used to be?"

"Edison and I broke it. We fell onto the concrete. Anyway, I'm mostly okay."

He takes a deep breath. "Abby. I think I owe you an apology."

"For what?"

"Last summer. When I came onto you. I wasn't trying to be a jerk."

"Dude. Please. You told me you thought I was ugly and then asked if I wanted to make out, that seems kind of like a jerk move to me."

"I didn't mean it. I was just negging you."

"Negging?"

"It's this thing in pickup artist philosophy, where you make a girl feel bad about herself before coming onto her, with the idea that she's more... uh... receptive?"

"That's ridiculous. Does it ever work?"

"Well, the pickup artists say it does. It never worked for me. I assumed I was doing it wrong."

"There's no right way to do that, it's just stupid. I mean, who's the most successful-in-love dude you know? It's Edison, isn't it?"

He sighs. "Well, yeah, he is. And I used to think it wasn't fair. When I met him in football camp, he was younger, smaller, less experienced—but, God, the girls just—went to him, like bees to a flower. What's his secret? I thought. Is he really so much better looking than me? How could anybody be that good? And why are women so shallow, always going for the best-looking guy around?"

"Um, because he's nice?"

He looks confused for a moment, then laughs. "Right. Sorry, I don't still think all that stuff. And I really am sorry for being a jerk to you."

Somebody needs the bathroom, squeezes past, interrupting our conversation. But I'm glad we had it, it feels like closure. I go back to Edison. Snuggle up next to him. Think I'm going to fall asleep like that and feeling pretty good about it.

I WAKE UP.

My mouth tastes like vomit and ashes. My sense of smell seems blunted, everything filtered through a terrible smell that reminds me of Bourbon Street.

The last thing I remember was snuggling next to Edison on the couch, not intending to have anything more to drink. But I get the sense that I must have... changed my mind. I have the distinct and frightening impression of having done things I can't remember. Just like when I got dosed with the berserker drugs.

I sit up in a panic. My head pounds and my eyes don't want to focus. I notice Brad draped in a chair, snoring. I'm wearing the T-shirt he gave me last night.

I look around at the morning light glowing on the party debris. A shockingly huge spider crouches in the upper corner of the wall. Probably a giant house spider and completely harmless, I make note automatically.

I stand up. I'm so sore I can barely unfold myself. Not just the bruises, but my muscles, like I overstrained them doing something athletic. Oh, no. A part of me flickers briefly to a terrifying but exciting possibility: did Edison and I have sex?

No, I would smell that. I think.

But my sense of smell is way off. The vomit that lingers in my nostrils is like a veil draped over my perceptions.

I head to the bathroom, legs bare under the large T-shirt and, being a bit taller means large T-shirts all by themselves are a bit less convincing as a dress.

Where are my actual clothes? Did I ruin Deena's cool velvet dress?

Downstairs restroom. That's where I threw up, I can tell, and I tried to clean it, although I missed a couple of spots, which I get to now.

Upstairs restroom. I find the black dress, draped over the edge of the shower, thoroughly damp, as if I showered in it. Well, okay. So, what, I came up here to take a shower and forgot that's usually done naked, until I'd already gotten my clothes all wet, and then I went, "oh, right?" and took them off?

How much time did I black out?

I leave the bathroom, almost collide with a yawning Deena. She does a double take, then smiles. "Oh, you're alive, good. I was hoping you would be."

"I... um... I think I kind of blacked out the last part of the evening?"

"Not surprised."

"But what did I actually do?"

She looks thoughtful. "Oh, you know, a little of this, a little of that. You wanted Edison to swing dance with you."

"That sounds... okay."

Grinning. "Maybe."

"What? What do you mean, 'maybe?'"

"Well. Your pop culture education is a little spotty, but apparently you have watched at least part of *Dirty Dancing* at some point because you were doing a pretty good re-creation of some of the dance moves from it."

"*Dirty Dancing*? You mean what I did was dirty?"

"No, that's just the name of the movie. It was pretty sexy though. Until you had to throw up. That's never sexy."

"Bon Dieu, I did all that in front of everybody?"

"Not quite. You turned green and ran to the bathroom. Eventually we peeled you out of there and marched you upstairs to take a shower."

"Where I tried showering in all my clothes."

"Yes. We brought you the T-shirt and a blanket and led you back to the couch. Otherwise I think you were prepared to curl up on some towels and sleep right there in the bathroom."

"That sounds like me."

"Well, that's it for your exciting blackout adventures. It could have been a lot worse."

"I'm really sorry. I had no idea—I mean, without the— you know, without the wolf, everything hit me a lot harder than I thought it was going to."

"I get that." She puts a hand on my shoulder. "I'm sorry, I don't want to mom at you too much, but it really seems like you need to be a lot more careful than you're used to being. I mean, in just one wolfless night, you tried to kill yourself by falling off a cliff and then tried to kill yourself again with alcohol poisoning."

"Oh, and I started off the evening failing to punch out Colin Ambrose."

"What? I didn't know about that."

"Yeah. It didn't last long. Edison told him to go away and he did. But it was still pretty humiliating."

She shakes her head, then gives me an unexpectedly fierce hug. "Look, Abby. I know there's still a part of your brain trying to tell you that you're indestructible. Don't listen to it, okay?"

11

ROMAN AND RUFUS

W hen we head out to Enumclaw, I'm still pretty hung over. Deena has dressed the four of us up in what she calls redneck camouflage: jeans, plain T-shirts, plaid flannel shirts, and knit caps.

Izzy is obviously amused by her outfit of yellow and black plaid, but her dark skin is very flattered by the right color of yellow and it looks good on her. "The flannel is how you can tell it's the Pacific Northwest, nobody in Louisiana ever wears flannel."

"What, never-ever?"

"Well. Maybe tourists." She tucks her long, fine dreadlocks up under the cap. "Do I look like a lumberjack yet?"

"Totally."

I sniff my own shirt, in dark blue and dark green. "Is this vintage?"

"It is! I go to the Highland Games out in Enumclaw every year. There's a vendor who carries this stuff."

"Highland Games? What is that?"

"See, she doesn't know either," Izzy says.

"Well, that's fine. Maybe they're only a northwest thing. Anyway, Edison and I go every year, we like the bagpipes and the sheep herding. So I'm going to play you my bagpipe mix on the way out there, just let me know if it gets to be too much."

"Babe, you're going to play bagpipes when Abby has a hangover?"

"I'm assuming she'll like it, that the bagpipe gene is linked to the red-hair-freckles gene, but I guess we'll find out." She glances over her shoulder at me with a smile. "If it sounds like the intolerable shrieking of a banshee to you, just let me know and we'll listen to a different playlist."

The music starts up. I must like bagpipes okay, since I don't instantly want to shut it off.

"I'm taking I-90, is that all right?" Deena says.

"Probably. I guess I don't know what that means?"

"The route. I'm heading east first. I like to drive past Mercer Island just in case the rich people are up to something."

"Rich people always up to something," Izzy says.

I don't think I've ever been this way before, east across Lake Washington. We're hit in the face with a hill full of mansions.

"Bill Gates lives somewhere over there," Deena says, waving her hand vaguely to the north. "I heard he burrowed into the hillside like a hobbit so from the water it looks like three normal size houses but on the inside it's an entire giant compound."

On the other side of the island we start heading south, at first through boring warehouses and shopping centers, but eventually we pull out into a green area where we're driving along a river, through what seems like the outskirts of little towns like Maple Valley and Black Diamond, toward some hills that are already covered in snow.

"What mountains are those?" I ask.

"Mount Rainier foothills. Oh, Flaming Geyser State Park!

Hey, Edison, remember when the church youth group went there?"

"Yeah." He grins. "We were the only kids who weren't sneaking away to make out."

"You want to stop?"

"Of course we want to stop, it's a flaming geyser," I say.

Deena snickers. "Oh, yes. Of course. Definitely."

"Why, what's so funny?"

"You'll see."

We pull into the park, use the restrooms, Deena smokes a cigarette. "Well, let's hike up to the flaming geyser, kids."

It's not much of a hike, but then, when we get there, it's not much of a flame. Or much of a geyser. In fact, it's a tube coming up out of the ground, encased in concrete. Methane gas is escaping through the tube, I can smell it, but the flame isn't even lit when we arrive.

Deena marches up to the tube with her lighter and gets the flame going again, then salutes it. "There you go, little flame. Godspeed."

"Is that seriously the flaming geyser?" Izzy asks.

"Yep. That's the flaming geyser."

"There's not another one somewhere else? With more flame? Or more geyser?"

"Nope. That's it. Apparently the flame used to be stronger, back in the day. You know, before any of us were born. The methane down below is petering out."

Izzy shakes her head. "Well, babe, this is the most underwhelming tourist attraction you've taken me to yet. Much more underwhelming than the Ballard Locks."

"Didn't you like the Ballard Locks? I thought you liked the Ballard Locks."

"I didn't dislike them. I just thought they were a little underwhelming as a tourist attraction."

"Hmm." Deena looks genuinely sad for a moment, then

brightens. "Well, just wait until we get to the Oregon City Municipal Elevator!"

"Did you say, 'municipal elevator'?"

"Yep. It connects the downtown to the uptown. And, get this, there's an elevator operator! Or at least there used to be! There's a person whose whole job all day long is to take people up and down in the elevator!"

Izzy smiles, shaking her head. "Wow. You really know how to show a girl a good time."

We get back in the car and keep driving south and east. As we start to approach Enumclaw, the landscape flattens out and we see ranches. Black cows, white sheep, horses, and other animals.

"Look, it's a llama! Or maybe an alpaca. Does anybody know how you tell the difference?"

"Deena, if you don't know, none of us are gonna know," Edison says.

"That's it, that road right there!" I yell, pointing, and Deena whips the car around, skidding on gravel, to turn down the side road.

She glances at the fenced off cattle field and sighs. "Of course, it had to be a bunch of Republican signs. I'm glad I wore the plaid."

"Not that ranch, I think it's the next one down. See? There's a sign." I point to a big wooden sign saying WELCOME TO HAMMER SPRINGS RANCH. In spite of the "welcome," the gate is closed and there's a NO TRES-PASSING sign.

Deena parks the car by the side of the road and we all get out. "Well. What do you guys want to do now?"

Edison eyes the gate. "I bet I could climb that. What about you, Abby?"

"Edison, don't be ridiculous. We're not invading. This is supposed to be a friendly visit. What if I stand around here at the gate and let them pick up on my scent?"

"You think that's going to work?"

"I don't know. Is there anything like a call box? Sometimes gates have a call box, don't they?"

We start examining the fence, then Izzy calls out. "Found it. There's a red button and a speaker. You want to do the honors, Abby?"

Feeling weirdly nervous, I press the red button, hear a buzzer, expect a voice. Instead, the gate starts rolling open.

"Oh. Huh." Deena seems taken aback. "I guess we just drive up then?"

"I guess we do." But we're all unsettled by this silent welcome.

We drive slowly on a road that goes fairly straight up to the main house, a vast white farmhouse with a wraparound porch. It looks like a "real" version of some of the "McMansions" in Meriwether.

"I guess the fitness chain must be doing well, huh?" Deena says, as we walk up the steps to the porch.

The main doors open outward, suddenly, revealing the whole pack all gathered together. Three born wolves, four bitten wolves, nostrils flaring, and two humans, one girl too young for a wolf to have appeared yet, and a woman who I'm pretty sure is her mother. It's the oddest thing, but she reminds me fleetingly of my own mother. Pale hair, very pretty, and something just a little sad about her.

The twins step forward as one, and the slightly shorter of the two shakes my hand firmly. "Sister."

"Abby. Roman? or Rufus?"

"Roman."

Rufus steps forward to shake my hand as well, but with less assurance. So, Roman is the dominant twin and never lets his brother forget it? I study the twins for a moment. Similar, but not identical, they do look very much like Pere Claude must have when younger: fair-haired, lightly tanned, tall and big, barrel-chested. But the twins are in even more impressive physical condition, possibly because they're young still, possibly because they run a fitness empire. They look massive, like body builders, and I get just a little apprehensive thinking about how much physical power they must have. Working together, they could probably remove my head from my body with their bare hands.

"I'm Abby. These are my friends Edison Kelly, Deena Santoro, Isobelle Quemper. I know they're all human, but you can speak freely in front of them, they know about, you know, all the wolf stuff."

"Hm." Roman grunts and turns toward the group gathered behind him. "This is our younger sister Kimberly and her husband Robert." Two bitten wolves come forward to shake my hand. Kimberly must have a different father, because she doesn't smell like a half sister. "My mother Noelle and my father William." More bitten wolves shake my hand. If he calls William "father," Leon must have left when they were fairly young. The twins must have been the ones to bite their other family members. I wonder when it happened. Is it weird to get bitten by your own son? I guess I bit my father, to restore his wolf. But I barely knew him, so it didn't seem weird at the time.

"This is Crystal, my wife, my son Raymond, and my daughter Sherry. Raymond is sixteen and newly a wolf, but Sherry is too young still."

"Nice to meet you," I say. Raymond gives me a "whatever" eye roll, apparently putting me in the category of "irrelevant adult" which is funny because we're technically the same age. He makes eye contact with his father, who nods, and he and Sherry take off to some other part of the house.

Roman says, "What brings you here, sister?"

"Well, we're trying to find out how this wolf from Meriwether got bitten. Or, not bitten, maybe some other thing, like getting saliva into a scratch." I hold up my phone with a picture of Andrew. "We're not sure, because he doesn't remember an incident that would explain it. When we found out you guys lived in the area we thought we'd find out if you knew anything. And, you know, I kind of thought it would be fun to meet each other?" I give my cheeriest, most optimistic smile. I guess I did think it would be fun, but so far, it hasn't been fun, it's been excruciatingly awkward. I can't quite put my finger on what's wrong though. Maybe the twins are just weirded out because they really didn't get any of our contact attempts, so it's like, hey, long-lost sister shows up out of nowhere. Or maybe they're worried I want money?

Roman takes my phone, shakes his head. "Well, I don't recognize him." He passes it to Rufus who also shakes his head. He passes it back to me. "What else?"

They're trying to get rid of us. What are they hiding?

"Well, maybe you don't know Andrew, but, obviously the two of you have made bitten wolves. Have you made any that —you know, that you lost track of?"

"Lost track of? You mean, uncontrolled? Accidental? Like your George?"

Oh, he does know about that. "Yeah. Like George."

"No." He shakes his head firmly. "My brother and I have never made any accidental, uncontrolled wolves. Anything else?"

I'm flustered. Roman might be telling the truth, but he's not very helpful. I glance over at Edison, try to communicate telepathically. I brought you along because you're charming, be charming, get him to talk!

And, amazingly, he does. A brief glance at me, then he steps forward. "Well, even if you can't help us, I'd love to see the ranch. I've been hearing amazing things about Hammer-fit. All the guys I know from the football team say it's the best gym. And they love your Untamed Snacks."

Roman relaxes a little. "It is a great gym, isn't it? And every one of them has become a kind of haven for the bitten wolves in their city. I think we're providing an important public service." He thinks for a moment, studying Edison in a way I'm not sure I like. Almost predatory. "You'd like to see the ranch? Let's see the ranch. Follow me."

Roman leads us off the porch, Rufus brings up the rear, and behind us, the doors of the house slam shut. We were never invited inside. Maybe Roman's pack is just very territorial and private, but I can't shake the feeling that something is being hidden from me. All those furtive glances and silent people. Even Rufus lets his brother do all the talking.

I follow Roman through the field, silently, and for a fleeting moment I'm reminded of what it felt like to follow Father Wisdom, his broad back in a dark suit, his hat, his long strides, his lack of concern for what was going on behind him. If he wants you to follow him, you follow him. And if later he finds out that you didn't follow him, there will be hell to pay.

I shake my head, try to clear my thoughts. This isn't helping, for me to have just met Roman and already be casting him as the villain. I don't really know anything about him. Think of this from his point of view, right? I show up out of nowhere, and sort of vaguely accuse him of irresponsibly biting people?

But I can't shake that sensation of uncomfortable similarity to Father Wisdom.

"This is a free-range organic ranch," Roman says, gesturing across the field. It's picturesque as can be, with peaceful-looking cows chomping on green grass, faded to yellow here in November, snow-covered hills behind them. "Because Untamed Snacks is still a fairly small operation, we harvest the meat for several of our protein bar recipes from our own stock. Of course, not everything grows here west of the mountains. We have a partner ranch on the other side of the Cascades that provides bison and elk."

"Oh, you have ostriches!" Deena exclaims.

"We do." Roman looks over at the fenced off area with ostriches. "We've been experimenting with ostrich meat for the Untamed Snacks. Ostrich meat is very low fat and nutritious."

"Oh, it's delicious," Edison says, encouragingly.

"Can I see the ostriches?" Deena says.

"I suppose. Let's go." Roman leads us to the ostrich pen. Ostriches, which I have never before seen in non-cartoon form, turn out to be giant nightmare dinosaur birds, with outrageously long necks that are constantly darting around like snakes, beaks snapping as if they catch invisible insects.

"Ohhh!" Deena exclaims, taking pictures, while Izzy folds her arms, looking skeptical.

"Those things gonna take off my hand?" she says.

"Any animal can take off your hand if you fail to respect it," Roman says.

Izzy gives him a sidelong glance, keeps her arms folded, keeps her distance from the ostriches, while Deena appears to be trying to make friends with them. The giant birds seem indifferent to all of us, just snaking those absurd necks out to catch those phantom insects.

I'm staring at the ostriches so intently that I don't notice the giant, pointed, blue tongue roll out of the cow's mouth until it's already snaking up my forearm. I yelp, turn toward the cow, a very pretty black and white cow, who looks fairly pleased with herself, all set up to lick me again, and also about three feet farther away than I expected.

"Yo, how are cow tongues so long?" I say out loud.

Deena laughs. "You got licked by a cow! That's good luck!"

"She licked you, did she?" Roman says, looking very amused. "Interesting. She must have noticed that your wolf was gone."

Wait, he knows about that? How does he know about that? "How do you know about that?"

"Word gets around."

"Are you in contact with Leon?"

"Not regularly. We know you restored his wolf." He smiles slightly, glances at Rufus, who hangs his head. Did Rufus try and fail to restore Leon's wolf? Is Roman needling his brother?

"Rufus, are you a trauma morph?" I ask.

He raises his head, squares his shoulders. "Fully mastered."

"What does that mean?" Deena asks.

Roman looks thoughtful for a moment, then shrugs. "Brother, you want to show them?"

"Sure." He disappears into a little shed. A few moments later, a distinctive smell of lightning and sense of pressure, like a storm coming. A huge yellowish wolf pads out of the doorway.

Deena yelps delightedly. "That's amazing! Oh my God! Can I pet him?"

Roman gives her a disgusted look. "He's a giant wolf, my dear. You can pet him if you like, but he can also take off your arm with a single bite."

Deena looks down, sheepish. "Sorry. I wasn't thinking." She looks from me to Rufus. "He's a lot bigger than your wolf, Abby, do you guys have conservation of mass?"

"I guess we must."

"And is your wolf fur always the same as your hair color?"

"No, Leon has red hair like me, but his wolf is white."

"Your wolf is red?" Roman says. "I hear our grandmother had a red wolf."

"I didn't know that. But I hear that I take after her." I kneel, low enough to make eye contact with Rufus-wolf. I notice, with my peripheral vision, that the other animals, the ostriches and cows and llamas (or possibly alpacas), are all moving away. Not rapidly, not in obvious alarm, but there is clearly some impulse driving them away from the giant wolf.

Rufus and I make eye contact. I feel like we're waiting for something. For one of us to flash and emerge as dominant? I'm not willing to try, knowing that I might fail. I nod, indicating I won't challenge him. He nods in answer, disappears again, lightning smell, and human Rufus emerges, smiling.

"Rufus, have you made any bitten wolves that carried your trauma morph?" I ask him.

"No." He shakes his head. "Not that I know of."

"Have you made any bitten wolves at all?"

"A few."

"Who are they?"

Roman answers. "I'm sorry. We can't tell you that."

"What? Why not?"

"It's a matter of privacy, my dear. Surely you understand?"

"But this is a matter of public safety."

"You have my absolute assurance that all wolves created by me or my brother were socialized properly and do not presently pose any threat of uncontrolled new bitten wolves. That should be enough."

Roman and I bristle at each other, hackles raised. I feel a strong urge to flash my eyes at him. But I can't. Not right now. Not knowing I might lose.

I look away, scowling, and realize how it felt, all those times Viv lost challenges against me.

"Was Hammerfit originally going to be called Savage Fitness?" Deena asks. Her tone is casual, but the twins startle, stress in their sweat spiking upward.

"It was," Roman says. "Why do you ask?"

"Oh, just a couple of typos in HAMMERFIT: THE DIETS." Her tone is still very casual. "Why did you change it?"

"We found the 'savage' branding alienated women. Also, we wanted to emphasize the signature sledgehammer workout."

"Was the Meriwether club ever called 'Savage Fitness'?"

"Not once it was built. Maybe in some of the early paper-work. I'm sorry, is this important?"

"Just curious," Deena says.

"It's a nice gym," I say. "The one in Meriwether. The Varger-style sparring room is a nice touch. How did you know about those, anyway?"

"Leon must have mentioned them, I suppose." He shrugs, in an exaggerated way that makes me think he's lying. "Hey! What are you doing in there?" he shouts at Edison, who has wandered over to poke his head into the shed Rufus used for cover when he changed.

"Who's this third guy?" Edison turns around, holding up a hardback book called THE SAVAGE WAY. It shows three men in various fitness poses—Roman, Rufus, and a third man, dark-haired, who doesn't look related to us.

"That's Flint Savage, our partner when we started Hammerfit," Rufus answers.

"Is that an earlier edition?" Deena takes the book from Edison and flips through it.

"There's a whole box of them in there." He points to the shed. "And some other things with the Savage branding, things like T-shirts and water bottles."

"We did make sample merchandise for trade shows," Roman says. "That was how we discovered women didn't like the 'savage' branding."

"Is Flint Savage a bitten wolf?" I ask.

"He was bitten at his own request and socialized properly."

"Where is he now?"

"We don't know. We had a bit of a falling out."

"Over what?"

"Vanity." Roman takes the book from Deena and flips through it until he finds a picture of Flint flexing for the camera, holds it up. "He asked for the gifts of the wolf, begged for them, but he was unhappy with the results. You see here and here and here? Implants. Body sculpting. But after the wolf came, the implants didn't sit right. We warned him that something like that might happen, but he still blamed us for it. By then we were able to buy out his shares in the company, and we did. It's been months since we heard from him."

"Where did he get his money?" Izzy asks.

Roman frowns at her, nostrils flaring. "I don't understand why that matters?"

"Maybe it doesn't." She shrugs. "Do you know where he got his money?"

"Inherited it, probably." Roman takes a studied pose of nonchalance. "Isn't that how most people get their money?"

"Did he deal drugs? In the mob or something?" I ask. "He wasn't Strigoi, was he?"

"Strigoi? What on earth is that?"

"Subset of the Russian mob. Last summer a bunch of them attacked us in New Orleans, trying to get bit. We still don't know if any of them succeeded."

"Oh, I heard about that. I didn't hear the name 'Strigoi' though." He rubs his chin thoughtfully. "No, Savage wasn't a mobster. Although, there are shadowy areas in the fitness world, illegal substances and questionable procedures."

"Was he involved with any of that?"

"I don't know. He didn't try to bring any of it into Hammerfit, certainly."

"Flint Savage wasn't his real name, was it?" Deena asks.

Roman shrugs. "I never saw any indication that he used a different one."

I ask, "Do you have anything that still smells like him? Clothing, maybe?"

Long pause. Eventually Roman answers, "You know, I think we do. He left some workout clothes behind and we put them in a box in case he ever came back for them. Rufus, would you?"

Rufus nods and goes back toward the main house. While

we wait, Roman studies Edison in a way I don't like. Clinical, but admiring. Sizing him up. "So, Mr. Edison, what's your story? You're not a wolf, are you?"

"Nope, just wolf-adjacent." He grins.

"But you are very athletic."

"Yeah. I guess. I mean, sure. I'm pretty athletic."

"Edison, you're going to the Rose Bowl as the Huskies' running back, don't sell yourself short," Deena says, punching him lightly in the arm.

"Have you ever thought about becoming a wolf?"

"I have. Abby even bit me last summer, but I took the cure instead."

"The cure?"

"For the bite. I don't think it works after the first transformation," I jump in to clarify. "We got it from the Cachorros."

"Hmm. Los Angeles, right? The Spanish-speakers?" And something about the way he says "Spanish-speakers," something scornful and dismissive, makes me hate him forever. As if Spanish-speakers are inherently worse than people who speak other languages.

Edison bristles too, I can feel it. I can smell it. He sort of hulks up, the same way he did when facing Colin Ambrose, stares Roman in the eyes, and says, "That's right. The Spanish-speakers."

They flash each other.

Roman, with his blue eyes, flashes red.

Edison, with his brown eyes, flashes gold.

Roman smiles and I swear it's the creepiest smile I've ever seen.

"You like them, don't you?" he says. "The Cachorros?"

"I don't know them." He shrugs. "But Abby likes them. And I trust her judgment."

"Hmm. She's your alpha, then? This little girl without a wolf?"

"Alpha is a human term," I say. "Based on overly anthropomorphizing the behavior of captive wolves in a highly unnatural environment."

Edison puts his arm around my shoulder. "Wolf or not, I guess you're right. She's my alpha."

Roman puts forth an effort, laughs slightly, speaks in a light tone. "Love, of course. It does make submissives of us all."

Rufus returns with a plastic bag, hands it to me. "This is everything I found that carried his scent."

"Thank you." I smile at Rufus. I don't know for sure, but I get a vibe like maybe he's not so thrilled with the way his brother uses personal dominance against him. Maybe he can be an ally. "I guess we have everything we need for right now."

"Can I borrow this?" Edison holds up the book.

"Just take it, boy, we've got hundreds." Roman sounds cranky for a moment, then masters himself again. "Good luck, children, I hope we were helpful."

"Oh, yeah, very much. Nice to meet you." I wave, force a cheery smile.

We leave, moving quickly, not speaking. But once we're on the other side of the gate, Deena explodes. "Was I the only one who thought that was hellaciously awkward and creepy?"

"You weren't," I say. "It was all weird. Like, did you notice how only Roman ever really said anything?"

"Or how he just plain didn't want us to go into the house at all?"

"Or how he sort of pretended like he didn't get any of our phone and email messages but you totally know he did?"

"Or how he wouldn't tell us what he knew about Flint Savage? There's no way he would have gone into business with him without having at least some idea of where his money came from."

"Izzy, you talked about the money, you think that's how we can find him?"

"Well, it's possibly how we can get the police to care about him. It's not as if 'being a werewolf' is against the law. Biting people without their consent is against the law, but if he does it in wolf form, good luck prosecuting that."

"What if he's exposing people on purpose to get back at the twins?"

Everybody gapes at me.

"You really think he could be doing something as messed up as that?" Deena says. "Seriously?"

"Well, why not? People do messed-up stuff all the time."

"But what's his end game?" Deena continues to frown. "If this is revenge it seems kind of indirect? How exactly is it intended to hurt the twins?"

"Maybe he doesn't know. But imagine the twins told him something like, 'whatever you do, don't expose people and then just let them go, you have to protect them through their first moon' and once he was mad at them he decided, 'forget that, I'm going to expose people all willy-nilly and see what happens.'"

Edison looks thoughtful. "But what's the mechanism? It has to be something you don't notice. And it's not like you can inhale it, right?"

"No. Everybody tells me saliva to bloodstream is the only way, but one of the Meriwether wolves was scratched, not bitten. So, I don't know, you could scratch somebody, maybe, without them noticing. Nobody knows how much saliva it takes. It's not like they've done a whole bunch of carefully controlled experiments."

Izzy says, "So, if this Flint Savage is exposing people on purpose for whatever reason, what can we do to stop him?"

I think about it. I tried to argue George into getting his wolf under control, and he wasn't interested in that, he just wanted to go out and kill more people. What if Flint is the same way? Will we have to kill him?

"I don't know," I say, finally. "I guess we'll deal with that when we find him."

We climb back into the car and drive away. Once we're on the road, Deena asks, "Edison, what was that between you and Roman? You gave him this fierce look like you were carrying the ball and he was the defensive line of the other team. Oh, hey, I just made a football analogy! Did I get it right?"

"You did. Yeah." Edison laughs. "I don't know, he just sounded kind of—racist, I guess? And it pissed me off."

I say, "It did more than piss you off, Edison. You eye-flashed him. Like a werewolf. You wanna tell me about that?"

"I did what now?"

"You know exactly what I mean. You've had lingering effects from my bite."

"But I don't change shape."

"Okay, but you did change."

He lets that sit for a moment, then makes eye contact with me, not a challenge at all. "All right. I did. I didn't want to tell you because I knew you'd worry, but honestly, it's glorious. If you could bottle this, you'd make millions. Every little thing about my body just, you know, works that much better. I mean, football alone—"

"And that's another thing, weren't you going to quit football this year?"

"I was. But the coach kind of pressured me into joining the team again. And that's part of what I mean. I didn't want to say anything, but last year the Huskies had kind of a bad year and I thought it was my fault. But this year we're going to the Rose Bowl."

"Yeah, I heard about that. What is it?"

Deena looks over her shoulder to make a turn and takes the opportunity to give me a shocked look. "You really don't know?"

"I was raised by religious fanatics, remember?"

"Right. Somehow I thought—but it's probably a West Coast thing anyway, isn't it?"

Izzy nods. "I hadn't really heard about the Rose Bowl before living in Seattle, babe. People in New Orleans care deeply about football, but it's a different scene."

"Never mind, we're getting off track. What about senses? Can you scent track?"

"Not like you can. But, yeah, kind of. Like, this guy—" He gestures toward the bag. "I think maybe I would recognize his scent if he were nearby. I'd be able to follow it if it were recent."

"Wow. This is incredible. Should we tell someone?"

"You mean the people at your maison? I guess. I'm already supposedly one of you, right?"

"Yeah, but—I don't know. I'm not sure I want to tell them. I still don't really trust the Varger with bitten wolves."

"No? Haven't they been handling the Meriwether guy's transition fairly well? And the Hammerfit wolves?"

"They have, but—I don't know. I guess I want to talk to the Cachorros first. It was their cure. I'll text Jaime. If he still has the same phone number he did last August, maybe we can talk."

> Jaime this is Abby I have some questions about the cure from August

Hopefully that will be clear to him, but vague enough to not cause trouble if somebody else has the number now. We're passing in and out of areas of good phone coverage, so I don't expect to hear back right away. Instead, I sink against Edison's shoulder, as much as I can while still wearing the seat belt. It's cold outside, but warm in the car, sunlight streaming in, and I fall asleep.

12

GEORGETOWN MAISON

*S*he stands on the far shore, wind stirring her ruff of red fur, nostrils flaring. She finds me with her eyes, flashes them brilliant poison-green.

Not yet, I tell her, and I turn to show her what I've found —

"Abby, we're at the maison." Edison shakes me awake gently.

"Wait, what?" I look around in confusion. "Where are we? This looks like a bunch of warehouses."

"It's the address they gave me," Deena says.

"Let's get out of the car, you'll know pretty quick if it's the right place," Edison says.

We do. And it is. Viv comes rushing out. "Abby! What did you find out?"

"There's a lot. Let's go inside."

The Seattle maison is a vast and mostly open space that used to be a warehouse, remodeled into a space for gymnastics of some kind, with padded surfaces and ropes hanging from the ceiling. The edges of the space have been carved up into smaller rooms. In the largest one of these, we gather around a huge wooden table marked with bright stains and deep gouges and other signs it's been in use as an art studio. It still smells faintly of linseed oil and turpentine.

The gathered group is fairly huge: me, Andrew, and Viv from Meriwether; Theo, Tabitha, Christophe, and Brenna from the Seattle maison; and my three loufrer hanging back, shyly, as if they're not sure whether or not to make themselves part of the meeting. Tabitha is a sister, one of Leon's children. Her wolf appeared near San Francisco and she was taken in by the maison there.

"Abby, welcome to the Seattle maison." Theo takes my hands. "Tabby, feet down."

Tabitha rolls her eyes, but puts her feet on the floor. "They're clean."

"And we're having a meeting. Abby, you and Tabitha haven't met before, but I'm sure you recognized each other."

We shake hands. "Nice to meet you, Abby. Until you came along I was the youngest sibling."

Theo continues, "This is Peter, Christophe, and Brenna, our immue full moon team. You might have seen some of us on the calls from Meriwether but this is the first time we've met in person."

We all shake hands. Theo says, "Abby, you and your loufrer have discovered something interesting?" I nod. "Great. Why don't you lead the meeting for now?"

I take a deep breath and go to the front of the table, dump out the contents of the plastic bag full of Flint Savage clothing. All the scent trackers (including Edison) flare nostrils.

"Several interesting things. First of all, the Hammond twins are confirmed as Leon offspring, my half-brothers. Rufus has a fully mastered trauma morph. According to them, they started the Hammerfit chain with financial assistance from a man named Flint Savage, but after making him a bitten wolf, at his own request, he didn't like the results, and they had a falling out."

Tabitha reaches for a T-shirt. "This stuff belonged to him,

didn't it? He totally smells like a guy who would call himself Flint Savage. What is that cologne?"

"L'Occitane Cédrat," I answer, without hesitation. Some of Babette's lessons must be sinking in. "Widely available, mid-priced."

"A jock strap, really?" Vivienne lifts it up with a pencil, look of disgust on her face.

"Good for scent tracking," Theo says with a small smile.

"Does he smell familiar to you?" Viv asks Andrew, holding up a pair of shorts.

Andrew takes the shorts, inhales them for a long time, then shakes his head with a frown. "I'm just not sure. It's possible I encountered him at some point in the last month, but nothing is jumping out at me. The thing is, until this happened—I wasn't really in the habit of thinking about what people smelled like, unless it was obviously bad, or unless I liked their cologne."

"Is Flint Savage his real name?" Brenna opens up her computer.

"No idea," Izzy responds, doing the same. "But I'm guessing no."

"There's a lot of stuff here," I say. "You think we can cut it up into smaller pieces, pass them out? Maybe share them with the Seattle and Meriwether Hammerfit packs?"

Theo frowns. "The Hammerfit wolves? Are you sure you want to involve them?"

"Well, why wouldn't we? The more scent trackers the better, right?"

He looks thoughtful for a long time. "We're not in the habit of involving bitten wolves, but I supposed it wouldn't hurt. They already know we're here, after all."

"We should check in with Pere Claude before doing that," Viv says sharply. "Don't you think?"

"Of course," Theo says. "Do you want to call or should I?"

"I will." Viv picks up her phone and leaves the conference room.

Izzy speaks up. "Last known location of Flint Savage, check it out." She turns around her computer to show a photo from a restaurant called Havoc. I'm not sure I'd recognize Flint from just the photo, since he's wearing dark glasses and a low hat, but the caption very helpfully gives his name and the description "fitness entrepreneur." He is not dining with either of the twins. Instead, he's accompanied by three very attractive women I've never seen before.

"Havoc!" Deena says. "That place is expensive." She quickly skim-reads the article, from a fancy lifestyle magazine called SEATTLE HIP. "This is from months ago; could you guys, you know, still pick up a scent from then?"

"No," Theo says, at the same time I say, "sometimes." We look at each other. "Not reliably," he says.

"Is it worth trying?" I ask.

"Could we get lunch out of it?" Deena asks, then facepalms. "Sorry, sorry, I know I'm just a loufrer, I shouldn't be saying anything."

"Never mind, I just figured out what's wrong with the idea," I say. "He drove there in a car and left in a car. All we would get from a scent trail is that he was there, which we already know."

Izzy looks thoughtful. "Your people, when you do scent tracking, how do you do it?"

Theo speaks up. "In what sense?"

"Let's say you want to map out a certain area of town to find out if a particular person has been there. How do you make sure you've covered everything with a minimum of backtracking? And what's your range? How close do you have to be to pick up on a scent?"

"Range varies, but we monitor our scent tracking with that." Tabitha points to a big map of Seattle tacked up on the wall, covered over with clear plastic and scribbling from dry-erase markers. It looks like the one we have at Meriwether, but much larger.

Izzy nods thoughtfully.

"Primitive, isn't it?" says Brenna.

"It is a little, um, old-fashioned?"

"It's ridiculous. We should do it on the computer."

"What about an app? That you all can put on your phones?"

There's a pause, while Brenna and Christophe exchange looks of shock and delight, then start typing on their computers. "Barney and Ricard are into it," Brenna announces a few minutes later. "Let's go!"

"Hold on." Viv enters the room again. "I just got the okay from Pere Claude to bring in the Hammerfit wolves, what are you all talking about now?"

"Developing an app," Brenna says. "You know, something where you can carry it around on your phone and use it to keep track of your scent tracking?"

"Don't you think we should consult Pere Claude about that?"

Brenna and Christophe exchange another look, this one just barely short of eye-rolling. "What's he going to say about it? Does he even know what apps are?"

Vivienne inhales, nostrils flaring in rage. The air in the room becomes dark and heavy, as if a thunderstorm is gathering. Viv turns blazing yellow eyes at them and, wolfless, they melt completely under her gaze. Her voice comes out in a deep growl and she smacks the table between every word. "You. Will. Respect. Your. Pere."

They smell scared. And it makes me feel angry at Viv, so I challenge her. "Come on, Viv, they weren't being disrespectful. Pere Claude isn't particularly computer-savvy and he knows it. I know for a fact he has you manage his email. If you asked him, 'Should we do an app?' he'd probably ask you to make that call. He's a good leader, he knows when to delegate."

A long moment while she inhales, tense and angry, but clearly without a reasonable response to the words I just said. She sighs, a long sigh that releases most of the tension in the room, although she continues to frown and sounds cranky when she speaks. "Fine. Work on your app. But when you finish it, we're going to test it thoroughly before use, and it had better be secure and reliable."

"Of course," Brenna says. "Of course. Isn't our conferencing app secure and reliable?"

Everyone nods. "Oh, yeah, it's great," Tabitha says. "Like, I was on a Zoom call with a group of my old Portland buddies and we got totally pranked by some masturbating weirdo. That never happens with the wolf calls."

A brief flurry of nervous laughter, then Viv says, "Let's take some of this to Hammerfit, then." She stuffs a few items back into the plastic bag, pointedly ignoring the jock strap.

Theo nods, slowly. "I think, Vivienne, it would be best if you and Abby went to do it. I'll text the members of the Seattle Hammerfit pack who I have contact information for, tell them to meet you there if they can."

Viv looks around at a bunch of frowning faces, closes her eyes and drops her head in a kind of surrender. "Very well. Let's go, Abby."

"So, what was that all about?" I ask, once we're the car headed to the Seattle Hammerfit, in the Green Lake neighborhood.

"Nothing. Turf wars. Here in Seattle, Theo is head of his own maison, but in New Orleans, my status is second only to that of Pere Claude. I become accustomed to acting as his agent. So, in my eyes, I was speaking on behalf of Pere Claude. But in Theo's eyes, we were in his territory, and I overstepped my boundaries."

"Viv, do you think Pere Claude would have done that? Responded with unbridled rage to a young person making a flippant comment?"

"No, of course not. I admit it, I lost my temper. I'm on edge. Something about this whole business doesn't feel right. How can you be exposed to the wolf essence and not know it? At first I thought Andrew was lying to us, and he was somebody with habits that would explain lost time, such as drug use. But that was wrong. And now we find out this man, Flint Savage, might be involved? But I still don't understand how."

"Uh. I have a theory."

"A theory? Oh, little one, your theories. What is it?"

"That he's exposing people on purpose to get back at the twins."

She gapes at me for a moment then laughs. "Oh, my. That's quite the theory, isn't it?"

"Do you have a better one?"

She sighs, shakes her head. "All right, I don't. It just sounds so absurd."

"But a lot of absurd things are true, right?"

She nods. "Say, Seattle has a pretty great independent radio station, KEXP. You ever listen to it? I think you'd like it."

"Viv, are you changing the subject?"

"I am. But, I'm serious, too. The radio stations available in Meriwether have not exactly been to my taste. Not yours either, I gather." She finds the station and the music comes up, as promised, very much to my taste. They go right from my favorite, Nina Simone, to Deena's favorite, David Bowie, both doing the song, "Wild is the Wind."

Our Hammerfit memberships from Meriwether get us into the Green Lake location. In the sparring room, three bitten wolves greet us warmly, introducing themselves with hugs and a brief backstory. There's a burly Asian man who introduces himself as "Mazaki. Maz. I was a guard at the jail that night."

Dan, a handsome, athletic Black man, is a "former police officer, tried to deal with what I now know to be a bitten wolf who was having a lot of problems."

"Why did you leave the force anyway?" Maz asks. "They wouldn't give you full moons off?"

"No, it's just—I didn't know how to hide all this from my partner, and I didn't know how to tell her either, so I just bailed. I bailed on my whole life."

Roberta, a short, sturdy woman with a crew cut, is a "nurse practitioner, leaving work after swing shift, intervened in what I thought was a mugging, but it turned out to be a werewolf, not a mugger."

"Are you the entirety of the Hammerfit pack?" Viv asks.

"Not at all. We're just the ones who responded to Theo's text. There's seven of us total," Maz says.

"Seven? What do you do on the full moons?"

"We have a cabin in the Cascade mountains."

Viv nods. "Similar to the Meriwether pack. Now, we're here to ask your help in locating a man named Flint Savage. He's suspected of exposing our friend Andrew to the essence of the wolf deliberately and without his knowledge, and without guarding him through his first full moon."

There's some grumbling, as everybody instantly recognizes that as terrible behavior.

Roberta asks, "What do we do if we find him?"

Viv says, "You have met with the Seattle maison, yes?"

"Maison?"

She shakes her head. "Pack. The other pack. Theo and the rest?"

"Oh, yeah, the Georgetown pack. We should contact them?"

"Yes. They're coordinating the hunt for this man, Flint Savage."

There's silence for a moment. I take a deep breath. "If you all are willing to help us find Flint Savage, his last known location was the Seattle restaurant Havoc, and we have some of his clothing. Could see if any of you recognize his scent?"

I overturn the bag onto the floor and everybody instinctively flares nostrils. They pick up the items and bring them to their faces, but shake their heads. The closest hit is Roberta, who spends quite a while with part of a strongly scented tank top, but eventually gives up with a sigh. "I'm so sorry, but if I ever smelled that dude, it was—you know, it was before all of this happened. So I'm just not sure. Maybe?"

I say, "That's okay. It was way too much to hope that any of you would go, 'oh, yeah, that guy, I totally know that guy.' But at least you might recognize him going forward, if he's still in town, or if he left a strong trail anywhere."

They all nod. Then Maz asks, "I'm sorry if you more experienced wolves think this is a silly question, but could you maybe go over how scent tracking is done a little more? I mean, obviously we've got the equipment." He taps the side of his nose. "But I still feel a little out of my depth."

Viv turns to me. "Abby, you're in training for this, you want to go over the basics?"

"Sure, I'd love to. But, like Viv said, I'm still in training, so I apologize in advance if you ask a question I can't answer. The first thing, um, do any of you get scent-related synesthesia?" Blank looks. "Okay, everybody, take one of the fragments of clothing and close your eyes. Exhale all your breath. Inhale deeply. Now, exhale on a count of ten. Pause for a count of five. Bring the clothing up right to your nose. Now, inhale through your nose for a count of ten. Hold it for a count of five. Let it sink into your brain. Now, inhale and exhale naturally, but keep your mouth and your eyes closed, and keep the cloth right there. Think about the scent. How would you describe it? Does it have a color? A texture? A shape? Does it remind you of anything?"

"Cologne," Dan says. "He wore cologne. Very—sharp and bright?"

"He did, that's good. Yeah. Sharp and bright. That's what I'm talking about, with the synaesthesia. Those are metaphors, right? A smell isn't literally sharp or bright. But it's part of how we make them clear in our minds. What do you get underneath that?"

Roberta grimaces. "Does it sound bad if I say, 'slightly spoiled lunch meat'?"

"No, that's good, that's perfect. Anyone else?"

"I get the lunch meat thing," Maz says. "But also a smell like a—like a burnt match sprinkled with black pepper?"

"Right! Some of you have fragments from before he was a wolf, and some after. He has a basic underlying person scent, but the ones from after that are going to smell wolfy. Notice the difference?"

Everybody nods.

Roberta inhales. "Am I being judgmental if I say, based on his scent, I don't think I like this guy?"

The door buzzes. Andrew is outside. The door buzzes again and he enters, reeking of tension. "Abby. Vivienne. Theo dropped me off here. He thinks the three of us should go investigate a place on the east side, Transformations in Kirkland, if it's possible to get there before they close. It might be where I was exposed."

13

TRANSFORMATIONS

"Andrew, can you navigate?" Viv pulls out of the parking space. Andrew nods and begins to give directions.

"How did you come to think this place was the likely source of your exposure? Did you remember something significant?"

"Well, the technical team had pulled up a list of Flint Savage's activities, and it turned out he had an aesthetics clinic in Florida that was also called Transformations."

"Aesthetics. That's plastic surgery?" I guess.

"But I didn't get plastic surgery," he says. "It was a weight loss treatment."

"And you didn't think to mention it until now?" Viv says. "We could have come here right away."

"Well, it was in Kirkland, I wasn't attacked by an animal, and I was never unconscious. I still don't know how I could have been exposed, but if we go there and find Savage, I hope we can figure it out."

"What treatment did you get?

"Mesotherapy."

"Which is?"

He chuckles. "Probably snake oil. Vitamins and whatnot. Meant to stimulate your metabolism. But a blogger I follow recommended this particular clinic. He seemed to think it actually did something, unlike most mesotherapy."

"How is it given?" I ask, trying to picture it. "Rubbed into your skin?"

"Oh, no, hon, it's administered by injection."

Viv gasps, so shocked that for a second I'm worried she's going to crash the car. "Bon Dieu," she whispers. "You don't think?"

"That the mesotherapy was full of werewolf spit? That's exactly what I think," I say.

"No." Andrew looks horrified. "Really?"

Viv growls. "Injection! Bon Dieu, that is both ridiculous and terrifying."

"The spit would have to be fresh," I say. "Maybe he got the trauma morph from Rufus after all. Or, are we absolutely sure that you have to be in wolf form to expose somebody? I mean, my loufrer and I were talking about it, and we all figured, there's a lot of stuff about transmission that nobody knows for sure because nobody's ever done any experiments."

"Well, no, because such experiments would be monstrously unethical and conducted on human subjects," Viv says.

"I know that, Viv. I wasn't suggesting that we should perform the experiments ourselves."

We slip into silence, listening to the radio. I hear a song that appears to be called "Jesus Christ Made Seattle Under Protest," which sounds plausible. But as I pay attention to the lyrics, the singer seems to be listing the downtown streets in order: Jefferson, James, Cherry, Columbia, Marion, Madison, Spring, Seneca, University, Union, and when they get to Pike and Pine, the streets where I used to hang out when I lived on Capitol Hill, I feel a clutching in my gut, an almost literal heartache. I miss the old neighborhood. I need to visit before we leave Seattle, even if I can't make it part of the official hunt for Savage.

Viv mutters, "I don't understand why you'd let somebody just inject some concoction into your body without knowing what it is."

Andrew sighs, heavily. "Vivienne, you've been a wolf for your whole adult life. You can't possibly understand how hard it is to stay in shape after thirty-five without a boost. I've only been pack for a couple of weeks and people are already noticing that my face is sharper, more defined." He rubs his chin. "You can't tell me it's not a weight loss advantage."

"Well, it is, but you shouldn't use it that way," I say. "Andrew, I got hurt very badly three months ago. I lost a foot in a leg hold trap, and a good portion of my head from a gunshot at close range. After healing those injuries, I was so weak I could barely move without assistance. I was okay, because my own people took care of me, I didn't have to hunt for myself. But if I'd been on my own, I could have gone into what they call a death spiral. Too weak to hunt, so you get weaker, so you can't hunt, so you get weaker. And eventually you just die. One of the rougarou sayings is that the only thing a wolf truly has to fear is hunger, and I believe it."

There's a vaguely horrified silence for a moment, then Andrew shakes his head with a slight smile. "Oh, hon. You are sweet to worry, but I do not live such a life that I have much chance of getting shot in the head or losing a foot in a trap. I'm an actor approaching forty. I worry about getting jowls." He sighs. "You do not want to know some of the things I've done to try to keep my weight down. Becoming a werewolf seems positively normal in comparison."

Viv gives him a chuckle. "All right, Andrew, I get it. I was in Hollywood for a while, I know first-hand what people are willing to do to lose weight."

We pull into a nondescript business park, and there it is:

TRANSFORMATIONS:
AESTHETICS FOR A MODERN AGE

We get out of the car and right away I notice a ghost of Flint Savage, which becomes very strong in the reception area. We flare nostrils, look around, nod. We're getting the same thing. He's definitely been here.

A young woman at the counter smiles at us, seems to recognize Andrew. "Mr. Collins, welcome. You look terrific, are you happy with your procedure?"

"Oh, I am, sure. But I have some questions for Dr. Strong, do you know where he is?"

"Dr. Strong?" Viv whispers.

"Dr. Strong." The receptionist frowns. "I'm afraid he's not here anymore. He left the clinic a couple of weeks ago."

All of us slump at once. Of course. It couldn't be that easy.

"Do you know where he went?"

"Another clinic, I assume. His departure was rather abrupt. He gave us an address to forward his final check, and that was about it."

"Can we have that address?"

"Oh, no, I'm sorry we couldn't possibly."

Viv steps forward, makes eye contact. "I think you can give us Dr. Strong's address."

Viv's eyes flash and the woman, name tag "Janet," wilts a little. But she shakes her head. "I'm sorry, I… I can't." But she sounds less sure than a few moments ago.

I step forward. If Viv already failed, I'll feel less bad if I fail. "Janet." She looks at me, meets my eyes with a look of confusion. "Janet, you were going to give us Dr. Strong's file?"

My eyes flash—I feel it, strong, for the first time in months. Janet relaxes, smiling. "Of course, it's right here." She opens a drawer, pulls out a manila folder, hands it to me. I put it behind my back so it's not there as a visual trigger, and she startles, as if shaking herself awake. "I'm sorry, who were all of you again?"

"We're Andrew's friends," I say. "My aunt and I were really impressed with his work and just wondered if we could get the same procedure."

"Oh, of course. The procedure you're looking for is mesotherapy, although I warn you, Dr. Than has a different formula than Dr. Strong. It's very typical for aestheticians to have their own patented blend. Here's Dr. Than's card."

"Thank you very much. We might be in touch. Thank you. Andrew, let's go."

I hustle everybody outside and for once, Viv doesn't fight me.

Once we're in the car, Andrew says, "What was that thing you both tried to do when you were staring at her?"

"You mean the flashy-eye thing?"

"Yeah, that. What was it? I've seen your people do it a couple of times and I don't get it at all."

Viv sighs, shoulders slumping. "We call it the stare of command, or sometimes the dominance stare. There's a concept we call personal dominance, or having a dominant wolf. If you have a lot of it, you'll be better at the stare."

"So it's like being more or less of an alpha?"

She winces. "We don't use that term. But, I suppose it's similar. When born wolves clash with each other, we often flash, and usually one emerges the stronger. But when we do the same thing to humans without a wolf, it can function more like hypnosis. For a moment, they do what we say. It's not a strong effect usually. You can't get someone to do something extreme or complicated. But you can say, for example, 'give me that file' and maybe they will."

"Wow. Can I do that to people?" Andrew asks.

"I don't know if it works for bitten wolves," Viv says.

"Only way to know is to try," I say.

"I wouldn't go around exploiting it," Viv says. She briefly

gives me a glowering look over her shoulder. "That woman is going to remember, later, that she gave us the file. It could make trouble."

"Viv. Don't get mad at me, I did the exact same thing you were trying to do. I just succeeded where you failed."

"Oh, Abby, you absolute bitch," Viv says, but she says it with affection. "You're really going to rub that in my face? Who got shot in the head three months ago, was it me? No, I don't think so."

"Viv is just annoyed that, even after three months without a wolf, my wolf is still more dominant than hers."

We continue teasing each other for a while. This is us, coming down from the tension. Now that we have the file, both of us want to imagine a quick path to finding Flint Savage, or Dr. Strong, or whatever he's calling himself.

But it can't possibly be that easy.

14

NEW MOON

Back at the maison, everyone seems to catch Viv's giddy mood, opening wine and ordering pizza. We've got Savage's clothes, we've got his file, he's practically caught, right? Plus, we've got a list of client names to check for wolfiness.

"And how are we going to do that, exactly?" I ask.

"What do you mean?"

"I mean, are we just marching up to the door and knocking and saying 'Hi, are you a werewolf maybe?' And what if they got exposed after the last moon and won't transform until next moon? Can we tell if somebody's been exposed?"

"We'll come up with a more definite plan tomorrow," Theo says. "It's been a long day, Abby."

"Plus, the app is almost ready to test," Izzy says.

Eventually Chez Lunatic goes home to sleep, and I curl up on a slightly ratty, paint-stained couch while everybody else is talking. My head aches in a dull way. I think I never fully got over my hangover.

Eventually I drop off to sleep, but it's a strange sleep, shallow, as if I'm asleep and awake at the same time. I seem to see everyone in the room without missing a moment, and then my wolf pads into the room, which seems both strange and entirely expected. The others don't notice her. We make eye contact, and with a gesture of her head, a flick of her ears, she indicates I need to follow.

I sit up, swing my legs over the side of the couch, stand up. I'm no longer wearing the dress and tights from earlier. Instead, I'm wrapped in a huge, loose garment, more like a blanket, no, a hooded cloak, and it's made from the pelts of my ancestors, the interior a butter-soft leather and the exterior fur in many different colors, with red dominating. It's heavy with the black pepper smell of born wolves.

"Where did I get this cloak?" I ask the wolf.

She doesn't make any noise to answer, but the knowledge speaks itself into my head like a whisper: *many generations gone, they all gave this power to you.*

"Power." I notice the cloak is very heavy, very hot. Too warm to be this close to the enormous fire. I think about taking it off, but then I'd be naked, and I don't want that either. "Not a burden?"

Power is one sort of burden. Lack of power is another. Path of needles. Path of pins. On the whole I prefer power, don't you?

"You only say that because you've never been haunted by your dead," I say. I inhale the fragrant smoke of the wood, that good roasting meat smell, but it reminds me of something unpleasant that I can't seem to remember.

The dead haunt the powerless too.

"It's not the same."

As you say. Things come anyway, ready or not.

My sister Ash, on her funeral pyre, sits up. That was her flesh making the roasting meat smell, and she is blackened, crackling, shreds of slow-roasted muscle falling off bones, as she shuffles toward me, smoked tissues peeling off and bones showing through, one eye still blue and full of accusation, as she takes one step and another step, and I'm paralyzed with fear, unable to move or look away, and when she reaches up her ragged burned hands to strangle me, I sink backward, accept it as my fate—

I STARTLE AWAKE, CHOKING AND COUGHING. I'M STANDING IN the middle of the large central room, naked except for a blanket, which is made of some cheap polyester and not the pelts of my ancestors. Morning light streams in through the high windows. I smell coffee.

The blanket will do for a kind of sarong and I shuffle toward the coffee smell, find Christophe in one of the other rooms, drinking a large cup. "Abby, good morning. The other scent trackers are all out testing the first version of our app, do you want to help?"

"Not really." Plunk down heavily in the seat, grab some coffee. When I hear myself say the words, it seems odd. I always want to help, don't I? I'm compulsively helpful.

"Well, that's okay," he says. "They had a big plan for how they were going to do it, so you'd just be out testing on your own."

"Right. Are those donuts?" I point at the pink box that smells like donuts.

"Oh, yeah, right, help yourself."

I do, but the chocolate ones are all gone. Grumpy, I settle for one that has some kind of sugary cereal sprinkled on top. It looks fancy, but it's not chocolate. As I bite into it and the strange texture of the cereal scrapes the top of my mouth, I wonder about that. I never want donuts. Sometimes I eat them, when the whole maison gets beignets, but I never just wake up and my first thought is, hey, where's the donuts?

Christophe notices that I'm not really dressed and asks, "If you're wondering, we do have a shower here. It's in a little cubby, I can show you."

"I know where it is, Christophe, I can smell the shampoo."

"Oh. Of course. Well. You know, you're welcome to use it."

"Thanks."

We stare at each other awkwardly for a moment and I realize that I'm acting really cranky and a little bit mean for no reason at all, but I can't seem to stop myself...

Wait.

It's been about two weeks since the last full moon.

"Hey, Christophe, is there a calendar in here?"

"Always," he says, with a grin, and points to the really obvious one on the wall that I should have already noticed.

Oh. It's not quite the new moon. Maybe this is just—

"Forgot," he says, and takes out a marker and crosses off what must be yesterday. "Oh, it's the new moon, no wonder you're so cranky."

"You noticed that, huh?"

He smiles sympathetically. "I know some of the wolves get that. I didn't know you'd get it without a wolf. You know what, you should take a spa day or something. Go to Hammerfit with that cute loufrer of yours."

"Thanks for the suggestion. I think I'll do that."

What I don't tell him is this: until today, for the last three months, I haven't had new moon depression. In fact, I kinda forgot about it.

I'm almost certain now, the wolf is coming back soon. And that thought fills me with terror.

CHRISTOPHE OFFERS TO DRIVE ME TO CHEZ LUNATIC, AND FOR some reason I turn him down. "No, I need the walk." He lets me, although he frowns. "Are you sure? It's a really long way."

"No, it's good, the walk will help."

But it's eight miles and takes me about three hours to walk

it. I periodically think about catching a bus the rest of the way, or even springing for one of those ride-share things, but then I feel stubborn. I said I'd walk, and I'm going to walk. Damn it.

When I finally get to the front door of Chez Lunatic, it's slightly open and I walk right in. Edison is inside, slumped deeply into the couch, unshaven, unshowered, surrounded by piles of paper. His eyes, glazed, stare at the television, which shows a low-resolution black and white image that jumps and skitters. Two people stand in a little alcove, tug on clothing, fix hair, rifle through bags. The images are accompanied by a toneless rhythmic mechanical noise. Scritch-scritch-hiss-pop. Scritch-scritch-hiss-pop. On the video, a door opens and the people disappear. The noise continues.

"What are you watching?"

"The door channel. Izzy found it while she was trying to hack us some free cable or something. I think it's the security camera from the apartment building at the end of the block. It's set up so that if somebody buzzes to get let in, you can see who they are."

"And what are we listening to?"

"I was playing some thrashed record I got at the thrift store and it reached the end and just kept going around in a circle. There's like this rhythm to it, listen. I'm thinking about writing a song around it."

"Uh. Okay." I listen for a few seconds to the rhythmic scritch-scritch-hiss-pop, then go over and start the record again. The music isn't bad, some kind of sixties soul, but the record is in such bad shape that it sounds dirty and lost and sad.

"And what are you doing with all these papers?"

"My mom dropped 'em off. They're basically my school career from kindergarten through first year of college. I guess she already picked out the ones she cares about, and everything else is, like, 'Edison, you're nineteen, I want my sewing room back.' So I'm supposed to be going through them all and recycling the ones I don't need, but I've been sitting here for a couple of hours and I've barely dented it and I'm starting to think I should just set fire to the whole pile."

"Don't do that indoors. Deena and Izzy will be very upset if you burn down the house."

"They would be upset. We're getting a major deal on rent. The owners are basically just letting this place sink into the mud until they're ready to sell the property to condo developers."

He picks up a paper, holds it up to the light, squints. "Oh, Economics 311, money and banking. I'd forgotten about that class. You know I've forgotten about half these classes. What was the point of teaching me all that stuff if I was just going to forget it?"

"I don't know." I pick up one of the papers. "You need this one?" and he shakes his head no. I rip it. In half, then in half then in half again until the pieces fall from my hands like confetti.

He joins in, and soon both of us are shredding the whole pile, like a couple of giant rats. I have a visceral sense of familiarity at the sensation of the paper tearing under my hands. I've done this once before, back in the summer, when I was hitchhiking back to New Harmony and experienced my first severe bout of new moon depression without knowing what it was. I thought my sense that everything was hopeless and there was no point carrying on was just an accurate assessment of affairs.

Edison—is he depressed? Is that why he's doing this?

"You want some pizza from last night?" he offers. "It's pepperoni but I guess that doesn't matter anymore—you eat pepperoni now, right?"

"Sometimes, but I have a complicated relationship with pizza."

"Why? What did pizza ever do to you?"

"Well, cheese pizza was one of my first outsider foods, you

know, when Steph picked me up when I was running away from New Harmony? She had no idea what else to feed a vegetarian teenager. And I had been kinda starving, and pizza is pretty great anyway, so pizza instantly became my favorite thing ever. But then, the night Steph's ex-husband George came over and tried to kidnap Terry, George posed as the pizza delivery guy. I found out later that he offered the actual pizza guy several hundred bucks to put on his uniform and deliver the pizza. But ever since then, pizza reminds me of that night. Sometimes more than other times. I'm in kind of a bummed mood today so it's really hitting me. The smell of the pizza makes me feel afraid. Apprehensive."

I get up to play the other side of the record. I come back. I inspect the pizza. Room temperature and dried out. I take a bite. It's stale and hard. I pull cheese, pepperoni, tomato sauce off the top, eat that. It's okay. I guess after walking eight miles I was sort of hungry, which I didn't even realize until I started eating.

Pause. Rip. Rip. Rip. "So, Edison, you're going to the Rose Bowl, isn't that good?"

He shrugs. "We're probably going to lose, though. That's what all the sports commentators are saying. But even if we win, and everybody treats it like the best moment ever, it's not going to last. Five years from now, who's gonna care?"

"I don't know, people still seem to care about that time the Seahawks won the Super Bowl."

He shrugs. Rip. Rip. Rip. "It's pathetic, really. I mean, football. Maybe people care, but why do they care? It's just a dumb game."

We rip. People show up on the door channel, tug on clothing, and disappear. Every time the record reaches the end of a side, I get up, flip it, play the other side. "Look, Edison, I mean, isn't everything in life kind of dumb? Is football any stupider than anything else?"

He chuckles a little. "I don't know. Good point I guess."

Rip. Rip. Rip. "So, uh. Edison? Are you depressed right now?"

He shrugs. "Maybe."

"I'm sorry. This is my fault, for biting you. I think I gave you my new moon depression. What the rougarou call the black moon."

"Oh yeah?" He looks interested. "I didn't notice the date. So this happens every month on the new moon?"

"It does. There's a variation with a red moon too, where you get mania during the full moon, do you have that?"

"Werewolf-specific bipolar, wow." He shakes his head. "I feel pretty up during full moons, but I don't think that counts as actual mania."

"I don't think it does. Not unless you have, like, delusions of grandeur and run around having a million kids like my father did."

He chuckles slightly. "Not so far. Anyway, thanks for telling me. Once a month is better than every day, right?"

"I guess it would be." I think about it. "Wait. Are you saying what I think you're saying?"

Shrug. "Probably."

"But you—you're like—you're the most perfect person I know, how could you possibly be depressed?"

He turns toward me with a scowl and spits out, "Congratulations on being my parents, who have expressed that exact sentiment to me many times, albeit in slightly less complimentary terms." He takes a thick pile of papers, several inches, and rips it in half with obvious effort, muscles cording and straining.

He's mad at me and my whole world crumbles in an instant and I start weeping uncontrollably. "I'm sorry, I'm sorry, I didn't mean it."

His anger breaks instantly. "Oh, Abby, no, I'm the one who's sorry, I didn't mean it like that."

"No, it doesn't matter, this is all my fault, you should hate me, everyone should hate me, I'm terrible, I screw everything up, I ruin everything, I should just go away forever."

He leans across the pile of shredded paper and interrupts me with a fierce kiss.

My body turns to water and rushes with a strong and unfamiliar tide, darkness surging, and I'm being pulled down, down—

Izzy's here.

Self-conscious, but a little slow to pull away, we're still together when she finds us, making out in the middle of our nest of shredded paper, in front of a big screen showing the door channel, listening to the abstract swish-swish of the inner groove of a thrashed soul record from the 1960s. She sighs loudly and Edison pulls away.

"Sometimes you people are so weird," she says, and heads into the kitchen.

Deena walks in carrying a bag of groceries. "Which one of you decided our living room needed to be more like a David Lynch movie?"

"That was me." Edison grins. "Don't blame Abby."

"No, it was my fault. I'm the one who started tearing up paper."

"Collaboration, okay." Deena carries the bag into the kitchen and then comes out again. "Is it the new moon?"

"Why do you ask?"

"Because, duh." She marches up to Edison, ruffles his hair affectionately. "I know you wolfy types get depressed on the new moon. But, hey, at least you can schedule it. And you know you'll feel better tomorrow, right?"

"Yeah. Yeah, we will." He smiles, although it's sad and small and not at all like his usual devilish grin.

"Not all wolfy types get depressed on the new moon. But my father does, and I do, and I guess I passed it on to Edison when I bit him. Um, the maison told me to take a spa day."

"Oh, that'll be great," Deena says. "Get massages and stuff."

"Yeah? But I should clean this up first," Edison says. "Shouldn't I?"

"No, absolutely not, I'm taking pictures first," Deena says. "Go on, get out of here, you two. Do something fun."

15

CAPITOL HILL

"Something fun" turns out to be Deena lending us her car. First, we go to the Green Lake Hammerfit, where I use a guest pass to get Edison in so we can check out their spa offerings. There's the Grotto, three mineral soaking pools in different temperatures meant to imitate a natural volcanic hot spring. There's the foot reflexology, which technically they're supposed to charge extra for, but they take one look at Edison and just wave us on in. Then there's the salt room.

"What's the salt room?" I ask the receptionist.

"It's a room. Full of salt."

"Okay, but why? Why is it a room full of salt?"

He shrugs. "I don't know, I guess you have to go in there to find out."

The salt room turns out to be a room fully lined with the same kind of pink rock salt that people make lamps out of sometimes, with the floor as a bunch of course salt in a cotton sack so you can lie down on top of it. But after twenty minutes in the salt room, I still can't figure out why there's a salt room. Restless, I suggest that we visit the old neighborhood on Capitol Hill.

We do, and eventually find parking near a tiny second-run movie theater. We go in, get espresso and popcorn, start watching. But the movie is a comedy. Modern comedies often leave me cold, when the humor seems to revolve around violation of social norms I don't understand anyway. At a certain point I realize I'm kinda bored and lean over to whisper "Are you enjoying this?"

"Yes." He looks annoyed.

"I'm going for a walk then. Text me when it gets out."

He shrugs. "Whatever. Suit yourself."

I wander the old neighborhood, following paths I used to know, looking for a trace of my old life. Map the routes I took to Saint Sebastian school, map the routes to my favorite coffee shops. Here's the thrift store we went to when we first arrived in town, the one where I got my first real outsider clothes and knocked over a bunch of housewares. It's been remodeled into a restaurant that has already gone out of business and now sits empty.

Of myself, I get nothing. A whiff here and there, maybe. I've been gone a long time, I guess. Too long. It's not my neighborhood anymore, is it?

But then, where is my neighborhood? New Orleans? Bayou Galene? Neither one feels like home the way Capitol Hill did, for a while.

I find Steph and Morgan's old house, now completely boarded up, NOTICE OF LAND USE ACTION billboard prominent and covered in graffiti.

Melancholy overwhelms me as I stare at it, but I stare anyway. Is there any trace of us here at all? Me, Steph, Terry, Morgan? Ghosts? Phantoms? Spirits?

And then, live, a familiar person smell. Two of them, plus one that isn't familiar.

I turn, and see our old neighbors, Paul Singha and Harold Davidson, walking past with slightly melancholy looks that match my own mood. And a baby! Mr. Singha has a baby girl in one of those front slings and I can tell he couldn't possibly be happier about that. I couldn't possibly be happier for him.

"Mister Singha! Mister Davidson!" I wave. They seem startled for a moment, then move to hug me.

Mr. Singha answers first. "Abby! I thought your people had all gone back to New Orleans."

"We did. But I'm in Seattle for a few days. What's up with you guys though? I mean, it looks like you're selling your house too?"

Mr. Davidson laughs. "We are. They needed both properties for the planned development, which means we needed to reach an agreement with both families."

"And you did?"

"We did." Smiles.

"What are you doing here now?"

"Just saying goodbye."

"Yeah? Me too."

"So, how've you been?"

"Pretty good. I connected with family on my biological father's side. But what about you guys? You have a baby?"

"Her name is Lucy. Do you want to hold her?" Mr. Singha starts taking her out of the harness even before I say yes. She seems excited to meet a new person.

"Hello, Lucy," I say, holding her close, and all of a sudden there are tears spilling down my face.

"Oh, hon, what's wrong?"

"Nothing, nothing's wrong, she's just so... beautiful. I'm sorry. I get really sentimental sometimes." I make a point of smiling at her, and she smiles back, and I hand her back to Mr. Singha. "I hope you're happy."

"We are. With the money, we're moving to Queen Anne, and I'm planning to quit my job and take care of Lucy full time while she's young. We can start a college fund for her."

"That's great. That's just amazingly great."

"What's your family doing with the money?"

"You know, we haven't decided yet. So many possibilities. It's overwhelming."

"It is, isn't it."

An awkward pause. I say, "You know, we weren't neighbors for very long, but it was memorable. That night with the dog? And Steph's ex-husband?"

"It was crazy, wasn't it? Have things been crazy like that in New Orleans?"

"No. Not crazy at all. Very normal."

"Well that's great. Really great to see you. Give our regards to your family."

We hug, move on. I'm briefly cheered up, but then my mood deteriorates again. I follow the route to the park where I woke up the morning after becoming the wolf for the first time. Here I get a trace of bitten wolf. Not recent, but I follow, until it terminates in a fountain that looks like tumbled rocks, smells of blood and stress and, yes, death. The wolf was killed here, violently. Somebody's scrubbed the blood away, but not well enough. And two familiar people smells: Dan, from the Hammerfit pack, and Officer Lou, the police officer who helped me on my first morning after the wolf came. Her smell is layered, as if she keeps coming back here.

In fact, she's here right now.

I turn around. She's not in uniform. Her hair has grown out into more of an afro, making a halo around her face, which is still dark and beautiful, but looks drawn, frowning, troubled.

"Officer Lou? Louanne Kaffa?"

She startles. "I know you. You were—"

"Abby, Officer Lou. Abby Marchande? You found me naked in this park one morning and showed me how to make a large T-shirt into a skirt?"

"Oh my God, that was you!" She laughs. "I'm sorry I didn't recognize you right away."

"Well, I'm wearing clothes."

She laughs. "Yeah, and you grew up a lot. It's funny how kids do that, huh? What's been going on? I heard you moved down to New Orleans?"

"That's right. I guess, Steph only left there because of her ex-husband, so when he was dead, she went back to live with her parents. Her mom helps with the baby. They sold the Seattle house to some developers and her brother Morgan went back home too. I lived with them in New Orleans for a while, but then my biological father's family caught up with me and I've been living with them for the past few months."

She smiles, sadly. "So, things are going well, then?"

"Well, I miss Seattle, but, yeah, things are mostly okay. What about you?"

She stares for a long time at the place where the bitten wolf was killed. "I'm fine," she says. She's about as convincing as Edison.

"Say, do you ever read *Teen Mode*? I name-checked you in an interview." I pull up the article on my phone and hand it to her. She reads the two-T-shirt-dress instructions and smiles.

"Hilarious, I had no idea." She hands it back to me. "Thanks for the laugh." But she sighs, as if "the laugh" was a very brief ray of sunshine in an otherwise bleak existence.

I want to ask her what's wrong, but we barely know each other and it's probably not appropriate. Still, she helped me when I needed it.

"What's been happening in Seattle? Are things bad here? I mean, in a crime way?"

She huffs out a small almost-laugh and shakes her head. "Well, that depends. Are you talking about the nights of the full moon, or every other night?"

My breath catches in my throat, a flash of phantom bony hands strangling me. "Uh. The full moon?"

"We've been told for years that the full moon thing is a myth, that there isn't really more crime or strange behavior. But it's not true. The full moon is—Abby. That morning you woke up naked in the park, did you ever remember anything more about the previous night?"

"No." Which is true, I never really did remember that first night very well.

"Did you ever find out anything more about what happened?"

"Did I? Um, our neighbor talked about, um, how he heard shouting and came in to take care of the baby? Is that what you mean?" I fumble, nervous, not prepared for questions this direct.

She can tell I'm nervous. She comes closer, leans in, like a cop interrogating a suspect. "What about the dog?"

"The dog?" My voice comes out in a guilty-sounding squeak. I was not prepared for this.

"According to the police report, your neighbor Paul Singha saw George fighting with a large dog. Morgan Marchande shot at a large dog who ran away and was never found. That dog bit George, who was treated for rabies. The next morning, you woke up mysteriously naked in a park after a night you can't quite remember. A month later, there's a riot and George busts out of jail. Again, everybody talked about seeing a large dog. Some people got attacked. A month after that? Another large dog, and this time, my partner almost gets killed by it."

"Oh no. What happened?"

"The attack was extremely violent, but the animal acted strange, not like any dog I've ever seen. Kept rearing up on his hind legs. Huge. When he reared up, I could see that he was just about the size of my partner. We're talking a two-hundred-pound dog. What do you think of that?"

"It sounds very unusual." I swallow, panicked. This is bad. This is sounding really bad. "What happened to your partner?"

"I killed the animal before he killed my partner, but I had

to shoot it so many times. I had to practically blow its head off before it stopped attacking."

"That sounds bad."

"It was bad. And the next month after that? My partner disappeared."

Oh, no. When a werewolf gets killed in wolf form, that's what it looks like: like the human just disappeared. "You haven't heard from him at all?"

"That's right. And I think you know something about all of this." She takes my hands, impulsively, a little aggressively. But it's her right. I did this to her. I bit George, I started this epidemic. "I think you need to tell me what you know."

"Not here."

"Let's go to my condo then. It's not far away, come on."

It isn't far away, she's right. We enter a nice townhouse, relatively new. In the summer I remember noticing that she lived with another woman and a couple of pets, but now she lives alone, only the slightest ghosts of another woman or any pets remaining.

"I saw that," she says. "Your nostrils flared. You were smelling my apartment." She punches in a security code and a vaguely British sounding woman tells us:

YOUR SYSTEM IS ARMED

"Go on, then. Tell me what you smell."

"I'm sorry. You, uh, you split up with your girlfriend? Roommate?"

"Girlfriend." Her expression is grim. "She didn't like the night terrors. Or the crazy obsessions."

She flips on a light that blazes onto a cork board wall that probably looked very chic, before it was covered over with pieces of paper, sticky notes, pages ripped out of notebooks and scribbled over in marking pen.

One piece jumps out at me, an article from a magazine called the *Fortean Report*, called:

THE ROUGAROU OF NEW ORLEANS

She marches forward, rips it off the wall. "I saw your eyes go right to this. You're one of them, aren't you?"

"One of the—rougarou?"

"Werewolves. I know it sounds crazy. But I also know what I saw. I see it in my nightmares over and over again. Teeth and claws like razors. Blood and brains spewing out, without slowing him down until half his head was blown off. He moved too fast for me to see, almost. And he was strong, much stronger than my partner. Dan was a big guy. This thing, it wasn't bigger than him, but it could have eaten him for lunch. It *tried* to eat him for lunch. It wasn't human. But it was no normal animal either. It was a monster. But that's impossible, right? Right?" She trembles, and I smell the distress in her sweat. "Go on, tell me I'm crazy. Tell me there's no such thing as werewolves."

I shake my head, choking on the words I want to say. I feel a strong internal pressure to tell her the truth, all of it, the absolute truth. But I can't. Then my brain catches on something else. "Wait, did you say 'Dan'?"

"I did. Why? Do you know something about him?"

"But he's okay. He made the transition and he's with the Hammerfit pack. Bon Dieu, he even said that he used to be a cop and I didn't make the connection. He talked about you, but I didn't know it was you. He said he had an ex-partner who he wanted to tell, but didn't know how, so he was avoiding her."

She stares at me in wonder. "Hammerfit? What is that?"

"Fancy gym in the Green Lake neighborhood. It was, um, it was started by a couple of werewolves so it's got, you know, wolf-friendly touches, like a sparring room?"

"A sparring room? What on earth are you talking about?"

"It's a padded, reinforced room where wolves can fight each other without worrying about—" I break off. I'm telling her way too much. Aren't I? But she already knows so much.

"Without worrying about what?"

"About wrecking the building. Werewolves can, um, throw each other with a lot of force."

"Oh my God. Really?" She exhales, anxiety rising, but also a kind of giddiness. "You're not bullshitting me, this is all real?" I nod. "So it's true, George was a werewolf?" I nod. "And he bit you that night?"

I don't nod, and she notices, turns sympathetic. "It's okay, Abby. I understand. It's not your fault."

It's not? I want to say. But I don't. I just hang my head. If she already believes a lie, why not let her go on believing it?

"But you said my partner Dan, you said he's going to the Hammerfit gym? With other werewolves?"

"That's right."

She exhales, a big, shuddering breath, drops onto the couch, rubs her face. "Oh, God. I need a beer. They're in the refrigerator. Get one for yourself if you want."

"You know I'm underage?"

"And I'm a cop. I won't tell if you won't."

The refrigerator is a stylish stainless-steel surface, and inside, there isn't much, some leftover takeout, a bunch of different kinds of beer, and two boxes of white wine, chardonnay and pinot grigio.

I pick out a beer called "The Freaks Come out at Night" from a local brewery called Hellbent, which all seems a little on the nose. The can shows a drawing of a zombie.

The beer turns out to be a dark and syrupy imperial stout, delicious, but high in alcohol. "It's strong. Should we split one?"

"Sure. Glasses are over there." The stout looks like motor oil as I pour it out. She clinks glasses with me, sips. "So, teenage werewolf girl, what's it like?"

"Um. The teenage part or the werewolf part?"

She laughs. "Either, I guess."

"I don't know. I don't really have anything to compare it to."

"Fair enough." She sips the beer. "How do we end this?"

"End? What?" Fear clutches at me as I picture her getting the Seattle Police Department to come after us with axes to take off our heads.

"We have to stop the contagion. Every moon, there's more werewolves. Right?"

"Not usually. George exposed a lot more people than usual because he was in prison when the full moon came. It's, um, apparently it's not really all that common for us to, uh, bite someone without killing them."

"Oh." She looks taken aback, thinks for a while, then nods. "All right, I guess I understand that. You bite like an animal does, because you feel threatened or trapped."

"Right. And we don't want a big outbreak any more than you do." I take a deep breath. "That's why I'm in Seattle right now. Getting everything contained again."

"Yeah? I want to help."

"Maybe you can help us find a man named Flint Savage?" I call up the picture on my phone, hand it to her.

"Why are we looking for this man?"

"He's a known werewolf, and we suspect he's deliberately injecting people with his saliva without telling them, which sometimes creates a bitten wolf."

Her jaw drops. "Why the hell would anyone do that?"

"We don't know." I think about the reading on serial killers I've been doing. "It's possible that he derives a kind of erotic satisfaction from exposing attractive people to the, uh, the wolf essence?"

She nods. "Right, okay. We can probably get some police resources behind this. There's no way to officially pin it on werewolves, obviously, but we're definitely feeling the heat for the uptick in violence. Having a name to go after, that helps. I can officially suspect him of being connected to dealing in howler."

"I'm sorry, did you say 'howler'?"

"New street drug. Like bath salts or something. Scary, but the rumor is even more scary than the reality. On most people it's just a cheap high, like meth, but some people get extremely violent on it. There are even reports of cannibalism. That's the official theory about George, that he was an early howler overdose."

"But why is it called howler?"

"Nobody's sure. It came out of Florida." She sips the beer.

"Florida? Oh, wow. Flint Savage was active in Florida. There really could be a connection."

"Say, you know what would really help me? You see my wall of crazy there?" She gestures at the cork board and I nod. "If you could, you know, clarify? What parts are real, what parts are a scrambled version of the truth, what parts are entirely made up?"

"Oh, sure. Sure." In order to have two free hands, I set down the beer. The *Fortean Report* article comes down first. "This? Entirely accurate, because it's about the rougarou folklore. Legends that grew up around a pack of real wolves. The mythology is real, but has very little to do with actual werewolves other than regional proximity."

She looks at it with a laugh. "I kind of figured the giant bats thing couldn't be real. But you've been in New Orleans, is there a connection?"

"There is an old and fairly large pack in the New Orleans area, yes. But they're not bad people, they just want to be left alone. They've got their own land, their own livestock they hunt. Mostly they don't make trouble. But trouble gets blamed on them anyway, you know?"

She nods. Next, I locate the articles about "howler" and skim. They're all from the last three months, which doesn't fit the Flint Savage timeline. "I just don't know about the howler. The timing doesn't seem related to Flint Savage. It could be wolf-related but I just don't know."

She nods. "I was looking for any clues at all. Grasping at

straws maybe." She gestures for the paper, I hand her the stack and she puts it aside.

Next, I notice a lot of articles about Seattle. Violence, strange incidents, people disappearing. Some of it I recognize as having to do with the wolves I've met at Hammerfit, or George's prison riot, but some of it I don't know about. I study it for a long time, sipping the beer, thinking. Then I make a decision.

"Officer Lou? I think I need to introduce you to the wolves who are in town trying to contain things. I think you all need to share information with each other."

"Yeah?" She looks uncertain, but tries to make it sound like a joke. "You want to take me into a den of werewolves? They're not gonna eat me, are they?"

"Of course not. I'll tell them about this conversation, and they'll reach out if they think it's safe."

"If they think it's safe? What about me thinking it's safe?"

"Officer Lou?"

"Just call me Lou, please, I'm off duty."

"Okay. Lou. Most of the time, werewolves are more in danger than dangerous. Think about the one you killed. He was terrifying, right, but with enough firepower, you killed him."

She bristles. "I had to. And it's not like I knew he was a person."

"I'm not trying to blame you for anything. I just mean, if the whole Seattle Police Department knew about werewolves, and decided their policy was to shoot us on sight until dead? We'd all be dead pretty quick."

She inhales deeply, exhales slowly. "All right. I get it. But think about it from my perspective. You tell the scary monsters that I know about them, they kill me in my sleep, nobody's ever the wiser."

My phone buzzes. Edison texting me:

`Movie's over, where are you?`

I text back:

`Busy, coming soon.`

"Officer—Lou. I don't know how to get you to trust the wolves or the wolves to trust you. But I'm serious about your partner, Dan. Do you still have his personal phone number?" She nods. "Text him that you know about Hammerfit. About the pack. Tell him you talked to me. Then the two of you can work it out however you want. If he can convince you to work with them, great. If not, you can all just leave each other alone."

She nods. "I'll accept that as a plan."

16

THE FLAMING SWORD

"I'm sorry, you did what?"

A couple of hours later, at the maison, Viv stands in front of me, arms folded, mouth sneering in rage.

"I told Seattle Police Officer Louanne Kaffa that werewolves are real and her former partner Dan is one and she should contact him to talk about it."

"I'm sorry. You did *WHAT?!?!?*"

"Viv, she already knew almost everything. She'd watched a rampaging bitten wolf almost kill her partner. Based on the scent layers in the park, she kept going back to the site, staring at it, bothered by it. That's where we met. She was about this close to deciding werewolves were a major threat to public safety and mounting a kill-us-all campaign. I had to talk her down somehow."

Viv makes a disgusted noise. "You could have come back and told one of us and asked us how to proceed."

"Sure, but the moment would have been lost. It felt really natural for us to start talking right then. But think about what would have happened if I'd excused myself abruptly, come running back here to tell you about it, waited for one of you to reach out. At that point, it would have just made her more paranoid."

Viv explodes a disgusted breath and turns away, but Theo looks concerned, interested. "And you think you convinced her not to fear us?"

"Well, I helped. Her ex partner Dan has said some things, I think he'll reach out if he knows he doesn't have to work to convince her about the whole 'werewolves are real' thing. Then you've got a bridge to Seattle law enforcement. Like your connection in New Orleans, Régnault." I turn to Viv, who explodes.

"It is not the same!"

"No? Because Officer Lou isn't sexually attracted to her former partner?"

She blushes, then gets even more angry. "Abby! This is—if you ever do anything like this again, you're off the team."

"What? What are you talking about, Viv?"

"You heard me. You basically made a new loufrer without any approval from senior leadership."

"Viv, I did not tell her anything she hadn't already guessed!"

"Which is the only reason you're not off the team yet."

"Viv, are you really telling me that I can't ever use my own judgment about things like this?"

"No! You're sixteen and you're an apprentice! You don't have any judgment!"

I sigh. Theo sighs. We exchange looks. I sense that he's on my side, but unwilling to cross Viv too directly. "Well, fine. I told you everything that happened. I guess you all have to take it from here. I'm going out."

"Going out where?"

"Going out on a date with a boy I like? We're planning to eat something, I think. In a restaurant."

"You're going out with your loufrer?"

"Of course my loufrer. Who else?"
I leave the maison, text Edison:

> I'm ready to go. Walking around the neighborhood, let me know when you're close.

I realize I've never walked around the neighborhood immediately surrounding the maison. It seems to be mostly warehouses and giant truck cabs, uninhabited except for the people obviously living long-term in motor homes and tents. I pass a rockabilly bar where the heavily tattooed female bartenders remind me of Steph, only wearing much less clothing than I've ever seen Steph wear.

Edison texts:

> Getting close.

I head back to the maison location. A few minutes later, he rolls up in Deena's car, pushes open the passenger door for me. We kiss, briefly, before he pulls back into traffic.

After a while I say, "This is our first real date-date isn't it? You know, where you pick me up and we go out to dinner?"

"Hey, yeah." He laughs. "Maybe I should have dressed up more?" He's wearing his Husky football workout gear, but the nice stuff, not the old worn-out stuff.

"That depends, where are we going?"

"Oh, it's just some place in the U-district. It's called the Flaming Sword, and they do kebabs. Like, you assemble one kebab, and they cook it for you, then you eat it. And you can just keep going until you get tired of eating. That's why the guys from the team like it, I'm not sure they ever get tired of eating. Don't worry, they have vegetarian options."

But when we get inside, we're greeted by a huge purple and gold banner:

CONGRATULATIONS HUSKIES
ROSE BOWL BOUND

The place is absolutely full of football players and cheer squad in uniform, decorations of purple and gold, little stuffed animals meant to look like husky puppies. I pick one up. "Cute. Edison, why were you being so coy, this is your going-to-the-Rose-Bowl victory party."

He looks embarrassed. "I was worried you wouldn't come if I told you that. That you'd think it was just for football types, and it's not. A lot of people brought dates."

But we do spend the first twenty minutes or so just circulating through the place while he says hello to people. Everybody is friendly enough to me, his "girlfriend from New Orleans," but they do spend an awful lot of time talking shop about football, which mostly goes right over my head. We find a place to sit at the edge of a big group table formed by pushing smaller tables together. Edison and one of the players both go off to get skewers, leaving me talking to the other girl at the table. I think I remember her from the party.

"Elaina?"

"That's right." She smiles. "And you're Hoodoo Abby."

"I didn't know you were a cheerleader." I indicate her uniform.

"Yep, I'm a cheerleader. The guy I'm with is Moose."

"Moose? That's really his name?"

"The name on his drivers' license is Mike, but the team already had two other Mikes. He's originally from Canada. That's why he's Moose."

"Montreal?" I name the only Canadian city I'm familiar with. Montreal is also the only non-US site of a permanent Varger maison.

"No, more in the west. Not a super big city. Saskatoon, maybe?"

We both watch Edison and Moose travel through the kebab station. I think of Edison as a big guy, and Moose as a big guy, but when they're together like that, Moose still looks like a big guy and Edison looks normal-sized. Tiny, almost. And when he plays football, he's dodging guys like that, built like a bulldozer, a battering ram, a truck. But Edison has a secret.

If you could bottle this, you'd make millions.

What if Flint Savage isn't motivated by revenge at all? What if he's trying to give people exactly what Edison has, the wolfy enhancements without the inconvenient monthly transformation? And maybe what happened with Andrew is that he miscalculated, got the dose or the mix wrong, and ended up making a regular bitten wolf?

What if he's still out there doing it?

The boys come back to the table with an assortment of skewers. "Abby, I made you falafel, that's vegetarian, but there's a salmon one too, I thought I remembered maybe you eat fish?"

"Sometimes I'm a pescatarian," I say, because I like saying the word, which I got from Deena. I take the salmon skewer. "It's my compromise between me and New Orleans food. According to the Catholic church, fish are basically vegetables."

"It's okay to eat fish 'cos they don't have any feelings," Edison sings, and everybody laughs.

We eat for a while and I don't know if Edison's new-moon depression has lifted, or if he's just really good at faking it, because he's playing "life of the party" pretty well, joking and talking and singing.

"Kelly!" An older man, slightly tipsy, stops to stare at him. "Congratulations on taking the Huskies to the Rose Bowl, I knew you could do it!"

"Thanks, Professor Stinson."

The man moves on.

"Professor? That was your professor?"

"Professors care about football too." He shrugs, slightly embarrassed. "Anyway, the pressure is terrible, and I'm kind of looking forward to the day when everybody forgets about it. You know, where I get to be that forty-year-old dude telling everybody about that one time I went to the Rose Bowl, and everybody else is like, Kelly, you did that when you were nineteen, get a grip."

I laugh. "Like, your kids are making fun of you?"

"Oh yeah. I definitely have kids who are making fun of me. They don't even like football. They're more like their cool Auntie Deena, you know? They think football is capitalist and exploitive." He pauses, with a thoughtful smile.

"What? Imagining all the dad jokes you're gonna tell?"

"What? I could tell a dad joke right now. But I'm not a dad, so it would be a faux pa."

Elaina groans and drops her head to the table. "That's terrible. Nobody as cute as you should tell jokes that bad."

"Terrible. You know, I bought a discount thesaurus, and it was terrible. Not only that, it was terrible."

Moose groans. "Dude. That's bad. You know, the other day I saw the coach yelling at a vending machine. He wanted his quarter back."

The entire table groans. Wadded up napkins and bits of kebab get lofted our way.

"I don't know if I'll make the game, Moose," Edison says. "I just got diagnosed with Tom Jones disease. It's okay, though, lots of treatment options. It's not unusual."

More groans and flying debris, and now all the dudes at this table are, seemingly, competing with each other to tell the worst dad joke or make the worst pun.

My phone buzzes. It's Jaime.

Abby. What do you want to know?

The cure. On my friend. It sort of worked and
sort of didn't. You ever hear of anything
like that before?

No. This is Reina. Bring your friend to LA
Venice Beach & we can examine.

My heart sinks. Bring him to LA? Like I can just do that?

Thanks. I'll see what I can do.

I wait for a lull in the dad jokes and say, "Edison, do you
want to go to Los Angeles?"

"Sure, that's where the airport is. I think they put us on a
bus to Pasadena. Is that what they do, put us on a bus?"

"Bro, they put us on a bus."

"Wait. Does that mean the Rose Bowl takes place in Los
Angeles?"

"Pasadena. They're close." He considers. "Well, close by
car."

"What about Venice Beach? Is that close?"

"Close enough. Why?"

"Never mind, I'll tell you later."

"Oooo, what've you got planned, Abby?" Elaina asks me.

"It's a secret. If I tell you, the hoodoo won't work."

Moose turns to me with a big smile. "Is that Hoodoo Abby
stuff for real then? I want in. Can you just give me whatever
you gave Edison?"

"No way, you guys play different positions, the same stuff
wouldn't work. I have to give you a gris-gris bag tailored just
for you."

"Gris-gris bag?" He looks intrigued. "Is that like a
spell?"

"More like a talisman. Let's see, you want something for
victory and strength, right? So, you find a few things that

represent that, you put them in a little bag, then you wear the bag."

One of the players, whose name I didn't catch, gives me an earnestly worried look. "Is that, like, devil worship? Because I don't think I can do that."

Everybody groans and throws napkins at him. "Pendell, you are really something," Moose says.

"I'm serious." Pendell gets pouty. "I'm a Christian, I don't think it's okay to do devil worship."

"What devil are we worshiping, Pendell?" I ask.

"What do you mean?"

"I mean, if it's devil worship, there has to be a devil we're worshiping, right? So, what devil? Give me a name."

He frowns. "You know what I mean. *The* devil, there's only one."

"What? And he's all by himself down there in hell?"

He frowns. "Well, I guess there are lesser demons. But if you worship them, that's still devil worship."

"Okay then. What demon are we worshiping by putting spices and semi-precious stones in a little bag?"

"You don't have to be rude about it, just because you don't believe," he says.

Moose rolls his eyes. "Let it go, Pendell."

Pendell stands up, face pale, eyes intense. "Stop it. Just stop it. I know you all make fun of me, but you're all going to hell!"

I look up at him. We make eye contact. I whisper, "This is hell." I feel my eyes blaze. He shakes his head, sinks to the seat, looking dazed. Then he recovers himself and points an accusing finger at me.

"Did the rest of you see that? Her eyes glowed! She really is a witch!"

Everyone laughs while Pendell, stress levels spiking into the red, scrambles to escape, holding out his cross necklace like somebody fending off a vampire. "Stay back, demon!" In his haste to escape, he knocks over one of the smaller tables that were pushed together to make this big table. Glassware shatters, people scream and jump.

"God damn it Pendell, what the hell?" Moose stands up, brushing Pepsi from his shirt. "Can't you be normal for one night?"

"Demon!" he shouts, a final epithet, then leaves the restaurant.

An awkward moment. One of the other team members says, "Finally" and pulls out a flask of vodka.

"That wasn't about you," Edison says to me. "He's been like that all season."

"I guess." I feel bad, though. What if I messed him up and now he's going to play badly and it's my fault the team loses? I just lost my temper. I'm not proud of it. "Maybe we should leave, Edison?"

"Sure, sure. Come on."

"Nice talking to you again," Elaina says, and the other people at the table wave at me vaguely. The restaurant has already sent somebody over to clean up the broken glass and spilled drinks.

In the car, Edison gives me a quick, reassuring kiss. "It's really okay, Abby. Don't let that guy bother you, he's just a weirdo."

"I did the flashy-eye thing at him, Edison."

"I figured. Since he accused you of having glowing eyes. Non-wolfy people don't usually notice, do they?"

"Not usually, but, he's a weirdo, as you said. But what if I messed him up? Like, what if there are lingering effects? What if he plays badly and your team loses?"

"Abby, he always plays badly, he's second string for a reason. It's not you."

"But what if it is?"

"What if literally everything that goes wrong in the whole

world is your fault?" His voice is mocking but gentle. "I know how you feel Abby, especially when you're depressed, but that's Father Wisdom talking. It just doesn't make any sense for you to think you're the only person who ever screws anything up. It's like, the world was really screwed up before you ever got here. It can't possibly be your fault. Anyway, happy— uh— December?"

He hands me one of the little stuffed huskies.

"Edison, you stole me a toy?"

"I didn't steal it, I asked the organizer if I could have it and she said yes."

I hug it to my chest. It's weirdly comforting. "This is literally the first children's toy I've ever had."

"Really? That's harsh."

My eyes prickle with tears. "It was. But that thing I wanted to tell you before, my brother Jaime says that you can find them in Venice Beach and talk about what happened to you."

He looks worried. "You want me to meet them without you there?"

"They're nice, Edison. Honestly, they are. Jaime and his girlfriend Reina are literally the nicest wolves I know except for Pere Claude, and you were okay with him."

"Okay. So how do we hook up?"

"When is the Rose Bowl?"

"January first. New Year's Day."

I double check my phone's full moon app. "That's after the full moon. I'll talk to them and give you the details about how to meet up. Is that going to be okay? You don't have to. I just thought you'd want to."

"I do want to. I'm just nervous."

We arrive at the maison and sit in the car, motor running. I say, "You know, until that one guy made it so awkward, I had a really nice time tonight. Especially considering it was the new moon."

"Yeah? Me too."

"Edison, I don't know how much longer we're going to be in town. Now that we know we're probably looking for this one guy, we're gonna throw everything into finding him before the next full moon if that's at all possible. I could get sent—I don't know, anywhere."

"I know." He kisses me. "And you know I'm part of this too. I want to help, as much as I can." Another kiss. And another. And then, for a long time, we're kissing, until Viv comes out and raps on the window.

"Abby, get in here," she says. "We have to talk about the hunt for Flint Savage."

"Well, duty calls. Goodnight."

"Goodnight."

Inside the maison, everybody is gathered in the main meeting room, including, wow, Dan and Officer Lou. It's loud and there's a lot of tension.

"Abby," Officer Lou says. "We're having a bit of a debate here. Do you think we should be looking for Flint Savage by sending every one of your—maisons?—pieces of his clothing and letting the wolves look for him, or do you think we should be doing it online, tracing money and social media and things like that?"

"Um. Both? Anyway, there's not really a conflict in resources there, since a lot of the computer people are immue and not scent trackers."

Theo smiles. "You know, I hadn't thought about it like that, but you're right, it's not pulling our resources two different ways. We simply need to have one person in charge of the cyber hunt, and someone else in charge of the physical hunt."

"Are we pulling in the Los Angeles wolves?" I ask, partly because LA is on my mind. I get a room full of shocked looks.

"Los Angeles?" Viv blazes at me like I've pissed her off again, but I can't imagine how.

"You know, my father's pack, the Cachorros?"

"No, we're not involving the Cachorros."

"Why not?"

"It's not our territory, Abby. We've got no business there."
She folds her arms, as if to close off the possibility for
discussion.

Theo frowns. "Doesn't Abby have a point, though? Especially if Savage is still working in the cosmetic surgery industry, Los Angeles seems an extremely likely place to find him."

"Also, Texas," Dan says. "Dallas and Houston are big
plastic surgery locations."

"Don't forget Miami and Atlanta," Brenna says. "I just did
a cross-referenced search for places with the most plastic
surgeons per capita."

Viv shakes her head in despair. "So many places we don't
already have a maison."

"So, why aren't we using a ready-made maison in a huge
metro area?" I say.

"I told you. It's not our territory,." Viv glares at me, not
quite a challenge.

"We don't have to show up and try to tell them how to do
things, all we have to do is give them the information we have,
plus a few Flint Savage clothing items."

"Contact them how? Do you have mailing addresses?"

I open my mouth, then stop. I have a phone number. And
I have a location, Venice Beach. Is it okay to give her Jaime's
phone number? Maybe not.

"What if I went down there in person? They know me."

"Absolutely not."

"Why not?"

"Because I said no. Abby, there is a chain of command
here, and, in spite of your very arrogant wolf, you are at the
bottom of it. She must be coming back soon, probably with
the next moon, for you to be so cantankerous."

A jolt of panic. "Viv, I'm always cantankerous."

Her smile turns gentle. "You might think so, little one. But, as an adult who often finds myself trying to give you instruction, I can say that you were fairly cooperative, if a little whiny, for quite some time. But you've spent the last two weeks growing more troublesome by the day."

"That's not fair, Viv, I did everything you told me to do."

She makes a noncommittal grunting noise and they all go back to planning and arguing. It goes late and mostly doesn't involve me, so once again I fall asleep on the couch listening to the others talk.

The wolf pads in, sits next to me.

They get everything wrong as usual.

"Is that it? I thought they were trying." I sit up. Once again, I'm naked except for the huge, heavy, hooded cloak made from the red fur of my ancestors. Only those who died in wolf form, I realize, with a chill of dread and awe.

Yes, that power is the greater. This has been largely forgotten. Now we die as other people do. In human beds.

"Is that important? We're looking for the Savage Rock Man."

He came to this northerly place seeking escape from the consequences of his past, but on the whole he prefers palm trees and sun.

"Are you saying that he is in Los Angeles? Or Miami? Anyway, how would you know?"

She tosses her head, arrogantly. *I know many things. The world speaks to me, and I pay attention.*

"But what am I supposed to do? Go to Los Angeles myself? Without Viv's okay?"

She snorts through her nose, a kind of sneeze or laugh. *You never called her master.*

"What about Pere Claude?"

What about him? She tosses her head again and begins to pad through the darkened warehouse. I follow.

It's important for you to see what happens if you fail. She nods toward the big picture window and I draw back the curtains.

Outside, an enormous full moon hangs low over a city in

flames. I hear screaming as the moon slowly turns red, an eclipse, and I realize from my high perch that I can see everything happening down below, the wolves and half-wolves devouring people, biting them, making more. Everyone they bite rises again instantly, not as wolves, but as misshapen wolf-people, in torment and driven to torment others. The pain in the head is why they bite, a terrible pressure.

A huge male wolf-thing rises over a little girl who looks like my sister Ash, fanged mouth open impossibly wide.

His head explodes, showering her in blood, bone, brains.

She screams, the small, high-pitched, helpless shrieking of a small child.

Terrified, I startle awake.

The room is dark, empty. I quickly pack my things, not entirely sure I'm ready to take dream advice from a wolf, but not sure that I'm not ready to do that either.

Viv didn't want me to go to Los Angeles. Theo wasn't so sure. Before, when Viv wasn't sure about something we were suggesting, she wanted to talk to Pere Claude. But tonight, she never even mentioned him. She shut me down herself.

She's hiding something.

Not just from me. From him. Pere Claude.

I grab a couple of Flint Savage clothing items, put them in a plastic bag, stuff the bag into my backpack. I leave as quietly as possible by the side door. Now I'm outside in a cold December night, walking toward downtown Seattle. Am I really doing this? There's still time to lose my nerve.

A car pulls up behind me. I remember this sensation, as I hitchhiked all the way from Seattle to New Harmony, Louisiana. But I had a wolf then. Nothing scared me. But tonight, at three in the morning, the sound of a car pulling up thrills me with panic. I stand my ground. If they mean harm, that ends this whole crazy scheme pretty quickly, doesn't it?

The passenger door opens. "Hey, sis, you need a ride to somewhere that's anywhere?" The driver smiles, friendly, with bright red lips. One of the bartenders from the rockabilly bar, the tattooed ones who all reminded me of Steph.

Wow. If anything in my life ever seemed like a sign that I'm on the right track, this is it.

"Thanks." I climb in. "Do you know a way I can get to Los Angeles really cheap?"

PART IV

LOS ANGELES

17

GOOD VIBRATIONS

The wolf is a dark silhouette against a huge red sun, pacing back and forth, waiting for me. But I can't get there, the mob has found me, all the peasants with torches. They decided I'm a vampire. The fangs. I tried to tell them the fangs were a costume, but I couldn't figure out how to get them out of my mouth and prove it. The mob is so huge, so many of them, they overwhelm me completely, holding me down while the vampire hunter, Wisdom, takes the wooden stake and pounds it into my heart —

○ ⚜ ○

"HEY KID? WE'RE HERE." MY SEATMATE SHAKES ME AWAKE gently. Over the last couple of days, I've had a variety of people in the other seat. The current resident is a grizzled-looking older man who got on in Stockton and spent the whole time sipping vodka from a flask whenever he thought I wouldn't notice.

"Thanks." I uncurl, feeling stiff and weird. I can see why people pay for planes when they can, the bus takes forever. I was curled around the stuffed wolf, put him back in my backpack.

I turn on my phone, ignore the many angry messages from Viv, text Theo:

> Safe in LA.

Then I text Jaime:

> Near Staples Center. My phone is almost out of juice, find me the other way.

The phone buzzes with a call from Viv, and I turn it off, put it into the backpack, shoulder the pack, step off the bus into Los Angeles. After the air-conditioned bus, the heat is shocking. The first thing I do is take the backpack off again so I can remove my wool coat.

"Wow, it's hot," I say, to nobody in particular.

A random person getting off the bus tells me, "There's supposed to be a heat wave through Christmas. You can't tell me global warming is a hoax, damn."

I nod. The air seems dry and smells weird. Dirty oranges? Is that a thing? I wish Etienne were here. I feel unsure of myself all of a sudden. When I left Seattle, I was certain I was doing the right thing. But now I just feel lost and vulnerable.

I start exploring the area around Staples Center, partly out of curiosity, partly to make sure to leave a fresh scent trail for Jaime to pick up on. Staples Center seems to be a sports stadium, and the area around it full of mildly upscale shopping and restaurants. It's decorated for Christmas, more lavishly than Meriwether, but without the more religious touches, the manger scenes and Bible verses. The cozy, wintery images seem particularly out of place here in the over-heated air of what seems to be obviously, underneath all the pavement and landscaping, a desert.

I stop at a Starbucks to get a protein bar, espresso, bathroom, and, to be honest, a feeling of being in known territory.

When I leave, sipping a big frozen latte, I notice a bitten wolf, not one of the Cachorros I know. Curious, I follow the trail and, as I follow, pick up more and more traces of unfamiliar wolves, most of them bitten, but a couple of born—born wolves who I don't think are half siblings.

Is this what Viv was trying to cover up? A pack of born wolves in Los Angeles who have nothing to do with Leon? But why?

I follow the wolf traces to the LA Hammerfit, adjacent to the convention center, in the base of a fancy hotel tower. I flash my membership. A bored and exceptionally tanned woman nods me in, air conditioning blessedly cool.

A bitten wolf, a tall, muscular woman, is working out on one of the weight machines. She drops the weights without a clang, sits up, nods in my direction. "You're new," she says.

"Just visiting. I have family in town. I go to the Seattle Hammerfit usually. I was expecting this to be the same, except bigger, but it's totally different." The one in Seattle has a very northwest flavor, with woods and evergreen bushes and fountains, while this one has a very beach sensibility, with tropical plants and tiki bar touches.

"The Hammerfits like to theme for the cities they get built in. I'm Kristen Aiken, stuntwoman." She towels off her hand and shakes mine.

"Um. Abby Marchande. Student?"

"Nice to meet you. I have to get ready for a night shoot, I didn't want you to think I was running off because of you."

"Oh, no, fine. That's totally fine."

"Enjoy your stay in Los Angeles." She heads off to the locker room. "Try some sushi while you're here."

I explore the Hammerfit for a while, but don't run into any more wolves. I consider texting Jaime to find me here and just waiting, since it's open twenty-four hours. But when I try relaxing in the salt room, my mind and heart won't stop racing.

I leave again, notice the sun going down, huge and red, just like it was in my dream. It seems ominous.

The bloody sun. Reminds me of something I can't place. The name of a movie? Maybe a line in a song?

I should text Steph, tell her where I am, tell her I'm visiting my brother. Just in case something goes wrong. But when I try to fire up my phone, there isn't enough battery to turn it on. I should have been charging it when I was at Hammerfit, why didn't I do that? I'm scattered. Not thinking clearly.

I've been wandering in a large, irregular circle around the big stadium, reached a place that seems to be in the middle of development into something else, sidewalks all torn up, no lights or people or open businesses.

Then I hear a scream.

A woman.

In a panic, I rush toward the sound, find a man and a woman arguing. He's got her by the arm. I shout out, "Hey, what are you doing?"

The man turns to me. He's afraid and angry. He waves a gun, dull moonlit gleam on metal, familiar sulphur-and-machine-oil smell. "What's going on? Who are you?"

Visceral rush of memory from last summer, when my sister Opal was arguing with a man named Dennis. I attacked him, beat him severely, but it was a setup. She paid him to attack her, because she wanted me to intervene, feel bonded, trust her.

Frozen, for a moment, I'm not sure what to do.

The woman runs away.

"I said, who are you, bitch!" the man shouts, trembling in rage and fear.

He has a gun.

It's pointing right at me.

It goes off.

The bullet goes in.

Just like that

THE BULLET GOES INTO MY CHEST. QUICKLY. NO PAIN, JUST A crushing sense of wrongness.

I collapse. My brain seems to be floating above me, watching this happen. Where's the wolf, can't she—there's so much blood.

The man walks away. Everything happens in slow motion. He shot me, now he's walking away, leaving me here. He's not robbing me. He's not anything. Does he think I'm dead?

Am I dead?

I don't feel my heart beating. Does your brain keep working after you're dead? Is that what it means to be a ghost? Am I a ghost?

Where's the wolf?

Damn it, I only got shot that one time, why am I on the ground like this, on this superheated sidewalk.

Is this hell?

Hell or Los Angeles.

I want to giggle. Angeles means angels, doesn't it? I don't speak Spanish. I don't speak French either. I barely speak English. Can I howl?

I can't howl. I can't make any noise. Where's the wolf?

The man is just walking away, the man who shot me. Just walking. Where is he going? Why isn't he running? Is he running, and everything happens in slow motion, so it looks like he's just walking?

I should sit up. Where's the wolf? No, I should stay down. Grandmother, are you there?

Do I feel her? A soft red shadow, fur, brushing against me. Distant howl, like a siren. I should howl so the wolves can find me. I don't have the breath for howling. I should call 911. He's walking away, where is he going?

Where is my wolf?

The world shimmers. Heat shimmer? No, a figure, moving fast, dark figure, a dark man. My father. I know his scent. But what is he doing? It happens so fast.

The man who shot me isn't walking anymore. He's on the ground. Like me. On the sidewalk in a pool of blood. Like me.

My father killed the man.

My father walks toward me, long firm strides as black cowboy boots strike the pavement, sharp noise that echoes off the partially constructed building next to us. He wears a silver wolf belt buckle like the one his father wears. Tinted glasses. His hair is a little shorter than mine. Dark red, graying at the temples. He's mad. Angry. I smell it on him, think for a moment he's angry at me, get angry back.

"It's not my fault" I try to say. I don't even know what I mean. It comes out as the barest whisper. He kneels down beside me, runs his fingers lightly over my chest, gets to the bullet wound and red pain sizzles along all my nerves. I shriek like a banshee.

"Good," he says. "You can scream like that, you're not dead." When he opens his mouth, I see that he has all his teeth. He pulls up my short dress, indecent, exposing the bullet wound.

"It looks like you still heal rapidly enough, I should take you to the Cachorros, not the hospital. It's going to hurt a lot. Are you ready?"

I nod. Barely moving.

He puts his arms under me, stands up. I gasp in pain as he carries me to the car, every shift in position bringing a fresh screaming along all my nerves. He lays me down in the back seat. "Just try to hang on."

I will I will I will. The car starts up.

That man who shot me, where was he going?

CHRISTMAS

I wake up.

I've been cleaned and dressed in a fluffy, freshly washed robe, placed on some kind of bed or couch that tilts me up enough that I can see through glass doors that open out onto a wide, sandy beach. It's still night. A gibbous moon hangs in the sky, reflecting off the waves. Leon is nearby but I can't see him.

Am I healed? I try to sit up and—

STABBED from the inside, I groan and sink back to the bed.

"You're awake?" Leon moves around to be in my line of sight. "I took the bullet out. How do you feel?"

In answer, I groan. Then I ask, "Where's Jaime? I thought I was texting with Jaime."

"No, that number you had is for whoever is leading the Cachorros. It was Jaime last summer because I wasn't well enough."

"You're well enough now?"

He shrugs, as if to say, well, I killed a man with my bare hands and carried you here, what do you think?

"But Jaime lives here, doesn't he? His scent is all around.

And Reina too. And… Andrea? The bitten wolf with a trauma morph?"

"Yes. But Jaime likes to spend the holidays with his mother's people. It's almost Christmas."

"Is that where Reina is? With him?"

"It is. They haven't said anything to me yet, but I think they're planning to get engaged."

"So, his mother's people—born wolves?"

He waits for a long time before nodding. "Yes. The Lobos are a pack of wolf-shifters who live in the Los Angeles area. They've been here for a long time, a hundred years or more. Similar to the Varger physically, so similar that we must share ancestry, but they have a completely different culture and history. They differ from the Varger in some genetic ways too. Trauma morphs are more common, for example. They almost always have somebody available to do what they call fighting the moon, triggering the wolf once or twice in the last week before full, then staying in human form during the moon."

"Wait, the Lobos—are they why the Cachorros are Spanish-speaking?"

"Yes. Core members of the Cachorros, including Jaime, are children of mine with Lobos women."

"They weren't raised by non-wolves, like me and Nic?"

"They were not."

"Wow." I think about that for a minute. "Why didn't Vivienne want me to come here?"

He raises his eyebrows. "You came here against her orders?"

"Um. Yeah?"

He shakes his head with a sigh and a small smile. "She's not going to like that."

"Nope. As soon as I charge my phone again, it's going to be full of angry messages. But I think Theo will back me up. They've been clashing a lot, I don't think he likes the way she just overrides him. I don't know if you know this, but there's a temporary maison in Seattle and Theo is the head of that, but Viv and I have been part of the Seattle maison for the past few days because of this other wolf named Andrew who showed up in New Orleans, but he was really from Meriwether Idaho, except that wasn't where he got exposed, where he got exposed was this place in Kirkland where they do cosmetic surgery, he got injected for weight loss of all things, and the guy who injected him is named Flint Savage, who's a bitten wolf and we have to find him because he could be infecting people all over, I'm sorry, I didn't mean infected, I meant—" I stop. "Did you give me painkillers?"

"I did. You consented, but you might not remember."

"Not berserker drugs?"

"No, those are used as painkillers when we want to stay awake. I gave you one with opioids. It put you to sleep. And apparently made you very talkative."

"I guess that's good. But look in my backpack, there's a plastic bag with Flint Savage clothes, and that's why I'm here, because we're trying to find him, and they were talking about bringing in all the maisons because we don't really have any idea where he is, and I said we should bring in the Cachorros because that's like having a maison in Los Angeles, but Viv said no, because it's not our territory, and I thought that was stupid, and I could tell Theo thought it was stupid too, and she didn't even call Pere Claude, because she called Pere Claude when they wanted permission to bring in the Seattle Hammerfit wolves, did you know about the Hammerfits? They're all bitten wolf havens and they have Varger-style sparring rooms and are you really where Roman and Rufus found out about the sparring rooms because when they said that it really seemed like they were lying, but that's why they brought me to Seattle, because Roman was ignoring the emails from the Seattle maison and they thought that because I'm family I could just go out there and visit them, and I did, and it was helpful because it's how we found out about Flint Savage, but they were so weird about everything and they wouldn't let us into the house even. Then they said something kind of racist about the Cachorros, and that made Edison mad, did you meet Edison? He's one of my loufrer. He's my boyfriend I guess, but it's kind of weird because we live in different cities, but he's a really good kisser, not like I have anything to compare, but that's why I texted Jaime, because when I bit Edison and then gave him Reina's cure, now he's got this thing kind of like partial wolfiness going on, and when Roman made him mad they actually eye-flashed each other. And it made him better at football! The Huskies are going to be in the Rose Bowl which is two weeks from now, I think? I wonder if I could go to that. How long does it take to heal from a gunshot wound when you don't have a wolf anymore?" I stop. "Bon Dieu, I feel like I was given truth serum. I can't stop babbling. Did any of that make sense?"

"Yes, but, mostly because not all of what you said was unfamiliar to me. My sons contacted me after your visit."

"You mean the twins? No kidding. What did they say? 'Wow, that Abby, what a bitch'?"

He looks amused. "Not in so many words. But Roman did seem to find you—troubling. He described you as pushy and domineering."

"Humph, he should talk."

"He told me about Flint Savage. Reading between the lines, I got the impression that Roman was only telling me because he was worried about how mad I would get if I found out through other means."

"Yeah, covering his butt, right? But why does he care? What does he think you're going to do to him?"

"I'm not sure he knows. But he does still respect me as his alpha. That's his word, I know the Varger don't use it."

"Haha, that's funny, you know, he accused me of being Edison's alpha and that's what it was like, an accusation, like, 'oh, this little girl, she doesn't even have a wolf, is she really your alpha?' and Edison said yes, like, 'you got a problem with that buster?' and you know you lied to me."

"About what?"

"My mother. Whether or not I was conceived by a rape. You said you didn't remember, because of the berserker drugs, but you do remember because Opal told me it was in your diary, that you sired me in wolf form and you were disappointed in the results, and you called me a runt, what was it, 'the one kid I sired in wolf form and she turns out to be the runt of the litter?'"

His look of horror seems genuine. "Abby. Opal told you I said that?"

"Well, yeah, I know she's a liar, okay, are you saying you never told her any of that? You didn't sire me in wolf form?"

He rubs his forehead, a genuine facepalm moment. "Abby. When I told you I didn't know if I remembered the specific incident when you were conceived, that was entirely correct. But in my diary, I assumed you were conceived when I was en loup because, with your mother, that's how we usually…"

"Wait. Don't finish that sentence." Instinctively I sit up, hold out a hand, then collapse back to the bed. "Ugh, that hurts."

"I didn't call you a runt, either. That was Opal's word. You aren't much smaller than my mother was. You may not trust me in much, but trust how I feel about my mother. She is still the strongest wolf I have ever known. Please understand that I would never discount a wolf's power based on her size."

"Yeah? What about an ex wolf?"

"My own wolf was gone for many years, you know this."

"But he's back."

"Yes."

"What if mine never comes back?"

"At your age that seems highly unlikely."

"Unlikely maybe. But possible. Do you despise the wolfless?"

"No, what makes you think—is that another thing Opal told you?"

I feel defensive now, realizing how much of my low opinion of him was driven by somebody who I now know to be an extravagant liar. "Maybe."

"Opal thought I rejected her because I was prejudiced against the wolfless, or at least, she accused me of it many times. But, as much as she didn't want to believe it, I was protecting her. You've experienced yourself how dangerous it can be for a person without a wolf to live as the wolves do. To navigate the world with the kind of utter fearlessness that gets you shot."

My gut churns. Anger? Fear? I'm not even sure. But I spit out the words. "What are you saying? Dad? Without a wolf I should just keep my head down, obey, submit?"

"Submit? I'm pretty sure I never said that. Abby, I know I'm far from perfect. There's a reason I have such a long string of failed romantic relationships. But I take a father's responsibilities seriously. If I had known where your mother went, when she was pregnant with you, I would have tried to stay in touch with her. And if I had known the circumstances you were being raised in, I would have taken you away from there."

"Yeah?" I sigh. "Maybe I believe you."

"If you don't, there's very little I can say to change your mind."

"I suppose." I turn away. "Those drugs you gave me, do you have any more of them?"

"Yes."

"Well. Lay 'em on me. Dad."

He hands me pills and a glass of water, and I have to sit up to swallow them, which hurts incredibly. "Bon Dieu that's painful, how do regular people deal with getting shot? This sucks."

"Regular people die, Abby. You were very fortunate."

"I don't know, I think a really fortunate person wouldn't have gotten shot in the first place."

I lie down, pass out again.

I WAKE AGAIN. SOMETHING'S BEEPING. LEON COMES OVER WITH my phone, fully charged. "Your Seattle loufrer are inviting you to a video chat, are you up to it?"

In answer I reach my hand toward the phone (ignore the muscle twinge) and he places it in my palm. I accept the call and now Deena's face is there, under tinsel-covered reindeer ears, flushed, and about as happy as I've ever seen her. "Check this out, I'm going to introduce you to everybody. Nonna, this is Abby, my friend in New Orleans."

"Ciao, Abby," says the white-haired woman.

"This is Nonna's lasagna." Deena runs her phone over the big pan of cheese melted over meat, tomato sauce, noodles, and it actually looks amazing.

"That looks fantastic."

"You hear that, Nonna? My friend likes your lasagna."

"You eat it someday, yes?"

"You bet. Maybe next Christmas."

"And, check it out, Izzy and my mom are talking."

Izzy, wearing her own tinsel-covered reindeer ears and a gorgeous dress of green stretch velvet, waves at me. "Hey Abby. Happy almost Mardi Gras. What's the weather like there?"

"I don't know, it's okay."

"It's been freezing here in Seattle. Like, literally freezing. As in, water turns to ice freezing." She shudders.

"Abby!" Deena's mom leans into the phone and makes a kissy face. "Nice to meet you finally! Deena, you should bring your friends over."

"Love to, Mom, except that Abby's in New Orleans."

Deena swings the phone around to her own face again, lowers her voice with a conspiratorial air. "Mom is a little in her cups right now. I think it's the warm spiced wine. Anyway, apparently several key members of my family just kind of knew somehow that Izzy was my girlfriend in a romantic way, and my mom made a point of telling me that she thinks that's okay—"

Her mom leans into the phone. "God is love! No qualifiers! I believe in Jesus, not the fricking pope!"

"Thanks Mom."

"Merry Christmas!"

"Merry Christmas to you too."

Deena's face again. "I think she's gone to get more wine. It's okay, Dad's always the one who drives to these things. And he's okay with it too. Me and Izzy, I mean. I don't know if my grandma is as cool as Izzy's grandma, nobody's willing to risk it, but my immediate family, they all know, it's good." Her eyes look a little glossy, as if she's about to cry. She makes a joke instead. "It's a Christmas miracle! Hey, Edison's family just got here, let's go say hi to them."

The phone trails through the party again. "Check it out, he's wearing the ugly Christmas sweater I gave him." Deena shows me Edison, panning the camera over his sweater which is, uh, not the most flattering look he's ever had. The black, red and green colors are okay, but the sweater is designed to resemble an advent calendar, and the front has twelve literal pockets with little knit representations of toys and candy sticking out of them. So, the sweater, which is resting on one of the most perfect torsos ever produced by humans, makes him look kind of lumpy.

"That is indeed a terrible sweater, Deena, a real find."

"It's vintage. I don't think ugly sweaters count unless they're from before ugly sweater parties became a thing."

The camera pans back to Edison, who laughs. "Thanks,

Deen, I wore this for you, but I think I'm going to overheat if I leave it on now that I'm inside the house."

And then he, uh, wriggles out of it.

On camera.

Which is phenomenally sexy as an activity even though the shirt underneath is very conservative, a button-up in black with red and green pinstripes. One of the tails comes untucked from his jeans. He tucks it back in.

"It's funny, isn't it?" Deena says. "Because it's winter, we wear sweaters, and then inside there's a fire so we have to take the sweaters off. But in the summer we wear tank tops and crank the air conditioning and when we go inside we have to put sweaters on."

"Hi, Abby." Edison waves at me. "I'm not much of a video chat guy, you know that, but it is good to see your face."

"You too."

"Oh, I should introduce, this is my mom and dad."

He obviously takes after his dad in looks, dark coloring and broad shoulders, and for a second I wonder, is that what Edison is going to look like in twenty or thirty years? Because it's not bad. It's really not bad at all.

Thirty years, what the hell is wrong with me?

"Nice to meet you," his father says.

"You're Abby," his mother says. She's very pretty in a heavily made-up, polished way. I can see echoes of Edison's bone structure, although her face is much narrower than his, almost foxlike. "I've heard about you. Ed, why have we never met this girl?"

"Um. Because she mostly lives in New Orleans?"

"Hmm. Well." She studies me intently for a moment, as if judging. "It is nice to meet you. Finally. Oh, Ed, don't eat the lasagna!"

"What?" The camera swings around to show Edison scooping a big slice onto a paper plate. He licks his fingers.

"No, honey, no! You're training for the Rose Bowl!" His mother takes the plate away.

Deena swings the camera back to her own face, speaks in a low voice. "We'll leave them to it. Seriously, the dude spends hours a day in the gym, never eats any sweets, and he still gets people like his mom and his coach policing his carb intake, it's ridiculous. It's Christmas Eve, my body is like 90 percent European butter cookies at this point, and Edison can't have one little square of my grandma's lasagna? Oh, wait, I've got it."

She turns around, confronts Edison's mom. "Hey, Mrs. Kelly, I know he's training and everything, but my grandma will be really sad if he doesn't eat any of her lasagna. You don't want to make Nonna sad, do you?"

This tactic appears to work. Deena briefly shows Edison eating the lasagna. Cousins and siblings arrive. For almost an hour, I continue to wander through the party with Deena, an entertaining guide. Eventually Izzy, Deena, and Edison all gather in the dimly lit coat room.

"What's going on with the investigation?" I ask.

"A lot of dead ends so far," Izzy says, shaking her head.

"Yeah, it's surprisingly challenging to locate a guy who's always changing his name and his appearance."

"But he works as a doctor, doesn't he have to—you know, register with—some kind of—doctor's organization?"

"You'd think that, wouldn't you?" Deena says. "But, thanks in part to recent federal legislation, many portions of the cosmetic surgery industry are almost completely deregulated. Certain types of outpatient procedures, like mesotherapy for example, don't have to be performed by an MD. I mean, we don't even know if this guy is actually a doctor."

"Or he could be a PhD in something unrelated," Izzy points out. "My calculus professor is a doctor, but I wouldn't want her injecting me with anything."

"What about you, Abby?" Edison asks. "How are you doing?"

"Great. Never better."

"Really?"

"Well, I miss you guys. But it's great. I'm basically on vacation. No job, no responsibilities, no wolf."

"That's good—what?" Deena speaks to somebody off camera. She hands the phone to Edison and disappears for a moment, then comes back. "Hey, Abby, we have to do party stuff right now, but it was great talking to you. Happy Christmas!"

"You too. Good luck in the Rose Bowl."

"Thanks. We're not favored to win, so I'm trying to be prepared for a noble defeat."

The conference stops, leaving me with a strangely flat, bereft feeling. "Wow," I say. "Why did they think I'm in New Orleans?"

Leon steps into the room. "That's what Viv told them. She's. Uh. She's here, Abby. In Los Angeles. If you're willing to talk to her."

"What? Oh, sure, I'll tangle with Viv."

He types something into his phone, and a few moments later Vivienne enters the house, stops. Stares at me, nostrils flaring. "Abby," she says, voice tight. "Merry Christmas."

"Yeah. Did you hear I got shot?"

"I did." She inhales a long, deep breath. "I—what you did was very rash and impulsive. But I—I accept that—you had reason to believe that—" She stammers, trails off.

"You can't admit you were wrong," I say.

"I didn't say I was wrong."

"I know. But you were."

Her temper flares. "You were also wrong, Abby! To run off like you did, without telling anyone?"

"I did tell someone." I gesture at Leon. "I told Jaime, I

mean, I thought I was telling Jaime, I was really telling Leon. And I told Theo."

"You didn't tell Pere Claude."

"No, and neither did you."

She scowls for a moment, looks like she wants to spit something at me, then closes her eyes, sighs, backs off. "You're right. I made a call that was maybe not the best call, and because of that you made a call that was maybe not the best call. Maybe we can just pretend that if you had asked Pere Claude, and he told you not to go, that you would have listened to him."

"Sure. But why didn't you want me to go to LA? I still don't get that part of it."

Leon speaks up. "I'm afraid that's my fault. When I left Idaho, I went to Los Angeles because it was the largest city in North America with no traditional Varger presence. The instant I arrived, I realized it was the territory of an entirely different pack, the Lobos. And, while we didn't know about them, they definitely knew about us." He sighs. "They were not fans."

"No? I think I heard about that. One of the Meriwether wolves was bitten in San Diego and he said the wolves there told him the New Orleans pack, the rougarou, that they were bad news."

"I don't know where that enmity comes from, but rather than try to change their impressions, I simply promised the Lobos that I would never tell the Varger about them. When Viv ran away and came here, I had her make the same promise."

"When Viv ran away? What are you talking about? Viv wouldn't run away from Pere Claude unless he gave her permission first."

She smiles slightly. "Maybe that's how it seems now, little one. But I was young. Nineteen and wolfless, sure I would remain wolfless forever. I came to Los Angeles for the same reason Leon did. A couple of years later, when my wolf came after all. I went home, but promised I wouldn't tell my father about Leon, or the Lobos, and never did."

"So, wait, you didn't want *me* to come to Los Angeles because of a promise *you* made decades ago? Behind Pere Claude's back, even! How can you be mad about me going behind your back just now when you went behind *his* back for years?"

She closes her eyes, sighs deeply. "You might have a point. But more importantly, you were right that finding Flint Savage is absolutely the most important thing for all wolves right now, far more important than me keeping my old promise. And I think the Lobos would agree. So I'm no longer officially mad at you. You might want to delete my messages without listening to them."

"Done. Could you say all that again? Specifically the part where you said 'you might have a point' and 'you were right'?"

"Don't milk it, Abby. You must be feeling better."

"I don't know. I thought the wolf was coming back, but now she isn't. I stopped dreaming about her."

"Because you got hurt?" Viv is sympathetic. "She'll be back."

"I don't think so, Viv. I think you can only get killed so many times before you stop coming back. Nine lives. Seven lives. Wait, that's cats, isn't it? How many lives do wolves get?"

"Abby?"

But I'm already slipping down into unconsciousness, dark and lonely, without the wolf pestering me.

A FEW HOURS LATER I WAKE UP. IT STILL FEELS LIKE THE middle of the night here, but it's late enough to be morning in New Orleans. I call Steph for a video chat.

"Abby! Merry Christmas. I heard you were in Idaho—then Seattle—then California? Where are you now?"

"California, Steph. I'm here with my, uh, this is weird. I'm here with my dad."

"Your dad—you mean Leon? Your biological father?"

"Yeah. We're, like, kind of—making friends?"

"Well that's good! Isn't it good?"

"Yeah, it's good, it's just weird. Oh, check it out though, he's got a house right on the beach."

I swing the phone around to show the beach behind me.

"That's lovely, sweetie, where is that? Malibu?"

"No, Venice. Are you having a good Christmas?"

"Yes, but this is New Orleans, Christmas is second fiddle." She grins and moves her phone to show me her sweater which says HAPPY ALMOST MARDI GRAS. "Do you think you'll make it back home for Mardi Gras?"

"I hope so. But I don't know. I'm sorry, Steph." My throat closes up a little bit. "I just don't know. Is Terry there?"

"Of course." The phone swings around wildly, picking up tinsel and ribbon and crumpled wrapping paper. "Terry, it's Abby, you want to say hi?"

The phone finds him. He points at the screen and says, "Bah-bie!"

"Hi Terry. Yeah. It's me, Abbie. Bah-bie. How are you doing? Do you like Christmas?"

"Bah-bie," he says. He gets a very serious look on his face, says a bunch of syllables I can't make sense of.

"Thanks Terry. Merry Christmas."

He points at the phone and looks even more serious. "Bahh-bie. Baaaaahhhhh-bie."

"I know, Terry. I know."

Steph turns the phone around to her own face, with a mixture of pride and frustration. "He's been doing that more and more lately. He'll say one of his words, but seems to be trying to make some bigger point with it, and none of us know what he's talking about. Then he gets frustrated that we don't understand."

We continue to talk for a while. I say hello to her parents. Then Terry needs changing, and we hang up with promises that I'll try to be back for Mardi Gras.

I realize I didn't tell her that I got shot.

I guess she doesn't need to know. It would just worry her for no reason, right?

19

VENICE BEACH

"Leon! I can't believe you left us celebrating the holiday in the mountains when this was going on!" Reina is frustrated. "We could have been searching for this man Flint Savage these past few days!"

Andrea shrugs, lights a cigarette. "Chill, Reina, it's not like they needed you, personally, trying to visit every plastic surgery clinic in the greater Los Angeles metro area."

"Put that out! Abby is still recovering from her gunshot wound!"

Andrea gives me a look. "What? My cigarette isn't going to make a difference, is it?"

"Take it out to the porch," Jaime says. "Otherwise you make everything smell like smoke. Father, Reina's right, we should have been helping."

"You are helping," Leon says. "Or, you will be. We're going to need to coordinate Lobos and Varger efforts for this. Hammerfit packs too. Los Angeles and San Diego. Jaime, I need you as an ambassador even more than I need you as a scent tracker."

They continue to discuss logistics, and I drift in and out. Now that it's not just Leon and me here in the house, it feels really awkward that my bed is basically set up in the middle of the living room. On the other hand, I enjoy feeling like I'm part of things, even if I'm just sitting here.

I need a bathroom, though. Swing my feet over the side of the bed and stand up—

OWWWWWWWWWW

All heads in the room snap toward me, nostrils flaring. I try to smile. "Whoa, the pain rush was that obvious, huh?"

"Abby, do you need medication?" Reina is very concerned.

"You know, I don't have a wolf right now, I actually do have to worry about things like getting addicted to painkillers. So, no thanks. I just need to be left alone to make it to the bathroom. Okay?" That came out sounding more angry than I meant. I put a hand on her arm. "Or, you could help me walk there?"

She smiles, pats my hand. "It's all right, Abby. Even with a wolf, a gunshot wound to the heart takes a lot of healing."

"To the heart?" I turn around, stare at Leon, who looks slightly embarrassed. "You didn't tell me I got shot in the heart. You took the bullet out, did you take it out of my heart?"

"It went through your heart, but it didn't lodge there."

"Damn. Really? When it felt like my heart stopped, it really did stop, didn't it? I really was dead?"

"Your heart probably did stop, yes. But you were never dead. Your brain never stopped, did it?"

"Not unless it's still stopped. Wait, maybe this is the afterlife. What do you all think? Heaven or hell?"

"You're at the beach!" Andrea shouts from the porch. "So, heaven, obviously!"

Over the next few days, there's a lot of activity in the Venice Beach house, and I often feel like I'm just in the way. I end up taking a number of very slow and careful beach walks with, of all people, Andrea.

"Look, I'm not really a planner type," she explains,

exhaling the smoke which is the other reason she keeps having to leave. "What, it's not like I'm going to get lung cancer."

"I didn't say anything."

"You didn't have to. Wolfy types say a lot with body language. I mean, regular humans too, obviously, but I think it's more pronounced with us. Anyway, I have my job already: fighting the moon, along with Leon and the other trauma morphs, and we're just going to be on call for the whole night. I'll go where they tell me to go, do what they tell me to do." She exhales smoke. "It's good that we're getting together, though. It's always been kind of ridiculous to have this whole big pack in Los Angeles, and this other big pack in New Orleans, and you never even talk."

"I wonder what's going to happen now that they are talking? Are we going to start having—I don't know—wolf conventions, where we all meet up somewhere?"

She laughs. "Don't get ahead of yourself, kid."

"Wait, my phone is buzzing."

"Yeah? Hey, mine too. Holy shit! They found him, come on!"

We rush back to the house, find it exploded in excitement. They located the Beverly Hills clinic where Flint Savage has been working, under the name Dr. Bliss, and they've got a client list.

"We don't have Savage himself," Viv tells me, with a sigh. "At the clinic they said he was out for the holidays. But with this client list, we can know all the people he might have exposed, and monitor them on the full moon."

"Which is tomorrow."

"Which is tomorrow We probably don't have time to contact everyone."

"Focus on the people who were treated within a couple of days of the full moon!" My brother Nic's voice, but not his presence. I realize they're on a big multi-site conference call. I find his face, wave. He waves back.

Viv says, "Nic's theory is that roughly five hundred years of thinking about how the wolf is transmitted is wrong and that it's the time of the month that matters, not the physical form of the biter."

Nic says, "I do have a PhD in epidemiology! Almost a PhD!"

"It makes sense though," I say. "When you consider the red and black moons, we've obviously got hormones or something that follow the moon cycle."

"Exactly right!" Nic says. "Abby gets it!"

"Hmmph. Abby is a teenager who hasn't even mastered algebra." Viv folds her arms, but her heart isn't in it. I think she knows Nic is probably right. "Well, now, we get to do something really fun: try to convince a bunch of random strangers to be in a certain place at a certain time for reasons that will only make sense *after* they become bitten wolves."

"After *some* of them become bitten wolves."

"Right. Even worse. After some of them become bitten wolves, watched by the ones who don't."

Leon strides into the room, phone in hand. "I've got it. We're inviting them to a party at the downtown warehouse."

Viv looks skeptical. "A party? That's your solution?"

"Jim has agreed to be there."

"Jim?" She frowns. "You mean James Warchesky? The director?"

"Yes. His Oscar win is recent enough, I think he'll be a draw."

"Wow." She nods thoughtfully. "I haven't thought of that name in years. But you're right. He'll be a draw. Except, even if he's available, we'll still be lucky to get everyone coming on such short notice."

"I know. Let's hope we get lucky."

20

AN EVENING WITH JAMES WARCHESKY, OSCAR-WINNING DIRECTOR

I t turns out, we do get lucky. Of Flint Savage's thirty mesotherapy clients, twenty-seven of them, including all seven who were injected within a couple of days of the full moon, are excited to accept a last-minute invitation to attend a swanky reception for James Warchesky, Oscar-winning director and, apparently, old friend of both Vivienne and my father.

The man they call "Jim" arrives at the downtown property early, with a small entourage, which includes bitten wolves, although he's definitely human. Viv and Leon appear to know most of the entourage, too, and they all hug, cheek-kiss, tell each other they're looking fabulous.

"I heard you were sick," Jim tells Leon. "But you look great."

"Old information," he says with a slightly uncomfortable smile. "My wolf was restored—" He looks around, gestures toward me. "By my youngest daughter, Abby. Abby, this is James Warchesky, he's been a, well, a loufrer, I guess you'd say, since the 1980s."

"Nice to meet you." I come forward, shake his hand. "So, you're a movie director? What's that like?"

"Like wrangling wolves," he says, and everyone laughs like it's an old joke. "I was an apprentice of Zara Sanders, a great filmmaker who never really got her due." All of them look sad for a moment.

"She died?" I guess.

"She was killed," Viv says, inhaling deeply as her rage ticks up. "But that's not important right now. Jim, we didn't go into much detail on the phone, but here's the deal: a man we're calling Flint Savage, although it turns out he goes by many different names, is a bitten wolf, possibly with a trauma morph, who has decided, for reasons unknown, to administer the cosmetic surgery procedure known as mesotherapy with a concoction that utilizes his own spit, sometimes resulting in a bitten wolf."

Jim looks blank for a minute and then bursts out laughing. "Oh, now, Viv, you have got to be kidding me. That's like something from one of Zara's films."

"Cinematic or not, it's real," Leon says. "Our current evidence suggests that people injected within a few days of the full moon have a very high risk of becoming bitten wolves. We haven't found the man himself, but we did find the Beverly Hills clinic he's been working at, and a client list. We have twenty-seven people showing up tonight, including seven who we think are at a very high risk of becoming wolves."

Jim nods. "All right, I get it. You said you wanted me to bring a movie?"

"Right. The plan is that, right before moonrise, you start screening a special exclusive pre-release cut of your next movie. Lights down, sound up. We'll have our people circulating through the audience, looking for signs of anyone in the kind of distress that might signal a new bitten wolf. These people will be escorted to the basement, drugged heavily, and restrained." He inhales. "The, uh, the basement is already set up for that. Restraints for up to eight bitten wolves."

"Leon, I didn't know you were into BDSM," Jim says, joking.

"It's not recreational, I assure you. We have enough of our people retaining human form during the full moon, we'll be able to guard them. Our people who shift will be guarding the exits, not letting any strange wolves leave the building. By the time the screening is over, anybody who's going to change shape, should have changed. Then we just guard them until morning, letting the others leave, hopefully none the wiser."

Jim looks thoughtful for a moment. "Let's see. It makes sense, but it all sounds a little too neat, don't you think? Like there must be something you haven't thought of."

Leon sighs. "Probably. But unless you can think of what that would be?"

"Oh, I don't know, if it were a movie script, I'd probably have an earthquake or something." He smiles. "Do you have extra restraints?"

"Well, there are eight installed into the walls, and seven likely suspects, but you're right, we should have backups in case we're wrong about the risk." He glances around, finds Andrea and one of the Lobos, a dark-haired young man named Manuel, busy setting up the bar. "Andrea! Manuel! Before the reception starts, make sure we have extra restraining materials on hand."

"You got it."

He looks at me. "Abby. In case Andrea and Manuel are late returning, are you feeling well enough to tend bar?"

"Tend bar? Am I allowed to do that?"

"Legally you're eighteen. You can serve but you can't drink. This is a private party anyway, so I'm not sure it matters."

"Sure, I'll tend bar. It'll be something funny to tell Steph later."

"Please, if you're not up to it, let me know. Jim, have you got everything you need?"

"Sure, I'll go get everything set up." He claps Viv on the shoulder. "It really is good to see you again, Roxy. You ever think about getting back into the business? Just, you know, a cameo or something?"

She laughs. "And ruin the mystery? Come on, Jim, you know Roxy's fans enjoy her films more without having to picture her as a middle-aged lawyer."

Jim and Viv both move on and I go to finish setting up the bar, which, based on what Andrea and Manuel were doing when they left, involves slicing a bunch of citrus fruit into wedges. This is something I am fully well enough to do, but before long I've sliced them all, and Andrea still isn't back, and the party still hasn't started. I take the opportunity to video-call Deena.

"Abby! Where are you? That looks like a fancy hipster warehouse."

"It is a fancy hipster warehouse! Apparently, in addition to owning a sweet beach house in Venice, my father also owns a fancy hipster warehouse in downtown. He rents it out for filming a lot. I think the main floor shows up in one of the Batman movies."

"No kidding. Is your dad, like, super loaded or something?"

"I asked him the same thing, but he says he just bought real estate at the right time. Early 1980s. But I wanted to ask you something. Remember when you said my aunt Viv looked like an eighties scream queen?"

"Yeah, Roxy Void."

"Well, get this, tonight's shindig features the director James Warchesky, and he's old friends with both her and my father, and he called her Roxy."

"No way! Warchesky was a protégé of Zara Sanders, the director who made Roxy's greatest films. It can't be a coincidence. Your aunt must have been, for real, Roxy Void." She looks concerned for a moment. "Wow, I do not know if I want to ask for an autograph or just feel really weird that I have such a huge crush on the younger version of my friend's aunt."

I laugh. "Is Edison around?"

"No, he and Izzy are both helping at the maison tonight. I had a paper due. And I don't know how much use I would be anyway. I'm not a computer whiz and I don't have 50 percent wolf powers."

"Well, all I'm doing is working as a bartender."

"You got shot a couple of weeks ago, it's not like you're up to wrestling new wolves into submission."

"Oh, it's starting, gotta go. I miss you guys."

"Yeah? You too. Have fun tonight."

It is fun. Mostly. I chat with people in an innocuous way and squeeze out citrus fruit and consult a bartending guide when people ask for specific cocktails. This is a hosted bar, and I've been told to give people as much alcohol as they want, since we picked them up in limos and we're sending them home the same way. The assumption is that drunk people will have fuzzier memories, and that's what we want.

One of the men, a fit, fortyish dude coming up for his third, confides in me. "That woman over there, the tall redhead, is she somebody? An actress or something?"

"She's a lawyer," I say.

"No, I know I've seen her somewhere else." The light dawns, a flash of lust. "Oh my God, that's her isn't it? It's Roxy Void?"

"Is it?"

"Oh my God!" He laughs, spills his drink. "I swear, when I was in college, every single guy in school had that one poster on his wall. You know the one." He laughs again.

"I'm afraid I don't."

"It's from that one movie. The zombie one, where she plays a stripper? She's coming up out of the mud in that bra and panties? My God. She held up pretty good, if it is her. You think she'd give me an autograph?"

"Can't hurt to ask," I say. He toddles off to pester Viv, who is obviously annoyed but makes an effort to be nice, signs a drink coaster for him. Maybe this is the real reason she avoids Los Angeles, all the Roxy Void fans.

"Miss?" Another man has come up for a drink and I'm struck: he smells different from the previous man. Spicier. Wolfier.

Bon Dieu, can I already smell it in the sweat, which of them is going to transform tonight?

"What can I get you, sir?"

"Gin and tonic."

"Of course."

I make him one and he inhales deeply. "This is good stuff," he says. "You guys throw a classy party."

"Thank you." He leaves, and I frantically look for one of the senior wolves to make eye contact. Reina notices me first.

"What is it, child?" Then she gets angry. "Andrea never relieved you, did she? She got back an hour ago!"

"I'm fine. That's not it. I think, uh, maybe——" I drop my voice to a whisper. "I might be able to spot by scent which of them is going to transform."

"Excellent!" She smiles, hugs me. "That could be a big help. Which ones?"

"Well, so far, that guy right there, the one with the blue jacket, he's a yes. And that other guy, the one with the martini who's boring Vivienne? He's a no."

"I'll relate that. Please keep us informed as you notice others."

By the time we're setting up for the movie screening, I've pegged four of the men and none of the women, which, if that's it, is a huge relief. The four most-likelies get seated in the back and watched more closely. Martini guy already seems about to pass out. If I were serving in a restaurant, I'd have cut him off two martinis ago.

The wolves who won't stay human all leave the room, nodding at me as they go.

Jim steps up to the front of the room and gives a brief talk about the movie people are about to see. It sounds really interesting. If I were here thinking it was a regular event, I'd feel pretty good about it—the meat skewers, the drinks, the charming host, the hip environment.

He turns around and lowers the screen. The lights go down. The movie starts playing.

Outside, the sun sets and the moon rises, bringing a rush of excitement all the wolves feel, and four men, the ones I spotted, feel for the very first time. It works exactly as we hoped. Their distress is spotted instantly by the watchers, all wolves themselves, and the men are escorted downstairs where, muffled by the sturdy wood and brick, my sensitive ears can still hear the howling. A few of the unchanged glance over their shoulders at the brief activity, but seem to go back to watching the movie with no undue distress.

Martini guy is fully passed out, snoring lightly.

Leon and Jim draw a set of heavy curtains behind the audience, approach me. Leon's relief is palpable. "Well, so far, it worked. We got them in the restraints, they're guarded, everyone else seems okay. I think we did it."

"That calls for a toast. Another Negroni, please. I was sure there'd be something you didn't think about, but it went like clockwork." Jim takes the drink from me and sips it, makes a cheers movement in my direction. "You're a good bartender, kid, you need a job?"

"Where?" I ask, at the same time Leon says, "No, of course not."

"Not at a restaurant," he says. "I often throw parties a lot like this one."

"Abby, you're still recovering from a gunshot wound, you do not need a job."

"Fine." I smile at Jim. "Maybe later."

"I will have a drink," Leon says. "Did you open any of the champagne bottles? We should finish those tonight, they'll be flat in the morning."

"You want a Death in the Afternoon? We have absinthe."

"Sure." He looks amused. "You've been a bartender for one night and you're already pushing the fancy stuff?"

"It's got literally two ingredients, it's not that fancy." I make one for me and Leon both, and all three of us clink glasses with big smiles. Job well done. Chaos avoided.

Then we hear the sirens.

21

BLOOD IN THE STREETS

L eon checks his phone. I smell the stress in his sweat. "Bon Dieu. We have new wolves appearing all over. Savage must have been working at more than one clinic."

There's a flurry of activity while everybody confers about how to re-allocate our resources. But it's a struggle. Just as with the Varger in New Orleans, more than a couple of new wolves in a single night strains the Lobos/Cachorros resources to cracking. The warehouse already has four new wolves who need to be guarded, the Lobos have captured three in Orange County, and one has appeared downtown not far from here. Leon and Manuel decide to go deal with that.

"Abby," Leon says. "I'm leaving you in charge here."

"Wait, you're doing what now?"

"Everyone else is either en loup, guarding the wolves in the basement, going out to deal with the wolves in the streets, or coordinating our efforts. That makes this—" He gestures at the reception. "Your job. Make sure the ones who didn't transform get home safely. Help James and his people as they need. When you've got everything shut down, check on the wolves in the basement to see if they need anything. None of this should require you to risk physical harm." He smiles. "In fact, it should be less strenuous than bartending."

"Okay, but, you know I'm kind of a chaos magnet, right? If you leave me in charge here, something bizarre and terrible is definitely probably going to happen."

"Definitely probably?" He looks amused. "I'll take that risk."

"Great! Okay! Fine! Good luck! See you tomorrow if we all survive!"

Within short order, all the wolves who were here in the party take off, leaving just me, the guests, and James and his people. James remains at the bar with me, sipping his cocktail. "So. You're Leon's youngest daughter. What does that make you, twenty?"

"Eighteen."

"You ever think of doing any acting?"

"Like, in the movies?"

"What else would I mean?"

"I thought you wanted me to tend bar for you."

"You could be an extra. And if you have good screen charisma, maybe more than that."

"Screen charisma? Don't I have to be able to memorize lines and say them?"

"Not always." He grins. "You could be the first girl who gets killed by the axe murderer, a lot of the time she doesn't have any lines at all, just screaming."

Now I laugh. "No way. I'm not doing horror unless I get to be the final girl."

He makes a cheers gesture toward me. "You know our genre, I see. You do have a certain final girl energy about you. What's your weapon of choice? Chainsaw?"

"Too noisy. I think I'm more of a sword girl. Or an axe. I can handle an axe pretty well in real life, and if it's an axe murderer, well, he's not going to expect me to take his own weapon away from him, now, is he?"

"Good thinking."

There's a pause. I offer, "You want another Negroni?"

"No, I want to sober up I think."

"You didn't drive here, did you?"

"Oh, no, I came in a limo. Leon made it sound like that was part of the deal, to really play up my role as recent Oscar-winning director."

"What did you win for again?"

"*The Light Through the Trees.*" He frowns. "You know, if you're a horror fan, I'm surprised you haven't heard of it. For a while, everybody wanted to make 'prestige horror drama' into a new trend, as if it had never been done before."

"My pop culture knowledge is wildly spotty. I was raised in a cult until last January and until then I'd never even seen a movie."

"A cult, seriously?" He frowns. "Wait, did Roxy mention that? I think she did. New Harmony, right? John Wise?"

"Yeah. She told you about that?"

"When she called to ask me to do this event. I can't remember why it came up, exactly. I'd be really interested in talking to you about it sometime when we're not dealing with a bitten wolf epidemic. I'm thinking about making another 'prestige horror drama' and I might do cults this time. Can I hook you up with my screenwriting partner? You met, but only briefly. She's in there watching the movie. Jayachandra, the lanky Indonesian-Caribbean woman in the designer dress?"

"Oh, yeah, I noticed her. Wait a minute, is there money in this? I mean, for me?"

"Of course. Zara would haunt me forever if I failed to pay you a fair rate for your participation. How much longer do you think you'll be in Los Angeles?"

"I don't know, maybe another week?"

We're interrupted by a scream of pure terror. I don't stop to think, just run toward the sound.

Outside the air-conditioned warehouse, unseasonably hot wind slaps me in the face, blowing smells and sounds of wolfy pain and human terror. There's so much agony in his howl, in his sweat. Is that what causes the berserking behavior? George talked about it hurting, to be a wolf, but Andrew never did. Maybe it only hurts some new wolves. But why?

I run toward the screaming and snarling, just across the street, find myself in a courtyard restaurant, the kind of place with tiki torches and a pretend volcano. People are dressed up, as if it's a nice place, the sort of place you'd go for a special evening. I notice a woman wearing a BIRTHDAY GIRL tiara, another woman in a BRIDE TO BE sash, both backing away from the wolf. He's snarling and snapping at everyone, terrifying for the size of his jaws and their frothing, foamy, rabid look. But he doesn't seem to be going out of his way to attack anyone. Maybe that's a good sign.

"Get back!" I shout. "I take care of rabid animals for a living!"

Everyone does get back. I approach the wolf slowly, as he snarls and snaps in my direction. "Come on boy, let's get you away from all these people. Come on. Does anybody have any meat?"

BIRTHDAY GIRL steps forward, hands me part of a roast chicken. I wave it in front of the wolf, who does seem interested. He darts toward me, as if he would take it out of my hand. But then he stops. Snarls. Moves backward, rolling his head around and snapping at nothing, like the ostriches eating their phantom insects. But the ostriches seemed calm, and this wolf seems incredibly distressed. I don't understand the behavior at all. I've never seen it before, in a human or a wolf.

"Come on boy, follow the chicken." I break off part of the

chicken and toss it to the ground in front of me. He snaps it up. I wave the chicken slowly back and forth in what I hope is a hypnotizing manner, backing away slowly the whole time. The wolf keeps seeming like he's going to follow me, darting my way, then shuffling backward as if some invisible assailant keeps chasing him off.

He rears up on his hind legs, as if he's trying to walk upright. Officer Lou mentioned that the wolf who attacked her partner did that, kept rearing up on his hind legs. It does make him look very much like the more humanoid wolf man monster of the movies. His shape is still that of a wolf, but his body language is disturbingly human.

"Come on, boy." I throw more chicken down at the ground. Once again he snaps it up, then backs away from me. I'm starting to feel desperate.

A small child at one of the tables breaks away, running, catches the eye of the wolf, who gives chase.

OH NO

I put on a burst of speed and dive for the wolf's back, just like I did on Bourbon Street, but this time I catch him, end up clinging around his neck. He starts bucking and prancing to try to get me off. It seems to be enough to keep him from chasing after anyone else, for now, but I don't have sedative, or a catch pole, or anything. Nothing at all to bring him down. So, what's my plan? Just ride on his back and hope I can steer him?

The wolf dashes off at top speed, only to crash into the harsh concrete surface of the artificial volcano. I get knocked to the ground, knees and knuckles bloody, hop to my feet, ready to run after the wolf again. But I'm starting to feel the exhaustion, partially healed muscles complaining, heart pounding.

He doesn't run. Instead, he knocks his head against the stones again. And again. And again.

Self-harming? I've really never seen that before.

Then his head explodes.

No, it can't be—

I'm covered in blood, brains, skull fragments.

A couple who were close enough to get showered scream and run away, and now everybody's screaming, running, crying, chaos and confusion everywhere.

I sink to my knees. The sense of failure and abrupt end to the combat have left me feeling completely spent. I'm not sure I can do much more than crawl forward on my hands and knees.

Leon is here.

He walks up behind me. Puts a hand on my shoulder. "Abby, you shouldn't be out here."

"What the hell was that? That explosion. Meltdown. Whatever it was. Have you seen anything like that before?"

"Not in person. I've heard about it. It's rare. But then, uncontrolled bitten wolves are usually rare." He sighs. "Manuel's taking care of the other wolf. I think this might be the last one in LA tonight. You shouldn't have had to do this. But it's good that you did."

"Is it?" I find myself weeping. "Is it good? Really? Did I do a good thing?"

"Yes, Abby, you did. And you're going to pay the price, I'm sorry."

I nod, as the fading adrenaline leaves me feeling how much everything hurts. He scoops me up in his arms, just like he did after I got shot. He carries me back to the warehouse, where the movie is only just now wrapping up. Leon stops briefly to tell James, "I'm taking her upstairs," before carrying me to the top floor of the warehouse, which is set up as an apartment, with beds and a kitchen and a couple of bathrooms. I think it's another maison, based on the overlapping variety of wolf person smells.

He takes me into a large, extremely fancy bathroom, and places me on a wooden bench inside a vast shower. "I'll find you some clothes and hang them on the outside of the door. Don't worry about using up all the hot water, we've got plenty."

He leaves. After half an hour sitting under the stream of warm water, I'm just barely starting to feel clean.

22

AFTERMATH

The December full moon, it turns out, was a nightmarish worst-case scenario. Not only did we get a dozen new wolves in the Los Angeles area, there were wolves in New Orleans, Seattle, New York, and Phoenix, all seemingly related to the activities of Flint Savage—either people he injected when they were in Los Angeles, or people bitten last moon by the people he injected previously. We also get three extremely public wolf meltdowns of the kind that hit me. The sheer number of strange, violent incidents attracts the attention of the mainstream news media, who go into panicked speculation about an alarming pandemic of "explosive rabies."

The uncontrolled bitten wolves kill two people that we know of. We have no idea how many they've exposed.

The Rose Bowl is canceled, based on health concerns. Edison claims to be relieved he doesn't have to play and lose.

I call Steph on New Year's Day. She's concerned about what's going on. I tell her that we have it under control. I don't know whether this is a lie. The investigation swirls around me, but I'm emphatically not part of it. Everyone seems worried that I'll go running off again, although I'm not sure where they think I'm going to go. There's not going to be a full moon until the last part of January, weeks from now.

I do pick up a few things. I know that we manage to identify two other clinics where Flint Savage was working, and get patient lists from them. But he never returned to those clinics. Does he know people are looking for him, and he's avoiding us? Difficult to say.

For my part, I seem to have pushed back my recovery from the gunshot wound by several weeks. I spend the first few days just lying in bed in the downtown warehouse. I was right that it's also used as a maison for the Cachorros, but here, my bed is set up in a small, private room. It's dark and cool and everyone leaves me alone. But after a few days I realize I miss the beach and Leon takes me back to Venice.

I stop feeling the wolf. Stop dreaming about her. The new moon comes and goes and I feel nothing, no change.

As promised, Jayachandra shows up to talk to me about New Harmony. We walk along the beach and she asks me questions, and I speak into her recording app. It reminds me of getting interviewed by Janelle Barker from *Teen Mode*, although Jayachandra ("call me Chandra") asks me very different kinds of questions. She's really interested in the way my older brothers, Great Purpose and Justice, served as enforcers to my father's will.

"Purpose, I think it bothered him to beat us, but he steeled himself against it, thinking it was the will of God. Justice, though, he really followed in my father's footsteps. He enjoyed it, I think. He had that sadistic streak. He didn't look like Wisdom, though. He was very blond. A literal golden child. I think his mother must have been blond. Chastity had kind of light brown hair, and Purpose looked more like Father Wisdom, he was dark. My mother had pale blond hair and several of us were blond. Sackcloth with Ashes, she had very pale hair."

"Any others with the red hair?" she asks, with her lilting Caribbean accent.

"No. Ash was a bit freckled, maybe strawberry? But nobody like me. I always took after my biological father."

"Right. Leon. The beast." She laughs. "I read the *Teen Mode* article before coming out to speak to you. He's an old friend and I find it most amusing to think about him being seen as a figure of evil."

"You don't think he's evil?"

Her golden-brown eyes twinkle. "He can be a bit wicked, no doubt. But I would not say evil. I have a question for you. Many times, when people tell the story of a corrupt preacher, they tell the story of a man who's a hypocrite, who shows the world a false face. He fakes his faith healing or secretly parties with the young people and sexually exploits them. Cult leaders are often the same—sleeping with the young people who follow them, even as they demand chastity from everyone else. But your Father Wisdom does not sound like that."

"Oh, no, he wasn't a hypocrite at all. Well, maybe in one way. He preached, and believed, that the only true job for a man of God was farmer, shepherd. So, he became a farmer, a shepherd, but he didn't know the first damn thing about it and he never grew enough food to feed his family, not without being subsidized by the income from his books or his guest preaching. But in everything else—he lived what he preached. And why not? He preached Christian patriarchy, so he preached his own self as like unto God on the earth, at least as far as his own family was concerned."

"But he didn't sleep around?"

"Oh, no. No, nothing like that. And he didn't cheat for his money either. He got paid for things he did do. Preach. Write books. Hold rallies. Now, you can say his books were frauds because he promised things that never came about, things like, 'God will bless you if you do this.' But that makes him no different from any other self-help or religion writer. They all make promises they can't keep."

She nods. Looks thoughtful for a long moment. "Abby. I have an idea for a way to tell this story, and I want to run it past you. Girl is raised in a cult, told she carries the taint of the devil himself. In this version, she always knows the cult leader is not her biological father. She runs away from the cult and finds her biological father on the streets of New Orleans. He is the devil. Maybe. Charming, amoral, alludes to having mystical powers, some hint that maybe he does. He offers them to her. She takes them. There's a ritual. Maybe she gets diabolical powers, or maybe it's just a hallucination. She goes back to the cult. Gets revenge on the ones who hurt her, frees the ones she deems to be innocent. Then burns the whole place to the ground. But in the end, her older sister, one of those freed, the innocent, rejects her, saying, 'You are the devil. That was the devil's power you showed.' The sister leaves with the young children who were all freed. The protagonist goes back to New Orleans. The end."

I think about it. I've seen enough movies now, that I can picture more or less how that would go. "Yeah, sure, I like it."

"But it does cast you as a bit evil."

"I probably am at least a little bit evil. Don't you think? I'm literally a monster."

"What do you mean, child?"

"You know. Werewolf? I thought you knew about all that. You were there on the full moon."

"Oh, I do, I do. I just hadn't thought of it like that. Are werewolves truly monsters then?"

"Well, they literally make monster movies about us, so…" I shrug. "Have you and Jim ever made a werewolf movie?"

"Oh, no, we have not done that." She smiles. "Thank you, Abby, I'll let you review the treatment, and then the script when I have the first draft ready. I'll give you credit as 'story by,' should this make it to the screen."

"That sounds good. Wait. The 'story by' credit—are you saying my name would be, you know, on the screen? My actual for-real name?"

"Unless you wish to use a pseudonym."

"And I'll get paid?"

"Of course. Speak to your auntie about it. Vivienne knows."

"You called her Vivienne, not Roxy."

"No." She shakes her head with a smile. "I am younger than Jim and the others. I never knew her as Roxy Void."

"My friend is a big fan."

"Is she? That's nice to know, that the impact continues on to the next generation." She stops. "What is it, Abby?"

She noticed my nostrils flaring. "Nothing except—are we done for now? I think I need to—run an errand?"

"Of course. Here, let me give you an advance of your payment. I'll give you a bit of cash, since I know you've been so dependent on your family with no money of your own." She hands me a wad of bills. "I hope we can make this work."

"Me too." I'm sincere, but distracted, because of what I noticed: Pere Claude is here.

23

PERE CLAUDE

I find Pere Claude standing awkward on the beach, frowning at the sand and the surf, wearing his cowboy boots. When I first see him he's looking down, scowling at the boots, but as I approach he looks up, embraces me. "Granddaughter. I am here to see how well you recovered from your injuries." He squeezes me again. "Your bones are far too prominent, don't they know how to hunt here in this concrete wasteland?"

I chuckle. "You don't like Los Angeles."

"I have only been here once before." He sighs. "I consigned my comatose son to a long-term care facility, thinking he would never wake up. Then I returned home and lied to my people that he was dead. I'm still not sure why I did that." He looks thoughtful, then bends down, a little stiffly, to remove his shoes and socks. "Walking on the sand is more pleasant in bare feet, as I recall."

"It's what I do." I point at my own feet, painted with sparkly green and purple toenail polish courtesy of Vivienne. "The beach is great, it's the only place you can go where nobody thinks you're weird if you don't wear shoes." We begin walking along the shore, in a leisurely way, as the sun is setting. "Sunset is my favorite time in Los Angeles. I like the way the sun turns into a big red ball and lights everything on fire."

"The bloody sun, I've heard it called."

"Are you here to make it up with Leon and merge your packs?"

"We've had a few discussions along those lines. Nothing has been settled yet." He smiles. "Something you should understand. When wolf groups get together, there is often a question of territory, of hierarchy. You are dominant in your own pack, no? The hunt leader? So, when you become part of a larger pack, who is the hunt leader?"

"Does there always have to be a single hunt leader though?"

"Perhaps not. That has been part of our discussion." He looks far away, over the ocean, toward the setting sun. "The world is changing, granddaughter. My son was right about that. We have lived in our own narrow space for so long, thinking ourselves the only wolf people in existence."

"But surely when you came to Los Angeles before, you noticed the Lobos?"

"I did." He nods. "And I did not know what to do about it, so I did nothing. It seemed to me they must be managing their own affairs as well as we managed ours, so I told myself they were not my business."

"But you could have been learning from each other. Helping each other."

"True." He sighs. "But there is, as I have said, the question of hierarchy and leadership. Dominance among our people is a complicated thing. It is not in a wolf's nature to be submissive, but it is in our nature to hunt together, as a pack. My people follow me only to the extent of their faith in my leadership."

With another sigh he slumps forward, and it seems almost

as if I can see a literal weight falling onto his shoulders. "Grandfather, what is it? What's wrong?"

"Feeling my age, granddaughter. It is our custom, that a pere retires well before any obvious decline in leadership ability. It would not be good for the people to lose faith in their pere."

"What? Are you thinking of retiring? Wait, are you going to turn things over to Leon? Is that why you're here?"

He shakes his head with a smile. "No, child, I'm not retiring right this minute. Within the next few years, though, yes, I think it will become necessary. But Leon is not my choice for the next pere."

"No? Is the pereship hereditary?"

"It is not. However, it is fairly common for a pere to be the child or grandchild of a former pere. The qualities we look for tend to run in families. Things like high personal dominance, or a fully mastered wolf."

"A mastered wolf is a thing you look for in a pere? But it's rare, isn't it?"

"Yes. It has, historically, been somewhat rare. But if one with a mastered wolf seeks to be hunt leader, they are almost certain to be accepted in that role."

"Is that why you don't want Leon to take over as pere? Because he never mastered his wolf?"

"He doesn't have the temperament to be hunt leader. He's smart, and has extremely high personal dominance, a lot of what you might call charisma, so he would look the part. But he's vengeful. He has a cruel streak. Some of that may have been tempered with age, but, still, I would not want the people to be led by Leon. His children, though? Several of you would make fine hunt leaders. But none of that is why I'm here." He stops walking, turns to face me. "I'm here about your wolf."

"She's gone."

"Is she?" He looks doubtful. "But I feel her. Her energy

surrounds you." He passes his hands in the air over me, near enough to make the hairs on my skin tingle.

"But how can you feel her when I don't?"

"You don't?" He folds his arms, gives me a skeptical look. "Are you sure you don't hear her calling you?"

She stands on the far shore, wind ruffling her red fur, nostrils flaring, eyes flashing green...

"I'm sure. For a while I was thinking she was getting ready to come back, but then I got shot. Now she's just not there at all. I don't think she's ever coming back. And I'm afraid."

"Afraid?" He cocks his head, like a dog listening to something unusual. "Afraid the wolf is not coming back?"

"Well. Yeah. I guess. I mean. I got shot, right? I almost died. Without the wolf, that's what I have to look forward to. A life of worrying about getting shot, or mugged, or being in a car wreck, or any of that stuff."

"So that's what you fear? That if the wolf never comes back, you will become terribly vulnerable, physically?"

"Of course. Who wouldn't be afraid of that?"

"You're not afraid of the wolf's return?"

"What?" I stop short, stub my toe on a discarded beer can. How could he possibly know about that? I never told anyone about that. He notices my reaction and smiles gently.

"What are you afraid of? If the wolf returns?"

"Well. Probably the trauma morph training?"

"Probably? You're not sure?"

"Well. I mean. I'm sure that's it."

"You don't sound sure."

"But what else would it be?"

He pats me on the shoulder. "Only you can say. Spend a moment thinking about your fear. Then tell me whatever comes to mind, even if it seems unrelated."

We walk along the beach. A volleyball sails overhead and almost hits me, but I catch it, turn around, toss it back to the game, where a bunch of impossibly fit, impossibly tan people wearing almost no clothing give me a cheery smile and a hand wave. One shouts out "nice throw, bro!" They seem so untroubled. So innocent.

"Pere Claude? Have you ever killed anyone?"

"Yes, child, I have."

"Were you human or wolf at the time?"

"It doesn't matter. Both are me."

"Okay, but—later on, did you feel like you did the right thing?"

"I did. But it still bothered me to have done it."

"Really? Even though you thought it was the right thing to do?"

"Yes. It troubled me. I worried it over and over in my mind. Was there some better choice I could have made, early on, that would have prevented things from getting to the point where I had to kill a person?"

"And was there? Did you end up thinking it was your fault?"

"My fault? No. I didn't. But it troubled me still, and I decided to let it. I think it should never become too easy for one of us to kill, don't you think?"

"I do. I do think that." I throw my arms around him, bury my face in his chest for a moment, try to keep from sobbing, fail. "But I don't think it matters now. The wolf is gone, Pere Claude, I know she is. She was getting ready to come back, I could tell, but now I can't feel her at all."

He strokes my hair. "Child, you are already very good at telling your wolf', 'no.' I believe you will learn to suppress your trauma morph in record time. But you are not good at telling her, 'yes.' You call her when you're afraid, when you need her strength, but you don't call her in joy."

"Joy? What kind of joy are you talking about?"

"The joy of the hunt. Oh, now, I know, that doesn't sound joyful to you. You think of the hunt as brutal and cruel. But the wolf is not cruel, child. There is a concept in the world

these days, my Evangeline often talked about it, of environ-
mentalism? An ecosystem? Where all the living creatures
within it work together and depend on each other?"

"Sure. Predators are part of a healthy ecosystem. I get it.
I've read about the wolves in Yellowstone. But I still don't see
how a hunt is joyful, when it always ends in blood and
screaming."

"It's joyful because we do it together."

For that, I don't have a ready answer. For a long time we
stand like that, me crying into his chest, him stroking my hair.

"My Leah," he says, and I hear the tears in his voice. "I've
missed you so much."

That—seems weird. I pull away, study his face, which
wears a distant, unfocused expression. "Grandfather?"

"Abby?" He blinks, seems to focus again.

"Did you just call me by my grandmother's name?"

"I'm sorry. But holding you is very much like holding her,
and it put me in mind of the past. I remember your story,
about what happened during the trouble in the taxidermy
shop, when you believe you were ridden by her spirit?"

"You think that really happened?"

"Of course I do. Why wouldn't I?"

"Because it seems kind of impossible?"

"More impossible than being a wolf-shifter in the first
place?"

"You got me there. But how do I know it was something
that really happened and not something I imagined?"

He shrugs. "I don't think it matters." We begin walking
again. "One thing you will learn, as you spend more time in
Bayou Galene, is that many of our people are very modern in
their thinking. They think of the wolf and her gifts as purely
physical. But you know she's more than that." He stops, takes
my hands, wraps his own hands around them, squeezes. "She
is your heart. Your spirit. And your connection to a larger
world, a world of life that surrounds you."

"Wait, Pere Claude, are you trying to tell me I'm a Jedi?"

He looks tolerantly amused. "You make jokes. But that notion of a mystical warrior is not so far off from what I'm talking about."

"I'm no warrior. Nic has tried teaching me to fight and I'm actually really bad at it. I get bored doing the same punch over and over again. Maybe I'm just not cut out for this."

"Granddaughter?"

"I'm just so tired." I sink my entire weight against him, and he takes it easily. "I can't be part of the track and chase teams for this moon. I can't trust myself. If that's why you're here. To try to get me to help. I just don't think I can. Not yet."

"I understand." He embraces me, strokes my hair. "It wouldn't do for you to injure yourself yet again."

"And it's not just that. I don't want to rely on my own strength if it's not there. I could get someone else hurt."

"Of course. Of course." He pulls back and gives me a big, enthusiastic smile. "Take all the time you need." We walk for a little way. "If you are not going to be in Los Angeles for the next moon, where do you wish to go?"

"Home, Pere Claude. I want to go home."

A long pause. "And where is home for you, Abby?"

"Steph. Where Steph is. That's what I mean when I say home."

PART V

NEW ORLEANS

24

DAY WITH STEPH

Steph picks me up at the airport wearing Mardi Gras beads, takes a few to drape around my neck before hugging me. "Abby! Welcome home! Happy Mardi Gras! Do you have any luggage to wait for?"

"Nope, just the same backpack as always." I shoulder it. "Let's go."

"Look at you! You're so freckled it almost looks like a tan. And your hair is so blond!" She brushes it away from my forehead. "Did you like the beach?"

"I like the ocean. And I like that at the beach I can go barefoot and nobody thinks it's weird."

She laughs. "Your family there? You got along with them? They took good care of you?"

"They did."

"Well, I'm so glad you could come back for Mardi Gras." She grins. "I have a surprise."

"What? No, Steph, I hate surprises, don't have a surprise."

"It's good, you'll like it. We're getting formal dresses. I have tickets to a krewe ball, do you know what that is?"

"No idea. Crew of what?"

"The krewes do the Mardi Gras parades. Each krewe does

their own parade. Krewe of Muses, Krewe of Orpheus. Anyway, the balls are very, very fancy, and it's not easy to get tickets. I have tickets from my boss at the restaurant who is a member of the Krewe of Oceanus, one of the newer ones. They have an early parade, just a couple of days from now."

"A fancy ball? Oh, no, Steph, I don't know how to act at a formal ball. Don't I have to know, like, etiquette and things? And how to wear heels? I'll have to wear heels, won't I?"

She laughs. "Not if you don't want to, honey. But you do have to wear something formal. I need a new dress too. I thought it would be fun for us to find them together. We can go straight from the airport, or if you're tired, we can do it tomorrow?" She looks at my face. "We'll do it tomorrow."

We walk to the car mostly in silence, pull out of the parking garage, drive down the freeway, still mostly in silence. Steph glances my way. "Are you sure you're okay?"

"Yeah, I'm okay. I guess I'm just tired. I wasn't able to sleep on the airplane."

"Okay. Sure. Well, your room in the attic is all set up for you, you can go right to sleep there if you want."

⚜

THE NEXT DAY I'M NOT AWAKE UNTIL THE DAY'S HALF OVER. I wander downstairs, yawning, find the household empty except for Steph, puttering around.

"Afternoon, kiddo." She smiles brightly at me. "My mama didn't want me to let you sleep so long, but I pointed out that you've been working graveyard shift and anyway it's Mardi Gras, what does she think you have to be awake for?"

"Thanks, Steph." I slip into the kitchen chair.

"Mom and Dad and Morgan took the baby out to have some family time—Morgan wanted to check out this place that supposedly has crawfish King Cake if you can believe it —and we're all alone to have fun for the day."

She pours me some coffee from a thermos, so it's still warm, and cuts me a slice of King Cake, which turns out to be a ringed cake sprinkled with sugar colored purple, green, and gold. "I know you don't eat a lot of sugar, but you should have some of the King Cake, it's traditional."

I take a bite. It tastes mostly like a cinnamon roll. I don't hate it, but I wonder what the big deal is. I take a second bite, and my teeth meet something clearly inedible. "Wait, why is there a plastic toy in here?" I take it out of my mouth. It's shaped like a baby, which seems ominous. I flash on months ago, when I had just figured out what I was, and Steph was telling me rougarou legends. She said unbaptized babies were a favorite rougarou snack and I got terrified that my wolf self might harm Terry.

"You got the baby! That means you have to buy the next King Cake!"

"The next King Cake? How many King Cakes do we eat?"

She laughs. "You have no idea. But we typically go through one every couple of days during the last two weeks of Mardi Gras."

"Oh. Where do you buy them?"

"Stop looking so worried. You have to buy the next one only in the sense of going to the store with me and helping me pick it out."

We head to a bakery, get a King Cake with chocolate filling, put it in the trunk. Next, we head to a store with discount formal wear, a small place stuffed with a bewildering array of fancy outfits, most of them dresses for women. The price of getting things at a discount seems to be that you have to put in the work to sort through all the chaos. I follow Steph's lead and start rummaging through the dresses right next to her.

"Oh, no, honey, these will be too big for you." She points to the tag that indicates she is looking through Womens 12-16. "You should go look at the juniors. Just pick out a bunch that appeal to you and try them on to get an idea of how they're going to fit."

Feeling banished, I go to the other rack and pick out anything where I like the color or the feel of the fabric. A lot of the fabrics feel weird and stiff or scratchy when I touch them, and one gives off a strange chemical smell that reminds me of the discarded prom dress I wore when I left Seattle after the wolf killed George, which reminds me of George, how he was at the end, a bitten wolf, a cannibal, threatening to kill Steph and bite his son Terry.

I shudder. Why does everything have to remind me of something terrible?

Steph comes over with her own armful of picks. "Let's see what you got." She scans through them. "Black, huh? And here I thought you'd moved out of your all-black phase."

"You told me to pick out the ones I liked, you didn't say 'pick out the ones you like except not the black ones.'"

She smiles. "It's okay, honey, I was just surprised is all. But this won't do, it's a cocktail dress."

"What's that?"

"A fancy dress that's short. For a cocktail party. Not formal." She plucks out the short dresses and hangs them back up on the rack. "Well, why don't you go try the rest on?"

"Even the black ones?"

"Even the black ones, of course."

Steph and I take side by side dressing rooms, so that we can easily examine each other's picks. I guess she was right, this part of it is pretty fun. Steph is looking for something that covers her tattoos, so she goes for long sleeves and high collars made from lace or translucent fabrics. The colors range from dark red through purple to dark blue, very deep, jewel-like colors.

My picks are all over the place. I discover quickly that some styles simply don't work on me at all, and also that the "size" listed on the tag is largely hypothetical. But when I finally try on the correct dress, both of us know it instantly. It's silk chiffon, in a bright yellow-green similar to my chartreuse coat, and makes my skin and hair look particularly vivid. The skirt is full, so it has a lot of movement, but the fabric is thin, so it doesn't take up a lot of space. A swirl of gold beads along the hem look pretty and also keep the skirt weighted to the floor. There's a leg slit in the front that keeps me from feeling trapped. The neckline hits at just the right place, but the best part is the asymmetrical design, where the right side of the bodice extends up to my shoulder and then flows out into a kind of cape that drapes behind and easily covers my shoulder scars.

"Well, that's perfect," she says, and I nod. "But we have to get you elevated shoes or you'll lose the effect of the beaded hemline."

"Shoot, you're right. Okay. I guess I'm wearing heels after all."

She finds me a pair of platform sandals that elevate my toes a couple of inches off the ground, then elevate my heels a couple of inches more than that. "These shouldn't be too hard on you."

They're not, during the five minutes I wear them here in the store. In fact, for those five minutes, I really enjoy being tall enough to look Steph in the eye, which makes me realize she's nowhere near as tall as Viv. It wasn't all that long ago that every adult in my life seemed uniformly towering.

She's picked out her dress too, deep blue lace over sheer fabric, long sleeves and a high collar, a combination that makes her tattoos look almost like part of the lace. She wraps her arms around me from behind, looks at us both in the mirror in our outfits. "Look at us. We're so cute."

I look. I guess we are cute, but what strikes me more profoundly is that I look normal. Like the people around me. Not shockingly thin or tiny, no shaved head that makes me resemble, as Morgan used to put it, a plucked chicken, no expression like I'm looking for an excuse to kill you. I could pass, unnoticed, in any New Orleans crowd. Just a teenage girl having fun.

I have a flash, remembering when I was young, sometimes Wisdom would take the whole clan into the outside world, all the pious little New Harmony girls with our matching pink dresses, aprons, little bonnets. People would stare and mock. We were supposed to hold our heads high because we knew that the mockers were going to hell. But I just hated it all. I hated the mockers for being cruel, hated my father for making us dress that way, hated myself for caring what I looked like or what other people thought about it. All I wanted was to be invisible, to go unnoticed.

"We are." My throat tightens up. I'm happy, why should that make me want to cry?

Once we have dresses and shoes, we go to another couple of boutique shops in search of sparkly necklaces.

"And earrings," Steph says, "don't forget earrings." She holds up a dangly pair in gold rhinestones, then does a double take. "Your ears aren't pierced."

"No, they're not."

"I can't believe I never took you to get your ears pierced."

I laugh. "It's okay, Steph. It's only been a year, remember?"

"A year! You're right, it has been just about exactly one year since I picked you up off Highway 61. Wow. So much has happened since then, huh? Let's see if we can get your ears pierced at the mall."

We go to the mall that still smells faintly of me and Barney chasing down Andrew back in November. It's been thoroughly decorated for Mardi Gras, with sparkling draped fabric in purple, green and gold, masks, and a jester motif.

"The piercing studs are going to be stainless steel." Steph holds them up against my ears, as if judging their size or color. "But we can get you something prettier to wear for the ball."

"These." I hold up dangly silver earrings that depict a crescent moon.

She frowns at them. "You want silver? Not gold?"

"I want silver."

"All right then." She smiles, leans into whisper. "I honestly couldn't remember if the silver thing was real, sorry sweetie."

"It's fine, thank you." I give her a little hug.

The piercing gun turns out to work kind of like a stapler for your earlobes. Quick, mildly uncomfortable for a moment, then a little itchy as the hole tries to heal.

"You want to keep turning them around in your ears to keep the hole open," the piercer says to me. "Enjoy!"

I finger the studs, wonder what happens if the wolf comes back. Do they stay put? My collar did, the one Morgan gave me to make sure I wouldn't get accidentally shot by a hunter. Viv has pierced ears, I think. When she goes to wolf form, if you look carefully, are the earrings still there? She must leave them in, otherwise they'll heal over. Or maybe she gets them re-pierced after every full moon? That seems like it would be annoying. I bet she's wearing them as a wolf, and now I want to make a point of looking for that on the next full moon, in Bayou Galene. A bunch of the wolves have piercings, what happens when they change shape?

"You're smiling," Steph says. "Is something funny?"

"Just having a good day, I guess."

We have lunch in a coffee shop in the mall, tomato-parmesan soup with a grilled cheese sandwich to dip into it.

Steph smiles. "You know, Abby, I really missed you, these last few months. I have friends in town, but so many of them are from my drinking days, and we just don't know how to relate when it's not over drinks. It gets hard to make friends when you're older, when you have a baby, when you have a past. It's harder to date, harder to—well, harder to do every-thing. I'm going to turn thirty on my next birthday, you know."

"That's not old, Steph."

"But it feels old sometimes. There are so many possibilities in my life that are closed off now. Things where, when I was your age, they could still have worked out a different way, but now it's too late."

I'm alarmed to hear her talking like this. "Too late for what?"

"Too late to have gotten a college degree in my twenties, for example."

"But you can still get a college degree, right? Why not? What about all that money in escrow or whatever it is?"

"Well, sure. That money is going to help a lot. But I'm not sure college is the right way to spend it. Not at this point in my life."

"Steph, what's this all about?"

She shakes her head. "I don't know, exactly. I guess I was just thinking about my first krewe ball, when I was around your age, and all the things I dreamed would be in my future, and all the things that ended up happening instead." She exhales and dabs at her eyes, which are glossy with tears. "Look at me, getting all sentimental."

"It's okay, Steph." I look down at my half-eaten grilled cheese, stained with tomato soup around the edges, and everything feels almost like it did a year ago, when it was just Steph and me. Terry hadn't been born, the wolf hadn't come, I didn't have all these relatives to deal with. And I guess I didn't notice it at the time, didn't make note of it properly, but looking back—it was the first time in my life I had ever really felt safe or happy.

She notices me tear up. "Sweetie, what is it now?"

"Nothing. Just getting sentimental myself."

"You're too young to get sentimental."

"Steph, you know that's not true. You're never too young to get sentimental."

Next, we go to the beauty shop to get our hair and

makeup done. The overwhelming smells are a little unpleasant, but it's still fun doing it with Steph. We head to the hotel where the krewe ball is happening, a very classy high-rise near the Superdome, change into our dresses in the women's restroom. We put our street clothes in shopping bags and check the shopping bags at the front desk.

"This way, we don't have to walk to and from the car in high heels without coats," Steph explains.

"We're going to need our coats? But it's been so warm today."

"It's going to start raining later. That happens a lot during Mardi Gras. It's nice all day, then in the evening, when the parades start, the weather turns nasty. That's why we're doing the daytime parades tomorrow." She leans in to whisper, "Don't tell my boss, his krewe rides at night. Anyway, it's better for the baby."

"The parades are for kids?"

"Families. Not just kids. Little kids don't get the naughty puns." She grins. "Terry has been to a couple already. He loves the horses. It's so cute. He calls them 'woof-woofs' which is his word for doggie and now, by extension, any animal he gets interested in. A dog is a woof-woof, a horse is a woof-woof, a squirrel is a woof-woof, a kitten is a woof-woof." She stops, gives me a grin. "Woof-woof. You don't suppose he's trying to say—"

"Wolf? I don't know. How much time has he spent around my grandfather?"

"Not too much, but as you saw at Thanksgiving, he's already a big fan."

"Me too. In spite of myself."

"You're a big fan of your grandfather?"

"Yeah." I sigh. All of a sudden I see the future as if it's a thing that already happened: the wolf will return, maybe as soon as the next full moon, just two days from now, and I will go out to Bayou Galene, and do the trauma morph training, because Pere Claude wants me to do it. I have to trust that all the experienced adult wolves can contain the bitten wolf outbreak and track down Flint Savage without me. And I guess it'll be okay. We hunt together. That's what that means.

"What is it? What's wrong?"

"Steph. I didn't tell you something about Los Angeles. I got shot."

Her jaw drops. "Shot with a gun?"

"Yeah. It was when I first arrived. There was a couple fighting—I tried to intervene—and the guy shot me. Without my wolf, it's taken me weeks to recover. It really scared me. I'm still not fully up to speed."

"Oh, sweetie. I knew something was wrong."

"You did?"

"Yeah. When I picked you up at the airport, I could tell something was bothering you, but I didn't want to say anything. I knew you'd tell me when you were ready." She hugs me, carefully, to avoid smearing our makeup. "You really do want the wolf back, don't you?"

"I do. I know I told you I was okay without her, that everything was perfect, but I was lying."

"Not lying. Figuring things out." She smiles, smooths back a single stray hair from my forehead.

"Steph, when she comes back, you know what I have to do."

"That trauma morph thing, I know. You'll be out living with your grandfather. And you just told me you decided that'll be okay."

"I guess that's it. But it means this may be my last party in town for a long while."

"In that case, let's try to have a good time."

25

MARDI GRAS

The krewe ball turns out to be fun, although not quite as much fun as it seems like it should be. I get exhausted talking to an endless stream of people I don't know, and it turns out that ballroom dancing, the process of being "led" by a male partner, doesn't come naturally to me at all. It's the first style of dancing I haven't thoroughly enjoyed. Steph and I leave at midnight and I drop off to sleep right away, without even bothering to take off the makeup. I wake with mascara smeared on my pillow.

Downstairs, everyone else is already up and running around getting ready for the parades.

"Sweetie, you're up! We were trying to figure out car logistics."

"Don't we all fit into Morgan's truck?"

"We do, but during Mardi Gras it'll be hard to find a place to park it."

"Without me, do you all fit into your car?"

"Yes, but don't you want to go?"

"I'll meet you there. I want to take a walk."

"A walk? But we'll be watching from the neutral ground at

Saint Charles and Josephine, that's miles away, in the Garden District."

"I know." I plug it into my phone. "About four miles. The weather is good. I want to walk. I want to really see the city." I make eye contact with Steph. "You know. Before going back to my grandfather's place."

She nods. "All right, sweetie. You can meet us there."

Walking through New Orleans during Mardi Gras turns out to be surprisingly fun. It's pleasant, not brutally hot like it was in August, and every little part of the city is decorated in a festive way. Beads hang from balconies and fences and the branches of the trees. Most people are dressed for the holiday, already wearing beads and costumes. Every kind of clothing you can imagine has been rendered in purple, green, and gold: hats and headdresses, feather boas, mini tutus, leggings, flapper dresses, sequined mini dresses, polo shirts, harlequin diamond suits. I start to feel positively drab, even though I'm wearing my fancy new silver earrings.

As I get closer to the parade route, I hear the hard, bright sounds of a marching band, people cheering and clapping and shouting. There's an air of excitement that's palpable and a bit contagious. The parade has already started, and walking along it, against the flow, I get a quick tour of the floats, dance groups, marching bands, and whatever you'd call the "Laissez Boys," men who dress up in fancy loungewear and ride around in motorized recliners, sipping cocktails and smoking cigars. They don't appear to have any women in the group, but I think Deena would really enjoy rolling with them.

I sniff out a few people I know, but don't stop to chat. I catch several strands of beads without even meaning to.

It eventually becomes apparent what "neutral ground" means, when I find Morgan barbecuing on the grassy, muddy area where the streetcars normally run.

"Abby!" He hugs me. "Happy Mardi Gras. You want a pork skewer?"

"Dead pig, sure." I take one. "Mmm, excellent pig corpse, very tasty."

He laughs. "You're always so complimentary about my cooking. You know I learned it from Charlotte Quemper."

"What, really? Grandma Charli taught you how to cook? That's cool. Isobelle is teaching my Seattle friends how to cook."

"Excuse me if I don't get up, I'm beat," Steph's father says, fanning himself, from a low folding lounge chair. "The band gets a lot of gigs around this time. The girls have got the baby down a little closer to the floats. That's better for catching the throws, if you want to go down and join them."

"Thanks." I hug him briefly. I realize I've never been entirely sure what to call him. Dad? Grampa? Mr. Marchande? Roderick? I've always called Steph "Steph" or "Aunt Steph" and Morgan "Morgan" or "Uncle Morgan" but I never did figure out exactly what to call their parents. I should ask Steph about that, I guess. Maybe it doesn't matter.

I push my way through the crowd and find Steph, her mom, and Terry all gathered together, cheering and clamoring for small items thrown by the people on the floats. I hold back for a moment, watching Steph in her Mardi Gras flapper dress, feathered tiara, beads clanking on her neck, holding out Terry, who adorably imitates her movements to reach out his hands for a strand of beads or a stuffed animal.

I have a strange moment of seeing her as if from a distance, like she's someone I don't know, just another young mother enjoying Mardi Gras. I wonder what I would think if we'd never made that connection out on Highway 61 when she picked me up. If I'd left New Harmony an hour earlier or an hour later, if I'd gotten more or less lost while trying to find the highway, if she'd spent more or less time packing to leave the city, any one of those things might have prevented us from meeting, and my life now would be very different. But what about hers? She would still have given birth to Terry, probably.

But without me, would her ex-husband George have succeeded in kidnapping his son? Would George have hurt her? Even killed her?

I know how much she helped me. I'd like to think I helped her.

I take a deep breath and plunge in through the crowd. "Steph, hey, Steph!"

"Abby!" We embrace, her and me and the baby. "How are you enjoying the parade?"

"Oh, it's fun. Really fun."

A float and a marching band go by. Now there's a group of women and men on horseback, wearing long blond wigs and body suits painted to look like a nude woman.

"Oh, the Lady Godivas!" Steph exclaims. "Wave at the horseys, Terry!"

She holds him out. He makes the hand grabby motions toward the horses that signal he's interested in something. The riders wave back. One of the horses stops for a moment, tosses her head, neighs.

"Woof-woof!" Terry says, excitedly, as the mare moves on.

Steph laughs, shaking her head. "See what I mean? Everything is a woof-woof."

He reaches his hands out to me. "Woof-woof. Bah-bee. Woof-woof."

"Oh, no, Terry, no, Abby isn't a woof-woof," Steph's mom says.

"But I am though!" I take him from Steph's arms and spin him around in a moment of fierce joy, while he laughs and laughs. "Woof-woof, Terry. Woof-woof."

And all of a sudden she's there.

My wolf.

Stirring, stretching, yawning. Waking up. Getting ready.

The full moon is tomorrow night and she's coming back.

I feel a powerful sense of urgency, that there's something I need to do before that happens.

Find Flint Savage, of course. Or whatever name he's using now.

Also, I need a bathroom.

"Hey, Steph? If somebody needs a bathroom during a Mardi Gras parade where do they go?"

"Well, that's a big question. There are porta-potties set up in a few places along the route. Restaurants will let you in if you buy something or pay a cover charge. Some schools and churches have a setup where they let you use a toilet for a small fee. Do you have cash? I have cash if you don't. Usually what I do is walk along the parade route until I find someplace that isn't too crowded. The last thing you want to do is wait forever for a free bathroom."

"Thanks, Steph."

Now that I'm actively looking for a restroom, I see exactly what she means. The porta-potties have lines outside them, sometimes long ones. Every business with a restroom has a sign in the window advertising a "bathroom pass" or something similar, and they still have lines out the door.

I can't believe my nose. Edison, Izzy, Deena, they're all here.

I follow the scent, find them gathered with several people who I assume are Izzy's family, although I haven't met them before. Like Steph's family, they've got a whole encampment set up on the neutral ground, with chairs, a canopy, a portable grill, a cooler of beers. At first they give me wary looks, clearly wondering why this strange white girl barging right up to their place. But then Edison turns around, cries out "Abby!" and comes to hug me, then Izzy turns around, and soon I'm meeting the whole family.

"Grammy and Chris are working the restaurant," Izzy explains. Chris is her younger brother, fourteen or fifteen. I've met him before. "We take turns helping Grandma Charli during the parades. She hates them and never goes."

"What are you guys doing here?"

"We're here for Mardi Gras, of course." She gestures at the parade route, where a man is pushing a cart of light-up toys and squid hats down the street during the lull between parades.

"Next question, why didn't you all tell me you were here?"

"Check your phone," Deena says. "I sent you a text message."

I look down. "Oh." She sent it about an hour ago and I've been distracted. "Fine. Final question. I need a toilet?"

"Right this way." Izzy beckons, and I follow her, Deena and Edison trailing behind, to a church school. "I'm paying for a one-time pass. I know it seems like you get more value out of an all-day pass, but I've never stayed in one place that long."

The toilets are clean and even have plenty of hand sanitizer, so I feel steered correctly. When all four of us are back out, Izzy says, "There's loup-garou business if you want to talk about it."

"I would. Yeah."

She turns toward Deena. "Hey, babe, have you had enough parading for a while? You want to go somewhere and talk?"

"Sure! We're here for two weeks, I need to pace myself. But I have to tell you right now, I have goals. I wanna be a Laissez Boy so bad."

"I knew it! I knew that was your kind of thing."

We start walking against the parade route again, eventually reach the point where the next parade is beginning, with police cars running their lights. I notice more familiar people smells: Babette and Barney.

"Huh, I wonder what they're doing here?"

Edison flares his nostrils. "One of your people?"

"Yeah, hold on."

"Babette, Barney, hey!" I push through the crowd, find her

decked out in her silver space-woman dress with the platform heels, him covered in Mardi Gras beads.

"Abby! Want a drink?" Babette holds out a flask that smells like it's full of King Cake-flavored vodka.

"Not right now, thanks. I just wanted to say hey. And why aren't you guys in Meriwether?"

"Because Meriwether sucks," Barney says, reaching for the flask, jostling one of his bead strands and making it light up.

"I don't understand, did you shut down the maison?"

"Not officially." Babette grins, taking back the flask. "But Meriwether is considered low-risk compared to New Orleans, and Barney and I are now considered experienced track and chase team members, so we are here at least through the full moon."

"How are things going in general? You know, with Snarlaway?"

"Terrible." She rolls her eyes, shakes her head. "We know there's probably going to be a big outbreak of—you know, explosive rabies—tomorrow night, probably in a major city, maybe more than one, but we still have no idea where. So, hey, tonight we might as well party, no? Sure you don't want a drink?"

"I'm sure. Thanks. Oh, do you know my loufrer? This is Izzy, Deena, Edison. They're all going to school in Seattle right now, but Izzy is the granddaughter of Charlotte Quemper. This is Babette and Barney."

"CharliQ's!" Babette exclaims. "Wonderful! So nice to meet you all. You're all very pretty."

"I'm not pretty, I'm just covered in glitter," Deena says.

"You're beautiful." Babette kisses her forehead and she blushes.

"Izzy, I know you, you were working with the Seattle team on the app," Barney says. "Good job."

"You too," she says. "Have we resolved our moral qualms

about inadvertently building the ideal tool for a werewolf-based surveillance state?"

He grins. "Not entirely." He looks at me. "Abby, hey. I heard you got shot, that sucks."

"Well, I got to recover on the beach in southern California, so it wasn't all bad. But, yeah, I don't know what it is, people just keep wanting to shoot me."

"Oh, tell him about the bullets!" Babette says.

"What? You mean how I can feel the bullets moving around until they find empty space in my digestive system, or pop right out of my skin? Like that?"

She giggles. "See, I told you."

"Wow." He stares at me. "I thought she was making that up."

"That happens to Wolverine in one of the movies," Deena says. We all look at her. She shrugs. "Uh, sorry, nerd talk."

Barney laughs. "I've seen the movie too. I just never thought about it being real. Wow."

"Well, it was nice talking to you guys, but we have to go," I say.

"Go do what?" Babette says, with a sigh. "I told you, we have no idea what city to focus on, no idea where Mr. Savage is."

"Not yet," I say. "But we're going to have a conference."

"Oh, a conference." Babette smirks at me. "Yes, of course. You go have that very serious, very important conference, darlings." She blows us a kiss as we leave.

Edison says, "Let's have lunch while we're at it. Are the rest of you hungry?"

"I can probably put it on my grandfather's credit card if we talk business," I say.

"In that case, I know a place, come on." Izzy leads us to a restaurant where they recognize her and, in spite of the long wait line, lead us right away to a secluded table.

"Wow, dating a scion of New Orleans cuisine has perks, everybody," Deena says. She and Izzy smooch.

We go through the process of ordering food and drinks. I get a text from Steph which reminds me that, as far as she knew, I was just looking for a bathroom. About an hour ago. Oops.

> Steph? I ran into my Seattle friends on the way back from the bathroom.

> That's great.
> Are you spending the rest of the day with them?

Oh no, did I hurt her feelings?

> We're having lunch right now, after that I don't know.

> All right. Have a good time.

The restaurant has to know we're not twenty-one but they bring Edison a beer anyway. More perks of being with Izzy, I guess.

"So, what've you guys found out?" I ask.

"Well, like Babette said, we've met a lot of dead ends," Deena says. "But we've found out a lot too."

Izzy pulls out a tablet computer, starts displaying visual aids. "You might wonder, how does Flint Savage keep moving on, changing his name, but still getting paid? Because he gets his money through a limited liability company he created. Health Transformations, registered in Florida. Florida has been deregulating like crazy and it's become *the* place for shady companies and scammers to hide their money. I think Flint Savage has always used his fitness clubs as a money-laundering scheme."

"Wow. Are the twins doing the same thing? Using their clubs for money laundering?"

"We haven't seen any evidence of it. Savage—under the name Barry Stark—got in trouble when there was a serious downturn in the value of Florida real estate. There was a cascade effect, and the chain, Transformations, went under. Articles about the bankruptcy sometimes brought up accusations of money laundering, but he was never charged with anything."

"We're going on the assumption that if you could be credibly accused of money laundering, hell yeah you're doing it." Deena says. "Apparently a lot of things are probably money laundering. Fine art, high end real estate, mattress stores."

"Mattress stores? Seriously?"

"Well, that one is more of a fringe theory. But think about it, how many mattress stores are there? And how often does anybody need to buy a new mattress? But the important thing—" She turns to Izzy. "What was the important thing again?"

"The man the twins knew as Flint Savage is shady as hell and the twins probably knew it, went into business with him anyway, and, extremely relevant here, made him a werewolf anyway."

I nod. "I think my father knows all that and has let them know he's pretty furious."

"Your father?" Deena frowns. "Oh, right, Leon. You saw a lot of him when you were in Venice Beach, didn't you?"

"I did."

"And what do you think of him after that?"

"Well, I'll be honest. Most of the things that made me think the worst of him are probably lies from people like Opal and Father Wisdom. But he's not exactly—I mean, Pere Claude himself told me that he thought Leon wouldn't make a good pere, because he's vengeful and has a cruel streak. And I saw that. When I got shot, he showed up to rescue me.

Good, right? But the first thing he did was kill the man who shot me."

"Oh my God," Deena says. "Just straight-up murdered him?"

"Yeah. That's what it looked like, although I was a little out of it at the time. Anyway, you could probably argue that it was strategic, to keep the guy from shooting me again, or interfering while he saved me, but I don't think Leon even considered that. It was his instinct to kill the guy, and he did. Revenge."

Edison looks down at the table, very uncomfortable. "But do you think revenge is always wrong, Abby? He shot you. If you didn't have some enhanced healing still, he probably would have killed you. Was Leon supposed to just let him walk away after that? What would you do to somebody who shot me?"

"Um." I look down, just as uncomfortable now, because the thing that leapt instantly to mind was: tear their throat out. "Let's hope it doesn't come to that."

Izzy says, "Here's something interesting. A few of the Los Angeles bitten wolves, the ones who were his mesotherapy clients? He contacted them a couple of days after the full moon. Acted like it was a standard follow-up call, but they thought he was clearly fishing for whether they'd changed shape during the moon. Then, when they tried to get information from him, about where he was, or what he was doing now? Nothing."

"So, do we think he knew and was doing it on purpose?"

"Whether or not he knew before, he knows now."

"Do we know what causes the meltdowns?"

"We haven't found a clear pattern, although your brother Nicolas thinks it might be an immune system response. Another weird thing though, almost all the ones who transformed have been male. He's given mesotherapy to female patients, so we assume either it doesn't work on women for some reason, or he uses a different mix, without his own saliva in it."

"It's the latter," Deena says, decisively. "Because he's a misogynist."

"How do you know that?"

"Reading THE SAVAGE WAY, mainly. It's not like one of those John Wise books, where he sets out the exact parameters of how he thinks God has decreed that the female shall be subservient to the male. It's more like a misogyny of absence. He writes a whole damn fitness book and never even mentions women or girls. It's all, 'a man' this, and 'a man' that. 'A man finds the modern world, with its rigid rules and high technology, offends his savage nature.' 'Men everywhere today are broken, flabby husks of themselves.' Which, if you've ever read anything from the world of online misogyny, is basically sidling up to it and rubbing elbows, without being quite as explicit at literally blaming all the woes of modern men on the supposed feminization of culture."

I think about it for a moment. "I've seen the comments on the *Teen Mode* article where they interviewed me, I think I know the attitude you're talking about."

"Yeah. Well, the second edition, the one called HAMMERFIT: THE DIETS? They took all that stuff out. There's almost no random philosophizing on the fundamental nature of men, and when there is, it makes a point, sometimes clumsily, of using gender-inclusive language. It's not just that the 'Savage' branding was off-putting to women, their original vision for the clubs was explicitly about excluding women."

"And the twins were good with that?"

"Up to a point, I guess. Obviously that wasn't their final business plan. Although, having met the twins, I suspect it's because they didn't want to turn down perfectly good money from women, rather than because they objected to the misogyny per se."

Our food arrives, and we spend a while eating and talking

about food. Then I think to ask, "If Savage is from Florida, and the twins are from Idaho, how did they meet?"

Deena says, "According to THE SAVAGE WAY it was in New Orleans during Mardi Gras."

"Wait, what?"

"Yeah, it's in his bio—Izzy, do you have it?"

"Sure." She scrolls through the tablet for a while, then hands it to me. I read:

> I started to develop the Savage Way to address the challenges of maintaining fitness during the nonstop bacchanal that is Mardi Gras in New Orleans. How much King Cake is too much? How does the body process alcohol calories? During one of my jaunts to the Big Easy I met the twins and we realized we had many things in common.

"That makes it sound like he goes to Mardi Gras all the time," I say. As I hear myself say the words, I'm overwhelmed with a sense of urgency so powerful I have to stand up. "What if he's here right now? He is! He's here in town!"

Deena looks skeptical. "That's kind of a leap, isn't it? Anyway, how would you find one single person in a city this crowded?"

"When we were walking along the parade route, I was scent mapping thousands of people. I found you that way, I found Babette and Barney that way, and I wasn't even looking for any of you. If we get every scent tracker mapping every parade route between now and the full moon, we might find him. We don't even have to find him, we just have to find a trace of him, somebody who shook his hand or grabbed the same parade throw. And if we do, maybe we can figure out what city he's been working in for the last month."

Izzy nods. "I think you're on to something, and it would be a good test for the app. As soon as we're finished eating, let's take it to one of your maisons."

26

THE HUNT BEGINS

The Garden District maison is just a few blocks away from the parade route, and it doesn't take long for us to get there on foot. Nobody is inside at the moment. Luckily the Garden District maison front door lock has the same code as the French Quarter maison, and we enter.

"Wow, high tech," Deena says.

"As soon as digital lock technology was developed, the wolves really favored it. For obvious reasons."

"Obvious?" She thinks about it for a moment. "Oh, right. Because you carry the key in your head, not your pockets. Which you might not have. Wait, do you guys memorize your credit card numbers and things like that?"

"If I had a credit card, maybe."

On the office computer I ping Pere Claude for a conference. He answers right away, expression concerned. "Abby. What is it? Any word of Flint Savage?"

"Not yet, but I have an idea. I think he's here in town."

"Really? Why do you think this?"

"In his first book, he tells a story about meeting Roman and Rufus—Leon's children—while in New Orleans for Mardi Gras, and describes it in a way that makes it sound like he goes to Mardi Gras regularly, might even be here right now. And I know it sounds crazy to try to find one person in a Mardi Gras crowd, but I noticed that if you walk all the way along a parade route, you pass a lot of people. Thousands. And they're from all over. What if we get every scent tracker we've got to trace the parade routes looking for Flint Savage?"

"We don't have long to find him before the full moon."

"No, we don't."

"Very well. The trackers will have to be those who are already here. We won't have time to call our people from other locations, and they will be needed to contain potential outbreaks tomorrow night. Do you have fragments of Mr. Savage's clothing there at the city maisons?"

"They should, just a second." I sniff around the maison until I find the garage, filled with weapons and a Flint Savage T-shirt. "Found it. I assume they've got one at the Quarter maison as well but if not, we can cut this up into fairly small pieces."

"Very well. I'll call a meeting with every trained scent tracker in or near New Orleans. I can also bring in some young wolves from Bayou Galene who are not yet trained, but have a knack for it."

"You're bringing people in all the way from Bayou Galene?"

"My dear. It's less than an hour's drive from New Orleans."

"Oh yeah. I don't know why I always forget that. Okay, that's great. We'll use the app. Izzy's here in town and she can help train people on it."

"Thank you. I'll let you know when we arrive." He pauses. "During Mardi Gras, gathering at the Garden District maison could be a problem. Why don't we gather at CharliQ's instead? There's private event space on the upper floor. Speak to Mrs. Quemper about it, she'll know."

○ ⚜ ○

A COUPLE OF HOURS LATER, A FAIRLY HUGE CROWD OF MOSTLY werewolves is gathered in a big room on the upper floor of CharliQ's. Chez Lunatic is showing people how to use the app, and Babette is uncharacteristically businesslike, carving up the city into areas to be scent mapped and explaining scent tracking basics to the wolves who haven't done it before. It's all fairly exciting. I think Deena is the first one to use the term "war room," and soon everybody else is doing it.

Pere Claude addresses the room. "Thank you all. I do hope this pays off. Remember, our goal is not just to find this man Flint Savage, it is to discover the identities of anyone he might have exposed to the wolf essence, in order to steer them through the full moon tomorrow more effectively. So, we do not want to kill this man unless it becomes absolutely necessary."

"Pere Claude? I didn't get an assignment," I say.

"That is because you are still not well enough to participate, granddaughter."

"What? But this was my idea!"

"And a good idea it was. But just days ago, you were still feeling that your recovery from the gunshot wound was not complete, and you were not well enough to participate on the track and chase teams. I believe that judgment was prudent."

"But Pere Claude, this is just scent tracking! I'm not planning on running Flint Savage down and pouncing on him!"

"You're not? What do you plan to do if you find him?"

I sigh. "Come on. Babette, you know I'm one of the best scent trackers we've got!"

"Of course you are, cherie." She stalks over with her silver space suit, drapes herself over me, kisses me on the cheek. "But of course, so am I. And I was not recently shot, with my wolf gone."

"Abby, you don't have to do everything yourself," Edison says. "You really don't."

"But if I'm not out there scent tracking, what am I supposed to do?"

"Have fun with your loufrer Miss Steph." Pere Claude hugs me, to take the sting out, but I still feel rejected. "We hunt as a pack, remember?"

27

THE JERK

The official scent trackers leave. Edison, Izzy, and Deena head back to the French Quarter maison to help coordinate the search for Flint Savage. I remain behind in the CharliQ's courtyard. Have fun, huh? That's my job? All right, I'll try to have fun.

I check my phone, notice a text from Steph. Lots of them, actually.

> I assume you're out having fun, Abby, but please let me know where you are?

Shoot. I wasn't thinking about that.

> Steph? Things happened. Find me at CharliQs & I'll fill you in.

> Be there right away.

Izzy's grandmother catches my eye, comes to sit at my table.

"Hey, Miss Abby."

"Ms. Quemper."

"You been taking care of my Izzy?"

"As well as I can, Ms. Quemper. You know my loup-garou powers are a little down right now."

"Oh, I know, I know." She gives me a quick one-armed hug. "We all do what we can, right?"

"I try, Ms. Quemper. I'm feeling a little left out right now. My people are doing a thing and I can't help because I'm still recovering from an injury."

"Well, child, you can leave them to it, can't you? They know their business. I know you don't want to hear this, because my Izzy never wants to hear it either, but adults aren't always wrong."

"I know."

"We aren't always right either. I guess in the end you have to make up your own mind, same as always."

"Yeah. Same as always." I pause, think about it. "Say, Ms. Quemper, what's the best place to watch a Mardi Gras parade?"

"From here."

"Right, you don't like them. Why not?"

"I just don't like being in big crowds."

"Okay. What's the worst place to watch a Mardi Gras parade?"

"That's easy, Canal near Bourbon. You get the whole rowdy drunk Bourbon Street crowd, plus it's the end of the route and everybody's tired. People on the floats are drunk. They're out of throws entirely or throwing the whole damn bag just to get rid of everything. That's where you get the worst tourists too, the rude ones who never leave the Quarter."

"Thanks, Ms. Quemper."

She nods. "Well, I have to be going now. You keep looking after my Izzy."

"I will."

Steph and Morgan enter the courtyard. Steph rushes up to

my table, very concerned. "Abby, what is it, what's going on?"

"Do you guys know what's been happening since Thanksgiving?"

"There's been a bit of an outbreak, right?"

"Right." I take a deep breath, and launch into the whole story from Thanksgiving all the way to about an hour ago.

"Oh sweetie, that's really a lot, isn't it?" Steph squeezes my hands. "Your grandfather made the right call though. You should stay out of it."

"You think? But I feel okay, I really do. Better than even a couple of days ago. I think the wolf is ready to come back tomorrow night."

"That may be. But she's not back yet, is she?"

"No. I guess not."

"So, you can let the others do it. Don't you think they're capable?"

"Of course I do. It's just…" I let the thought trail off. I'm not sure what I want to say. Maybe I just hate feeling left out. "Okay, since I'm not otherwise occupied, are we watching the evening parades?"

"Not me, I've just about reached my limit for today. Are you sure you've got the energy for a parade? You seem a little tired yourself."

"I'm too stressed out. If I went back to the house, I'd just pace around all night."

"I'll watch the parades with you," Morgan offers. "I can take 'em or leave 'em, but the weather's pretty good tonight for a walk."

Morgan and I leave Steph drinking an iced tea and chatting with Ms. Quemper. We walk along Chartres (pronounced "charters"), the one way I know for sure to get from Bywater all the way to Canal Street. Thankfully, Morgan doesn't object to the distance. I don't think of walking five miles as a big deal unless I'm in a hurry, but I've learned other people often do.

He has a flask of the same King Cake vodka that Babette was drinking, and we pass it back and forth.

"I miss doing this with Steph," he says. "Back when we were teenagers, we would just wander around the city sometimes, drinking and talking."

"You guys are close, huh?"

"Pretty much. We've had our conflicts, of course. Mostly about politics."

"I don't think I understand the outside world well enough to have any politics yet."

He snickers. "You're a lefty, kid. I hate to break it to you. You're already about as political as anybody I know."

"But I haven't even registered to vote yet."

"You will." He sighs, passes the flask back to me. "I used to think I was conservative, because I like guns, and all the other guys I know who like guns are conservative. But a couple of years ago they all started getting—religious, I guess?"

"Always a bad sign." I take a sip, pass the flask.

"You got it." He takes a sip, passes it back. "I'd known these guys for years, and we were always joking about how being out on a hunting trip on Sunday morning was our version of a worship service, just kinda, you know, making fun of the really pious people we knew? But then they started to —" He stops, thinks about it, takes the flask from me. "It's a little hard to explain, because it wasn't like they actually started going to church. But they started to get really offended when I made fun of church. They completely lost their sense of humor about it. Then they started to lose their sense of humor about other things."

"Very bad sign." I take the flask back for a sip. "Cults do that to people. Kill their sense of humor. In New Harmony I used to get in so much trouble just for laughing at stuff."

"Laughing? Wow." He frowns. "But I don't think these guys joined a cult or anything like that. I mean, they didn't mention it."

"Could be online. There's a lot of weirdness out there. Like, people who seem more or less normal in real life, but then you look at their favorite online forum and it's all about how world leaders are secretly lizard space aliens? Izzy told me her werewolf-hunting online algorithm has turned up some really bizarre stuff."

"Space aliens, huh." He shakes his head. "I don't think these guys are into space aliens, but who knows? Say, Abby, your people, do they hunt?"

I burst out laughing so hard I spray King Cake vodka, have to wipe it off my lips with my sleeve. "Morgan, we literally call our top wolf the hunt leader, what do you think?"

"I don't mean as wolves, obviously. I mean, in human form."

"Sure. But they don't use guns. Too noisy."

"What do they use?"

"Bow and arrow, knives, sometimes they run something down and snap its neck bare-handed."

He looks intrigued. "Really? Bare-handed?" He smiles. "Maybe I should explore bow and arrow hunting. Steph hasn't outright told me to get rid of my guns or anything, but it's obvious that she really doesn't like me having them around the baby."

"You'd do that? Stop being a—gun guy—for Terry's sake?"

He takes back the flask, sips. "I don't know. I still haven't fully processed all of—this. Everything. I'm an uncle, but because Steph and I have been living together and she's single, a lot of the time I feel more like a co-parent. It matters to me, keeping that cute little crazy person alive."

"Crazy person?"

"Abby. You know kids. They're basically tiny insane drunk adults. Before this, I never thought of myself as a kid guy, right? I didn't think I wanted kids. I probably still don't want kids of my own. But Terry? He's a big hoot. I really like having him in my life." His eyes get a little glossy, all of a sudden. "And I do not want anything bad to happen to that kid. Oh, God, that is such a strong feeling in me. And I used to think of guns as being a protection, right? Like, you shoot the bad guy. That's protection. And Steph told me I was wrong about that, and I argued. But now I think that argument wasn't really mine. It was borrowed from those other guys I knew. Those guys who are getting so weird now."

I jump in. "Heck, the one time you shot at a bad guy, that I know of, you hit me instead."

He laughs. "I did, didn't I? In my defense, you were a wolf at the time. But, damn it, I shot you, you didn't finish killing George, he went away to become a bitten wolf and bite all those people in prison—this outbreak is my fault, isn't it?"

"Morgan, most of this outbreak is the fault of Flint Savage. Anyway, the other one wasn't your fault either. It's not like you knew that wolf was me."

We finish the flask. And here we are at Canal Street. Instantly I see what Izzy's grandmother was talking about. It's crowded, people are drunk, and there are a lot fewer families. We push through the crowd hoping for a spot with a good view, but settle for a mediocre one. The bead situation isn't good either. On Saint Charles, I was catching beads without even trying, but here, I can't seem to get any. After we've been watching for a while Morgan says, "That was a long walk, I already need a bathroom. You want me to come back with a drink?"

"I'm not twenty-one."

"And this isn't Seattle." He grins.

"Sure. Come back with a drink."

Morgan leaves. I go back to trying to catch beads, but feel short and overlooked and it isn't fun.

A whisper of scent moves past me. Not Flint Savage himself, but a trace of him on someone else, as if he's recently touched their hair or clothing.

It's faint enough that it could be an illusion, a fantasy, but I have to follow it. I text Morgan that I'm moving on and never mind about the drink, then call up the scent tracking app, drop an anchor, identify it as "flint savage, secondary" hope they'll know what that means, hope I don't get in trouble for doing this. But he's just right there, what am I supposed to do?

I follow the scent, spot a large, beefy, dark-haired man wearing a baseball cap for the Houston Oilers. I instantly dislike him. His body language is domineering, and he's aggressively trying to catch all the beads that come anywhere near him, not letting anyone else get a chance. Another man says something to him, and I don't catch the exact words, but I can tell the other man is mad. A teen girl, blond, younger than me, is particularly getting abused by him—she keeps catching part of a bead strand, then he catches the other end and rips it right out of her hand.

The girl's mother, I think, turns around and says, in frustration, to the crowd, as if asking for help, "This guy keeps taking her throws right out of my daughter's hand!"

Everyone sort of nods, looking uncomfortable. The big guy folds his arms and manages to take up even more space. Another collection of beads sails our way, a dozen strands bound together with a bit of cardboard, and he catches it by reaching his arms up higher than all the rest of us. He puts all of them around his own neck with a satisfied air.

One man steps forward and says, "You could let other people catch some beads, you know."

The man makes a scoffing noise. Puffs himself out to take up more space. Looks at the girl and her mother. "She's just white trash anyway," he says.

The girl looks stunned, as if she's been slapped across the face.

"Hey!" her mother says sharply.

"Whoa!" I say, and stumble wildly as if drunk, crashing right into the big man, knocking him off balance. I let loose a shrill giggle. "Sorry, man, I had a really… big… daiquiri, I'm kinda wasted." I clutch his arm. "Scuse me, sorry." He looks down, annoyed, then, intrigued. That's right, you big dumb jerk, you can't resist a girl who seems too drunk to make good decisions.

"God, I need a place to lie down," I say, and give a little hiccup, like I'm about to vomit.

"Hey, you wanna go back to my room?" he asks.

I sigh. "Okay, whatever." I cling heavily to his arm as he starts to lead me out of the crowd. I turn back, see the girl's mother looking concerned, give her a wink. She nods. I watch the girl catch another collection of beads and then distribute them to everyone in the vicinity. People are smiling and it seems like a palpable weight has been lifted from that little section of the parade route.

"Oops." I stumble again to cover how long I spent looking back over my shoulder. I giggle. "Oh my God, I have never been this drunk before." I frown up at him as if I'm having trouble focusing. "Wait, who are you?"

"I'm Chucky, sweetheart."

"Chucky." I laugh. "Like the killer in the *Child's Play* movies!"

"You like horror movies, doll?"

"I love horror movies, they're my favorite. What's your favorite horror movie? I like *Ginger Snaps*."

"Yeah? I like the *Texas Chainsaw Massacre*."

"Oh, me too! Are you from Texas?"

"Why do you ask?"

"Your hat." I giggle, take the hat off his head, put it on my own head. A strong dose of Flint Savage, is this his baseball cap? "Are you an Oilers fan? What do they play?"

He laughs. "The cap is vintage, babe, the Oilers used to be the Houston NFL team but they moved to Tennessee and the new Houston team is the Texans."

"Vintage? Where did you get it?" Shoot, what if he picked it up in a thrift store?

"Oh, this guy I work with." He says it dismissively. "Say, you want a drink?"

"Sure," I say, although anybody actually as drunk as I'm pretending to be has no business getting another drink.

I turn. A flying pole slams into my forehead.

I reel backward in shock and pain, and a second later realize what happened: I got hit by a whole sleeve of plastic cups. One of the people on the floats must have been trying to get rid of their throws here at the end of the route. Exactly what Izzy's grandmother warned me about.

"Oh my God," the man says. His face goes pale, like there's something horrific about me, and I reach up to my face, discover that the left side of my head is covered in blood. Other people give me similar horrified looks.

"You've got to put a bandage or something on that, come on, my hotel is right here."

We stop at the front desk and I get a now-familiar look of abject horror. The concierge takes a brief look at my face, rifles through a drawer, hands me a cotton rag and an assortment of adhesive bandages in various sizes. "You should sit down, miss."

"I will."

"Over here." The man, Chucky, directs me to a corner near an ice-water dispenser. He gets the rag wet, starts wiping blood off my face.

"Why don't we go to your room?" I ask.

"We need to get this taken care of right away," he says. "The bleeding is slowing down, I think, but you got blood everywhere."

I use my phone for a quick selfie, see blood drying in my hair, blood dripped onto my dress. I look down. Blood on my shoes.

"Hold still." He applies a bandage. "After an ordeal like

that, you need a drink. Let's go to the hotel bar, Cafe Adure."
He touches my arm to steer me forward and it hits me: of
course, this isn't actually his hotel. So why...?

But I don't have long to wonder, because as soon as we
start approaching the bar, I realize Flint Savage is here. In
person. Waiting for us.

28

SAVAGE

C hucky, not his real name I'm sure, steers me to the table, not that he needs to. I'd know that person-scent anywhere: I've been chasing it for months.

"Please sit down." Flint Savage gestures toward the empty chair across from. him, but I remain standing, arms folded. He's sipping a sazerac, dressed as plainly as can be, in a pair of jeans and a gray T-shirt under a white linen sport coat.

Chucky takes off the hat, puts it on Savage's head. Savage gives him a wad of cash. "Thank you."

"My pleasure." Chucky gives me a smug half-smile. "You little bitch, you almost had me going, you know? But no real drunk chick likes the Chucky movies. "

He walks off. I sigh. "Wrong. I do like the Chucky movies, even when drunk. So, he was bait?"

"Yes. Although you're not exactly what I was fishing for." He smiles, gestures again toward the empty chair. "Please, sit down. I won't attack you in a public place like this. Not unless you force my hand."

I sigh, plop into the chair. "Fine. What were you fishing for?"

"Your alpha. Or his alpha. Anyone high enough in the pack to make a deal with me."

"You actually want to talk to Pere Claude?" I'm incredulous. We spent all this effort hunting him and he's just going to walk right up to Pere Claude and surrender? That seems anticlimactic.

"Is he the alpha around here? Then, yes." He continues to wear a self-satisfied smile and shows absolutely no sign of being terrified.

"But, Mr. Savage—is that your real name?"

"Real enough."

"Mr. Savage, Pere Claude is very upset with you. You understand that, right? He's got the whole pack out hunting for you, and it's not because we want to pat you on the head and tell you that you've been a good boy."

He chuckles. "I know that. Once I realized I was being hunted, that's when I decided to turn the tables." He tugs on the baseball cap for emphasis. "Many of your people were not at all subtle about it."

"Do you know why we're looking for you?"

"My progeny, I assume. A month ago they made quite a splash in Los Angeles, I hear."

"Did you know what was going to happen to them?"

"Not exactly." He shrugs. "It was an experiment. Which made any result a success."

"But you just—you just left them to fend for themselves! You didn't tell them what was happening. You didn't protect them and you didn't protect people from them. People died. Wolves who didn't make it, and people they killed."

"Regrettable," he says, without sounding at all regretful. "I still need to speak to your alpha. Contact him for me. Tell him I have a weapon pointed at your heart."

I glance down, under the table. He's got a surgical knife coated in silver, pointed vaguely in my direction. I decide to play up being alarmed.

"Mr. Savage, if you kill me, there's no way you're getting out of this town alive."

"I know. That's why I'll only hurt you if it looks like I'm not going to survive anyway. It's in the interest of both you and your alpha to make sure I don't start to believe I'm not going to survive this meeting, wouldn't you say? Now. Contact him."

I'm angry and disgusted, but also a bit amused. He really wants to talk to Pere Claude? Okay then. I text:

`Found him. Meet us at Cafe Adure`

"Show me what you just texted."

I hand over my phone and he scrolls through the texts. "Grandfather?"

"Hey, give that back."

"No, I'm keeping this. I want to make sure you don't contact anyone else."

It galls the wolf, but I let him keep the phone.

Wait. Is that true? Is it the wolf who can't stand to defer to him? Is she really that close?

A waitress comes by our table. "Can I get y'all a drink?"

"I'll have a vodka martini, and whatever the little lady wants."

She gives me side-eye. "You twenty-one, hon?"

"What happens if I say no?"

She laughs. "I bring you a Coke."

"Iced tea?"

"You got it."

She leaves. For an awkward moment Savage and I stare at each other. I have an urge to eye-flash him just to find out what happens, but with Pere Claude on the way, I don't want to escalate things until he gets here. Instead, I start asking questions.

"I heard your plastic surgery went all wonky after you got

bit, what was that like? Did you have, like, implants traveling all over just under your skin?"

"Yes, until I removed them. You have pierced ears, do you have to re-pierce them after every full moon?"

"I don't know, I just had it done yesterday. Where did you meet the twins? According to the book it was here, during Mardi Gras, but where?"

"The gym on Rampart."

"The wolf gym? I knew it! I knew they'd seen a Varger-style sparring room before putting them in all the Hammerfits. But why were you there?"

"I heard it was a good gym. You seem awfully young, girl. How old are you?"

"Eighteen. And my name is Abby."

"Abby. When were you turned?"

Turned? Did the twins not tell him about the born?

I play along. "About six months ago. Why are all your clients male?"

"I have many female clients. I just don't give them the special mesotherapy."

"Why not?"

"Well." He exhales in a little half-laugh. "I wouldn't want to give a woman my own wolf essence, now, would I? But eventually I will need a female wolf. Someone like you, maybe. Small and feminine-looking. Interested?"

"Absolutely not, but you act like I should know what you're talking about, and I don't."

"Well. Obviously, a woman wouldn't want a masculine wolf, a fierce and deadly predator, like me, or the twins. But the wolf brings healing, too, sometimes weight loss, and women will want that."

"I'm sorry, do you think the wolf itself is different some-how, depending on whether you get bitten by a male wolf or a female wolf?"

"Of course. How could it not be?"

I sit for a moment in stunned silence trying to figure out a coherent response, but before I do, Pere Claude arrives.

I stand up. Savage stands up. Pere Claude joins us at the table, his body language thunderous, the crowd parting around him. He's not only as mad as I've ever seen him, he's about as mad as I've ever seen anybody. It radiates off him in thick red waves.

But he masters himself. He sounds quite civil when he says, "Mister Savage, we must go somewhere private to discuss what you have been doing."

"No." He shakes his head with a small, satisfied smile. Is he just indifferent to the rage coming off Pere Claude? He must smell it, same as I do. But he isn't afraid. "I am quite certain that if we venture outside of this very public area, you'll kill me."

Pere Claude looks thoughtful, nods. "Very well. I can understand why you would think that." He pulls an empty chair from a nearby table, sits down. We sit down. The waitress comes back. She gives Flint his martini, me an iced tea, and Pere Claude a shot of single malt Scotch.

"Mr. Claude, welcome."

"Thank you, Miss Fayette, you always remember my favorite brand."

"Enjoy." She leaves.

Flint Savage frowns. "She knows you?"

He sips, eyes twinkling in spite of the underlying rage. "I tip well."

Savage gets nervous for the first time, maybe starting to sense that he's in way over his head, confronting a senior wolf who's deep in his own territory.

He directs his attention to me, goes into a totally different mode, straightens up, tugs his coat, gets a slick smile on his face.

"Miss Abby, you're young, you probably want to go to college? A top school? But where is that money going to come from? College is so expensive these days. Your generation is facing unprecedented hurdles for the most basic features of adult life. But your grandfather has a gold mine running through his veins and doesn't even realize it.

"When the twins made me what I am, it was an old-fashioned, messy process. Positively barbaric. There were drugs, and pain, and a lot of uncertainty. A chance I wouldn't be able to get the wolf to bite me. A chance he'd rip out my throat. A chance it wouldn't work at all. I realized that the whole process needed to be much more scientific and predictable. And if it is, we can monetize it. Assume you didn't already have all the enhancements of being like we are, how much would you pay for them? For the healing? The strength? The metabolic boost? The stamina? What would it be worth to you? A thousand? Five thousand? Ten thousand? My injection procedure is close to being perfected. And when it is, I think we can charge up to ten thousand dollars, maybe more, for a guaranteed transformation."

A pause. I can't believe what I just heard. "You want to charge money to make people werewolves? Like it's a cosmetic procedure?"

He nods. "Correct."

I burst out laughing. "That's the stupidest damn thing I ever heard."

His mood shifts instantly, becomes glowering. "You think this is funny, bitch?"

Which, naturally, makes me laugh harder. "Oh-ho, I have surely never been called a bitch before, this insult has devastated me to my very core! I shall never recover."

"Very funny. Maybe your alpha has a different opinion? Sir. You've heard my proposal?"

"I have." Pere Claude slams back the Scotch, slams down the glass, meets the other man's gaze with a flash of pure hellfire red, voice a low rumbling growl. "You are, surely, the lowest creature I have ever encountered. To take the gifts of the wolf and make them a thing to be sold in the market-place? The very idea is an abomination beyond anything I could have imagined a person to be capable of."

Savage wilts under the fire of Pere Claude's gaze, but recovers quickly. "So, that's how it's going to be, is it? All right. You don't want the money, it's your loss. But you will let me leave here alive, and you will let me continue with my project. Because otherwise——"

He raises the knife, not to my heart, but to his own throat.

"Like my sire Rufus, I have the gift of pain transformation. If I slit my own throat, I will transform right here, right now, in front of all these people, and I will begin attacking them. Do you want that? Here? In your hometown? During Mardi Gras?"

"Of course not."

"Then give me what I ask for. Safe passage and freedom to earn a living as I see fit."

"I need to consult with other senior members of my pack," Pere Claude says. "Excuse me a moment." He takes out his phone and heads toward the bathrooms, but I'm pretty sure he's not planning to chat with anyone: he's planning to come back in wolf form. The Varger prohibition against public transformations doesn't prohibit the wolf from being seen in public after the shift is complete, especially a fully mastered wolf like Pere Claude's.

That should end things. Make Savage's threat meaning-less. But Pere Claude doesn't come back right away. I don't smell the distinctive ozone sharpness of a transformation. A minute goes by. Two minutes. Three minutes.

Savage looks at me with an evil smile. "I don't know what your grandfather is up to back there, but I'm pretty sure it's not drawing up a contract."

He slits his throat.

29

THE FINAL PARADE

O zone tickles my nose and I know what I have to do. If Pere Claude is in trouble for some reason, the only way to stop Flint Savage is to summon my own wolf.

I pick up the dropped knife, drive it into my gut with a shock of pain, hit places still not completely healed from the bullet more than a month ago.

It occurs to me this might be a very bad idea. How can I be sure the wolf is there?

I inhale, gathering, searching, reaching—the wolf was so close before. I felt her, like a predator breathing down my neck, chasing after me.

I find it. A moment of stillness. A moment to let her catch me.

She's here.

We're here.

Together.

Stop briefly to shake off the clothes that cling to us, sniffing out where the enemy has gone. His trail is bold, offensive, leading right into the middle of a crowded street. People were having fun, and now they're afraid. Their fear swirls around us, a thick yellow fog, not sharp or intox-

icating like the fear of an enemy, but foul, poisonous, wrong. These people, here, right now, should not be afraid.

The Enemy invades a group of young people, carrying objects that make noises we like (marching band, Fluffy, that's a marching band). *He snarls at them, showing his teeth, making them his enemies, his prey. This is wrong. These people are under our protection.*

We charge in, ready to bite out his throat, but he catches our approach, begins to flee. Instead of a clean killing bite to the throat, we get his leg and start a brief, awkward tussle.

One of the large prey animals the humans like to sit on (horse, that's a horse) *gets scared by our fight. He wants to run but is penned in by the thick crowd, and instead begins screaming and rearing. The human on his back gets thrown off, and other humans react in fear, running from his stomping hooves.*

We need to get the Enemy away from all the people.

We chase the Enemy, nipping at his legs, and he runs. But after a while he stops, roars, enraged, turns to challenge us. Fool, does he think he's going to win? We fight, and nearly get another killing bite to his neck, but he realizes his danger at the last moment and flees.

We chase. And hear: Grandfather howls the hunt is on, he's coming to join us, thick spicy smell drawing closer.

We stop for a moment, howl back: Should we wait for you to arrive?

Another howl: Protect the people first, always.

Enemy darts after a woman as if to attack her, and we charge again, get his throat, bite, shake. Any human enemy would be dead. But this Enemy is a wolf like us. He continues to fight.

Grandfather joins us now, and together we seize hold of our Enemy, my jaws around his leg, preventing him from running, Grandfather's jaws around his neck for the killing bite. He seizes, shakes, snaps the neck bones. Enemy seems dead, but a wolf needs more, to be sure. Grandfather bites down harder and harder on the Enemy's neck, gnawing and worrying, as blood spurts out, stains his white fur. We rush in to help, and between us, we remove the Enemy's head from his neck.

Now there's no coming back, not even for a wolf.

Grandfather touches noses with us, to say, well done, my kin, my packmate, my Granddaughter, we have protected the people.

He takes the head of our slain Enemy in his jaws and begins to run, back to the den, where the rest of our pack waits. We follow.

Wait, was that big white dog carrying the head of a totally different dog?

As we reach the entrance to the den, Grandfather drops his burden. He rises on two feet, unfolding, human again.

We do the same.

He hugs me, with arms, human skin that still smells like the head of our enemy. "Granddaughter, we did it."

"We did."

Edison flings the door open. "Abby! Pere Claude! What are you doing here?" He looks down at the wolf head. "That's him, isn't it? Flint Savage? Wait, you're naked, you fought in wolf form, didn't you?"

Barney shouts from inside, "You bet they did, and the footage is all over the internet, parades are shut down, city's going nuts. Pretty much maximum chaos." He sounds more excited than alarmed.

Edison takes another look at me, then blushes hard, sweat turning sharp and green with lust. "Um, you guys need clothes." He turns away, rushes to where we keep the stash of generic gray sweatsuits, begins pawing through them. We enter the house and Pere Claude sets the bloody wolf head on the big wooden Snarlaway desk.

Edison returns with two sweatsuits: one not quite big enough for Pere Claude and one not quite small enough for me. We don them with practiced swiftness. At last I can stand up straight and stop using my arm as a pretend sports bra.

"Thank you," I tell him.

"No problem," he says, and blushes again. "Um, hey, yeah, wow, good fight?"

"Successful," Pere Claude says. "Our enemy is dead." He gestures toward the wolf head. Everyone gathers around to marvel at it, all admiring, even though it is, let's face it, a bit macabre. A big, bloody, severed, wolf head.

"But the crisis isn't over," I say. "We don't know if Savage was injecting people here in town. We need to get his stuff, hack his phone, find out who he's been talking to."

"Hack his phone? You think that's easy?" Izzy says.

"I didn't say it would be easy."

She grins. "Good. Because I didn't say I couldn't do it." She gives the head a sidelong glance. "That's really him, huh?"

"It is. Yeah."

"Where's the body?"

"Somewhere on Burgundy, between here and Canal."

Pere Claude says, "Abby and I need to retrieve our own personal items from Cafe Adure. I imagine they have put Mr. Savage's personal items aside as well. That's where his phone is likely to be."

"I can drive you," Etienne offers, but Pere Claude shakes his head.

"No, we go by foot. It's not far, and the traffic will no doubt be very troublesome still." He turns to me with a smile. "You may accompany me or not, granddaughter, as you wish."

"I do wish. I'm still kinda wired. Let's go."

We walk in silence for a while, nostrils flaring as we retrace our own extremely strong scent trail. Emergency vehicles blare in the distance, a wailing that sounds almost like the howling of wolves. "The city remains tense," he says. "But it will pass."

We continue, until we reach the location of our final battle. Burgundy and St. Peter. Somebody has already picked up Savage's headless body and chucked it into an alley dumpster. I peek inside and instantly wish I hadn't.

"Ewww, that smells bad."

Pere Claude chuckles. "It seems a fitting end."

"It's weird, though, isn't it? They just threw his body in there. Like he was a rat that got hit by a car or something."

"I suppose it does seem strange. When we die as wolves, we die as wolves."

"Or as dogs."

"Or as dogs." He sighs deeply. "Granddaughter, you summoned your wolf on the day before the full moon."

"I did. Guess I'm doing that old trauma morph training after all, huh?"

"It was terribly risky. Until she had appeared for the first time during a natural moon, you had no assurance she would be there."

"But I did know. I felt her. Otherwise I wouldn't have done it."

He smiles. "Ah. You finally knew what I knew. That she was ready to return, and all you had to do was call her."

"I guess so."

"And you needed to do it because my wolf was delayed."

I look down at the sidewalk, where the drying blood might be mistaken for a spilled daiquiri. "I meant to ask about that. Are you okay? Did something happen?"

He sighs. "I was… not able to summon the wolf instantly. It has happened to me before, but never under such important circumstances."

"Does it mean anything? What does it mean?" I hear the panic in my own voice.

"Perhaps nothing. Perhaps advancing age. But it emphasizes the importance of hunting as a pack. We need each other. I could not have done it without you."

He squeezes my shoulders and I lean into him briefly, a moment of affection.

Then I overhear, "It sucks about the parade, but that dog fight was awesome, have you seen the video yet?"

I turn, see an obviously drunk man, under a heavy collar of Mardi Gras beads, holding up his phone for the other members of his group. My heart sinks, as I realize just how many people must have filmed a portion of our fight, must have already uploaded it to the internet.

"This is bad, isn't it? We had a big wolf battle on Canal Street during a Mardi Gras parade and it's already gone viral. Hundreds of people have seen it already. Thousands."

Pere Claude gives me a troubled smile. "My dear. We must brace for the worst, of course, but there is still hope. You heard that man call it a 'dog fight.' Such videos have become popular before. As long as the moment of transformation itself was not captured, we are likely to weather this storm as we have weathered so many others."

"Sure. It's probably fine."

At Cafe Adure, the same waitress, Miss Fayette, is ready for us, waiting, with three plastic bags of clothes and personal items. She smiles. "Mr. Claude, you left without paying your bill. But you left your wallet behind."

"Did I?" He smiles. "Well, I know the amount of cash that was in my wallet, and I believe that should be sufficient, am I correct?"

"More than sufficient, thank you very much."

"My deepest apologies, Miss Fayette, I had an extremely urgent matter to deal with. Please forgive me."

"Oh, I always do." She pats his hand. "I always do. Now, is this little girl your granddaughter, did I hear that right?"

"You did."

"Well, isn't that something. Is the trouble all dealt with?"

"I believe it will be. Very soon." He takes the three bags. "My items, my granddaughter's items, and the items belonging to the—the other man?"

"That's right. Is everything there?"

I quickly lean over to check the Savage bag to make sure it has his phone. It does. And also a silver-plated surgical knife with the blood still on it. "Everything is here, thank you," I say.

We leave. "Does she know?" I ask Pere Claude. "I mean, she seemed pretty unsurprised that we left all our clothes behind."

He smiles. "She knows, and she doesn't know. As so many here do. In New Orleans, during Mardi Gras especially, no event is too strange to be accommodated."

We hustle back to the maison and help the tech team start unraveling Savage's phone. At the same time, other members of the tech team are busy creating "noise" around the inevitable "wolf attack" videos getting shared online. Luckily, most people can't, at a glance, tell the difference between a dog and a wolf. On the bad side, there's a lot of public worry that the animals suffer from rabies—possibly even explosive rabies—and not only are evening parades shut down, but tomorrow's parades might be shut down as well.

Fortunately, the worst-case scenario from the Varger point of view, clear video evidence of the transformation itself, seems mercifully absent. In the moment when Savage and I transformed, apparently, nobody was paying attention to us yet.

Régnault, Vivienne's cop friend, steps up onto the porch and Pere Claude opens the door. "Mr. Régnault."

"Mr. Claude. Please tell me you all have this under control now. "

"We do. We're still trying to determine the risk for the full moon tomorrow."

He turns toward the tech team. Izzy gives a thumbs up. "No phone appointments for the last few days," she says.

"Bon Dieu." Régnault comes inside and sinks heavily to the couch. "These last few months have been a trial, hey? Vivienne told me there is a single rougarou exposing people by the dozens?"

"He was developing an injection technique," I say. "He thought he could charge money for it."

The look of horror on Régnault's face matches the look of

rage when Pere Claude heard the same thing. "Bon Dieu, that is the most appalling thing I ever heard of. The kind of man who would pay money to have the power of your people? Is the kind of man who should be kept from it by any means."

"That's what we thought," I say. "But it's over. The man is dead."

"Oh, no, do I have to deal with a body?"

"Not a human body."

"Ah." He exhales in obvious relief. "That is somewhat better news. I suppose he is the third wolf in the videos? The very large white wolf, I know him well." He smiles at Pere Claude. "And the small and very fierce red wolf, I believe that was you, cher?" He smiles at me and I nod. "So the gray wolf who menaced the girl in the marching band, that was the man who was doing all this?" We both nod. "And now the outbreak should stop, yes?"

"There might be a few moons of secondary exposure, from people bitten by the original injected wolves," I tell him.

Pere Claude nods. "Abby is right. Mr. Régnault, we should discuss a few logistics, hey? I have a private office upstairs."

Régnault nods, and the two men disappear up the stairway.

Babette and a couple of wolves who work at the Garden District maison burst in the front door. Babette greets me. "Abby! We saw everything on the news! Your wolf is back!"

More and more wolves pour into the maison, as they get word that the man they were hunting has been caught and killed. It's turning into a big party. But I'm starting to feel exhausted. I curl up on the couch next to Edison and lean into his shoulder. In spite of being tired, I also feel better than I have in a long while. I don't feel like somebody who recently got shot, anyway.

Pere Claude and Régnault come downstairs again. Régnault says some things I don't catch, and the name, "Vivienne," then leaves. He has a huge crush on her, but I'm not sure how much she reciprocates. Pere Claude sits down on the couch, so now I'm sandwiched in between Edison and Pere Claude.

"Things are not as bad as they might be, granddaughter," Pere Claude says. "The transformation itself was not caught on video. A relief, no?"

"Definitely a relief."

Edison strokes my hair and that's it, I think I'm going to turn into a puddle right—

Wait.

Pere Claude stiffens and we turn together, the first to pick up on a new, but familiar scent.

I unfold from the couch, throw open the door, Pere Claude coming up right behind me.

"Father." Leon stands on the porch, hanging his head with a penitent air. "I came to help if I could. I submit myself to your leadership. I hope you will accept me."

AFTERWORD

Although the general outline of this book has been in place for some time, writing the final draft was a strange experience, because I did it during the pandemic lockdown of 2020. Some days I would be really productive because, well, it's not like I had anything better to do. On other days I would be paralyzed by doubts, like, "when I finish writing this, will airports even still *exist?* And what about Mardi Gras? Is New Orleans ever going to have a traditional Mardi Gras again?"

Eventually I decided it doesn't matter, since this is probably the book where the timeline of the rougarou universe starts to diverge significantly from our own — a major bitten-wolf outbreak starts to push us from a world where almost nobody knows werewolves exist, to a world where werewolves are kind of an open secret.

This book covers a lot more physical ground than the first two — from New Orleans, to Meriwether, Idaho, to Seattle, to Los Angeles, then back to New Orleans again. New Orleans, Seattle, and Los Angeles all exist in the real world, and I have spent considerable time in all three. Los Angeles is a new location for the series. I grew up in southern California, Orange County, but have two brothers who live in Los Angeles proper.

The Los Angeles Abby encounters is based on my visit in 2017, to my brother who lives in the downtown area. It was Thanksgiving, but freakishly hot.

Meriwether is a thinly disguised version of Lewiston, Idaho, where my grandparents lived for the last twenty years or so of their lives. Why did I make up a fake town? I joke that it's because I was less than flattering in my depiction, but really, I think it's because when a town is small enough, it's harder to get away with things like businesses and housing developments that don't actually exist.

The werewolves' own little town, Bayou Galene, follows the same rules: situated more or less in the location of Montegut, Louisiana, and based loosely on what I saw when visiting there, but also, fundamentally fictitious.

In 2019, my last major trip anywhere was to New Orleans. On that trip we went not only to Voodoo Fest (God, I miss live music) we also went to Rougarou Fest, which happens out in Houma — if you're in Montegut, Houma counts as "going into town," so I figure the werewolves in Bayou Galene think of it that way, and that's going to inform Book 4 (working title: *Hunting After Ghosts*).

Also, for "book locations" nerds, I went to Hermann-Grima house and decided it was the perfect location for the Varger's French Quarter maison. The Seattle maison in Georgetown is based on the School of Acrobatics and New Circus Arts (SANCA), if you ever want to check that out.

Writing is weird. Sometimes it's hard to convince yourself it matters. Sometimes it's hard to feel like anything *else* matters. I hope you enjoy this book and I hope for better times to come.

ACKNOWLEDGMENTS

A big thank you to:

- Carol and Ulysses, my first readers, who gave me a fantastic critique in a park, masked, from six feet away, because that's how we do things in 2020.
- Paul, for driving us around in Cajun country during our October 2019 trip to New Orleans, pretty much the last time anybody went anywhere.
- The Ladies Who Drink and Know Things, for reasons which, er, well, I think wine was involved, but I know they were very helpful and I mentioned on the last virtual meeting that I would thank them in the book.
- Carol again, who gave me the name "grandfather-heart-sausage."
- All the KEXP DJ's who kept me tethered to reality during 2020, especially Eva Walker of The Black Tones, who may or may not remember me gushing after a show about how much I love her band, but they totally have that Seattle-New Orleans

connection going on. Listen to their album, *Cobain & Cornbread*.

ABOUT THE AUTHOR

Julie McGalliard is a writer, data scientist, and occasional cartoonist. She lives in Seattle and has traveled to New Orleans a lot.

Follow her adventures at https://www.gothhouse.org/author/juliemcgalliard/

Photo by Andrew S. Williams

CPSIA information can be obtained
at www.ICGtesting.com
Printed in the USA
LVHW082308240221
679892LV00035B/819